Outcast

D1347800

Chronicles
of Ancient
Darkness

Outcast

MICHELLE PAVER

Illustrated by Geoff Taylor

Orion
Children's Books

First published in Great Britain in 2007
by Orion Children's Books
Paperback edition first published in Great Britain in 2008
by Orion Children's Books
Reissued 2011 by Orion Children's Books
a division of the Orion Publishing Group Ltd
Orion House
5 Upper St Martin's Lane
London WC2H 9EA
An Hachette UK Company

1 3 5 7 9 10 8 6 4 2

The Orion Publishing Group's policy is to use papers that
are natural, renewable and recyclable products and
made from wood grown in sustainable forests. The logging
and manufacturing processes are expected to conform to
the environmental regulations of the country of origin.

A catalogue record for this book is available from the British Library

Printed in Great Britain by Clays Ltd, St Ives plc

ISBN 978 1 84255 115 8

Ӌ

www.orionbooks.co.uk

ONE

The viper glided down the riverbank and placed its sleek head on the water, and Torak stopped a few paces away to let it drink.

His arms ached from carrying the red deer antlers, so he set them aside and crouched in the bracken to watch. Snakes are wise, and know many secrets. Maybe this one would help him deal with his.

The viper drank with unhurried sips. Raising its head, it regarded Torak, flicking out its tongue to taste his scent. Then it coiled neatly back on itself and vanished into the ferns.

It had given him no sign.

But you don't *need* a sign, he told himself wearily. You know what to do. Just tell them. Soon as you get back to camp. Just say, 'Renn. Fin-Kedinn. Two moons ago, something happened. They held me down, they put a mark on my chest. And now . . . '

No. That wasn't any good. He could picture Renn's face. 'I'm your best friend – and you've been lying to me for *two whole moons!*'

He put his head in his hands.

After a while he heard rustling, and glanced up to see a reindeer on the opposite bank. It was standing on three legs, furiously scratching its budding antlers with one hind hoof. Sensing that Torak wasn't hunting, it went on scratching. The antlers were bleeding: the itch must be so bad that the only relief was to make them hurt.

That's what I should do, thought Torak. Cut it out. Make it hurt. In secret. Then no-one need ever know.

The trouble was, even if he could bring himself to do it, it wouldn't work. To get rid of the tattoo, he'd have to perform the proper rite. He'd learnt that from Renn, whom he'd approached in a roundabout way, using the zigzag tattoos on her wrists as an excuse.

'If you don't do the rite,' she'd told him, 'the marks just come back.'

'They come back?' Torak had been horrified.

'Of course. You can't see them, they're deep in the marrow. But they're still there.'

So that was the end of that, unless he could get her to tell him about the rite without revealing why he needed to know.

The reindeer gave an irritable shake and trotted off into the Forest; and Torak picked up the antlers and started back for camp. They were a lucky find, big enough for everyone in the clan to get a piece, and perfect for making fish-hooks and hammers for knapping flint. Fin-Kedinn would be pleased. Torak tried to fix his mind on that.

2

It didn't work. Until now, he hadn't understood how much a secret can set you apart. He thought about it all the time, even when he was hunting with Renn and Wolf.

It was early in the Moon of the Salmon Run, and a sharp east wind carried a strong smell of fish. As Torak made his way beneath the pines, his boots crunched on flakes of bark scattered by woodpeckers. To his left, the Green River chattered after its long imprisonment under the ice, while to his right, a rockface rose towards Broken Ridge. In places it was scarred, where the clans had hacked out the red slate which brings hunting luck. He heard the clink of stone on stone. Someone was quarrying.

That should be me, Torak told himself. I should be making a new axe. I should be doing things. 'This can't go on,' he said out loud.

'You're right,' said a voice. 'It can't.'

They were crouching on a ledge ten paces above him: four boys and two girls, glaring down. The Boar Clan wore their brown hair cut to shoulder length, with a fringe; tusks at their necks, stiff hide mantles across their shoulders. The Willows had wovenbark strips sewn in spirals on their jerkins, and three black leaves tattooed on their brows in a permanent frown. All were older than Torak. The boys had wispy beards, and beneath the girls' clan-tattoos, a short red bar showed that they'd had their first moon bleed.

They'd been quarrying: Torak saw stone dust on their buckskins. Just ahead of him, he spotted a tree-trunk ladder notched with footholds, which they'd propped against the rockface, to climb up to the ledge. But they were no longer interested in slate.

Torak stared back, hoping he didn't look scared. 'What do you want?' he said.

3

Aki, the Boar Clan Leader's son, jerked his head at the antlers. 'Those are mine. Put them down.'

'No they're not,' said Torak. 'I found them.' To remind them he had weapons, he hoisted his bow on his shoulder and touched the blue slate knife at his hip.

Aki wasn't impressed. 'They're mine.'

'Which means *you* stole them,' said a Willow girl.

'If that was true,' Torak told Aki, 'you'd have put your mark on them and I'd have left them alone.'

'I did. On the base. You rubbed it off.'

'Of course I didn't,' said Torak in disgust.

Then he saw what he should have seen before: a smudge of earthblood at the base of one antler, where a boar tusk had been drawn on. His ears burned. 'I didn't see it. And I didn't rub it off.'

'Then put them down and get out of here,' said a boy called Raut, who'd always struck Torak as fairer than most. Unlike Aki, who was spoiling for a fight.

Torak didn't feel like giving him one. 'All right,' he said briskly, 'I made a mistake. Didn't see the mark. They're yours.'

'What makes you think it's that easy?' said Aki.

Torak sighed. He'd come across Aki before. A bully: unsure if he was a leader, and desperate to prove it with his fists.

'You think you're special,' sneered Aki. 'Because Fin-Kedinn took you in, and you can talk to wolves and you're a spirit walker.' He raked his fingernails over the scant hairs on his chin, as if checking they were still there. 'Truth is, you only live with the Ravens because your own clan's never come near you. And Fin-Kedinn doesn't trust you enough to make you his foster son.'

Torak set his teeth.

Covertly, he looked about. The river was too cold to swim; besides, they had dugouts on the bank. That meant there was no point running upriver, either – or back the way he'd come, he'd be trapped in the fork where the Green River merged with the Axehandle. And no help within reach. Renn was at the Raven camp on the north bank, half a daywalk to the east; and Wolf had gone hunting in the night.

He set down the antlers. 'I said you can have them,' he told Aki. He started up the trail.

'Coward,' taunted Aki.

Torak ignored him.

A stone struck his temple. He turned on them. 'Now who's the coward? What's brave about six against one?'

Beneath his fringe, Aki's square face darkened. 'Then let's make it even: just you and me.' He whipped off his jerkin to reveal a meaty chest covered in reddish fuzz.

Torak froze.

'What's the matter?' sniggered a Boar girl. 'Scared?'

'No,' said Torak. But he was. He'd forgotten the Boar Clan custom of stripping to the waist for a fight. He couldn't do that, or they'd see the mark.

'Get ready to fight,' snarled Aki, making his way down the ladder.

'No,' said Torak.

Another stone whistled towards him. He caught it and threw it back, and the Boar girl yelped and clutched a bleeding shin.

Aki had nearly reached the bottom of the ladder, his friends swarming after him like ants on a honey trail.

Grabbing one of the antlers, Torak ducked behind a pine, hooked the tines in the nearest branch, and swung into the tree.

'We've got him!' shouted Aki.

No you haven't, thought Torak. He'd chosen this tree because it grew nearest the rockface, and now he crawled along a branch and onto the ledge they'd just left. It was littered with quartz saws and grindstones, a small fire, and an elkhide pail of pine-pitch, planted in hot ash to keep it runny. Above him the slope was less steep, with enough juniper scrub to make it climbable.

Throwing stones and dodging theirs, he raced to the ladder and gave it a push. It didn't budge. It was lashed to the ledge with rawhide ropes, no time to cut it free. He did the only thing he could to stop them coming after him. He seized the pail and emptied it down the ladder.

There was an outraged roar – and Torak dropped the pail in astonishment. Aki was faster than he looked – he'd nearly reached the ledge. Without meaning to, Torak had just dumped hot pine-pitch all over him.

Bellowing like a stuck boar, Aki slid down the ladder.

Torak clawed at juniper bushes and hauled himself towards the ridge.

⫟⫟

He ran north-east through the trees, and their cries faded. He *hated* running away. But better be called a coward than get found out.

After a while the slope became gentler, and he was able to skitter down it and make his way to the river again, keeping off the clan trail and sticking to the wolf trails which he could find almost without thinking. Once he reached the ford, he could get across and double back to the Raven camp. There'd be trouble, but Fin-Kedinn would be on his side.

In a willow thicket on the bank, he came to a halt, the breath sawing in his chest. Around him the trees were still waking from their long winter sleep. Bees bumped about among the catkins, and a squirrel dozed in a patch of sunlight, its tail wrapped around the branch. In the shallows, a jay was taking a bath. No-one was coming. The Forest would have warned him.

Shaky with relief, he leaned against a tree-trunk.

His hand moved to the neck of his jerkin and touched the tattoo on his breastbone. The Viper Mage hissed in his mind. *'This mark will be like the harpoon head beneath the skin of the seal. One twitch, and it will draw you, no matter how hard you struggle. For now you are one of us . . .'*

'I'm not one of you,' muttered Torak. 'I'm *not!*'

But as he'd lain awake through the storm-tossed nights of winter, he'd felt the mark burning his skin. He dreaded to think what evil it might do. What evil it might make *him* do.

Somewhere to the south, Wolf howled. He'd caught a hare, and was singing his happiness to the Forest, his pack-brother and anyone else who was listening.

Hearing Wolf's voice lightened Torak's spirits. Wolf didn't seem to mind his tattoo. Nor did the Forest. It knew, but it hadn't cast him out.

The jay flew up, scattering droplets, and for a moment, Torak followed its flight. Then he pushed himself off the tree and began to run. He left the thicket – and Aki head-butted him in the chest and sent him sprawling.

The Boar Clan boy was almost unrecognisable. His reddened eyes glared from a skull that was black and slimy with pitch, and he stank of pine-blood and rage. 'You made a fool of me!' he shouted. 'In front of everyone, you made a fool of me!'

7

Struggling to his feet, Torak scrambled backwards. 'I didn't do it on purpose! I didn't know you were there!'

'Liar!' Aki swung his axe at Torak's shins.

Torak jumped out of the way, then side-stepped and kicked Aki's axe-hand. Aki dropped the axe. He drew his knife. Torak drew his too, and they circled one another.

Torak's heart hammered against his ribs as he tried to remember every fighting trick Fa and Fin-Kedinn had taught him.

Without warning, Aki lunged. He mistimed it by a heartbeat. Torak kicked him in the belly, then punched him hard in the throat. Choking, Aki went down, grabbing at Torak's jerkin. The throat-lacing ripped – and Aki saw it. The mark on Torak's chest.

Time stretched.

Aki released him and staggered back.

Torak's legs wouldn't move.

Aki glanced from the mark to Torak's face. Beneath the pine-pitch, his features were blank with shock.

He recovered fast. He pointed one finger at Torak, aiming straight between the eyes. He made a sideways cut of the hand: a sign Torak had never seen before.

Then he turned and ran.

丰丰

Aki must have regained his dugout and paddled faster than a leaping salmon, because when Torak finally reached the Raven camp by mid-afternoon, the Boar Clan boy had got there first. Torak knew at once from the stillness of the Ravens as he ran into the clearing.

The only sounds were the creak of the drying racks and the murmur of the river. Thull and his mate Luta, whose shelter Torak shared, stared at him as if he were a stranger. Only their son Dari, seven summers old and Torak's devoted follower, rushed to greet him. He was yanked back by his father.

Renn burst from a reindeer-hide shelter, her dark-red hair flying, her face flushed with indignation. 'Torak, at last! It's all a mistake! I've told them it isn't true!'

Behind her, Aki emerged with his father, the Boar Clan Leader, and Fin-Kedinn. The Raven Leader's face was grim, and he leaned on his staff as he crossed the clearing; but when he spoke it was in the same quiet voice as always. 'I've vouched for you, Torak. I've told them this can't be so.'

They had such such faith in him. He couldn't bear it.

The Boar Clan Leader glared at Fin-Kedinn. 'Are you calling my son a liar?' He was a bigger version of Aki: the same square face and ready fists.

'Not a liar,' replied Fin-Kedinn. 'Simply mistaken.'

The Boar Clan Leader bridled.

'I've told you,' said Fin-Kedinn, 'the boy is no Soul-Eater. And he can prove it. Torak, take off your jerkin.'

'*What?*' Renn turned on her uncle. 'But you can't even *think* –'

Fin-Kedinn silenced her with a glance. Then to Torak, 'Quickly now, let's clear this up.'

Torak looked at the faces around him. These people had taken him in when his father was killed. He'd lived with them for nearly two summers. They had begun to accept him. Now he was going to end that.

Slowly he took off his quiver and bow and laid them on the ground. He untied his belt. There was a ringing in his ears. His fingers belonged to someone else.

He said a prayer to the Forest – and pulled his jerkin over his head.

Renn's mouth opened, but no sound came.

Fin-Kedinn's hand tightened on his staff.

'I told you,' cried Aki. 'The three-pronged fork, I *told* you! He's a Soul-Eater!'

Two

W hy didn't you tell me?' said Fin-Kedinn in the voice that made grown men blench.

'I wanted to,' said Torak. 'But I . . . '

'But you what?'

Torak hung his head.

They were alone in the clearing. The Boar Clan Leader and his son had left to gather their people, and messengers had been sent to clans camped within reach. Fin-Kedinn – who'd been scraping a reindeer skin before Aki burst in – had returned to his work: a sign to the others to get on with theirs and leave Torak to him. Some had gone hunting, or to spear fish upriver. There was no sign of Renn.

The Raven camp was eerily calm. Torak saw a deerhide canoe drawn up on the bank; a wovenbark net draped over a juniper bush. Around him the birch trees were a brilliant green, the undergrowth bright with blue anemones, yellow celandine and silver fish-scales. Nothing to show that a storm had broken over his head.

He watched Fin-Kedinn fling the hide over a log and stretch it taut. The veins on the Raven Leader's forearms bulged, and his movements – usually so measured – were savage. 'If you'd told me. We could have found a way.'

'I thought I could get rid of it without you knowing.' Torak realized how that sounded: covering one lie with another.

Fin-Kedinn took a deer's rib-bone and started scraping fat from the hide with short, vicious strokes. 'You brought that evil mark into my clan.'

'I didn't mean to! Fin-Kedinn, you've got to believe me! I tried to fight, but they were too many!'

The Raven Leader flung down the scraper. 'But *you* sought them out! *You* got too close!'

'I had to! They'd taken Wolf!'

'Ah, there's always a reason!' The force of his anger made Torak step back. 'You're just like your father! I warned him not to join them, but he wouldn't listen. He said they meant to do good, he went on calling them the Healers even after they'd turned evil.' He broke off. 'In the end it killed him. And it killed your mother.'

Torak saw the deep lines at the sides of his mouth, the pain in the fierce blue eyes. This was his fault. He had hurt this man whom he'd come to love.

The Raven Leader went back to work. Torak smelt the stink of dead reindeer, and watched the bloody fat bubbling over the edge of the rib-bone. He pictured a knife slicing into his own flesh to rid it of the Soul-Eater tattoo. 'I'll cut it out,' he said. 'Renn says there's a rite.'

'Which can only be done when the moon is full. We're in the moon's dark. You've run out of time.'

A gust of wind brought the smell of rain, and Torak shivered. 'Fin-Kedinn. I'm not a Soul-Eater. You know this.'

The scraper stilled. 'But how will you prove it?' He met Torak's eyes, and his own were filled with a sorrow that was even more frightening than his anger. 'Don't you understand, Torak? It doesn't matter what *I* believe. It's everyone else you've got to convince. This is out of my hands. Only your own clan can vouch for you now.'

Torak's heart sank. He was Wolf Clan, but his father had kept him apart from them, and he'd never even seen the rest of his clan. Few had. The Wolf Clan had been deeply ashamed when its Mage – Torak's father – turned Soul-Eater. Since then, it had stayed hidden, becoming as shadowy and elusive as its clan-creature.

Torak touched the tattered scrap of wolf fur sewn to his jerkin. Fa had prepared it for him, so it was precious. It was also his only link with his clan. 'How do I find them?' he said.

'You don't,' said Fin-Kedinn. 'Not if they don't want to be found.'

'But what if they don't come? If they don't vouch for me –'

'Then I'll have no choice. I'll have to obey clan law and cast you out.'

The wind strengthened, and the birch trees lifted their branches – as if Torak was already outcast, and they feared to touch him.

'Do you understand what it means,' said Fin-Kedinn, 'to be outcast?'

Torak shook his head.

'It means you would be as one dead. Cut off from everyone. Hunted like prey. No-one could help you. Not

13

me. Not Renn. We couldn't talk to you, give you food. If we did, we'd be outcast too. If we saw you in the Forest, we'd have to kill you.'

Torak went cold. 'But I didn't *do* anything!'

'It's the law,' said Fin-Kedinn. 'Many winters ago, after the great fire which scattered the Soul-Eaters, the clan elders made this law to stop them coming back. To stop others joining them.'

The first spots of rain pattered onto the reindeer hide. 'Go to your shelter,' said the Raven Leader without looking up.

'But Fin-Kedinn —'

'Go. The clans will gather. The elders will decide.'

Torak swallowed. 'What about Thull and Luta and Dari? It's their shelter too.'

'They'll build another. From now on, don't talk to anyone. Stay in the shelter. Wait for the clans to decide.'

'How long will that be?'

'As long as it takes. And Torak . . . Don't try to escape. You'll only make it worse.'

Torak stared at him. 'How could it be worse?'

'It can always get worse,' said the Raven Leader.

Torak learned the truth of that two days later, when Renn finally came to see him.

Until then, he hadn't caught a glimpse of her. His shelter faced away from camp, so he couldn't see much except by peering through gaps in the hides, or when he went to the midden. The rest of the time he sat and watched the small fire before the opening, and listened to the clans gather.

Late on the second day, Renn stalked up to the shelter. Her face was pale, the blue-black bars of her clan-tattoos livid on her cheekbones. 'You should have told me,' she said stonily.

'I know.'

'You should've *told* me!' She kicked the doorpost, and the shelter shook.

'I thought I could get rid of it in secret.'

Squatting by the fire, she glowered at the embers. 'You lied to me for two whole moons. And don't tell me that keeping silent isn't lying, because it is!'

'I know. I'm sorry.'

She didn't reply. Over the winter, she'd developed a tiny freckle at the corner of her mouth, and he'd teased her, asking if it was a birch seed and why didn't she wipe it off. He couldn't imagine teasing her now. He'd never felt so bad.

'Renn,' he said. 'You've got to believe me. I'm not a Soul-Eater.'

'Well of course you're not!'

He drew a breath. 'So – can you forgive me?'

She picked at a scab on her elbow. Then she gave a curt nod.

Relief flooded through him. 'I didn't think you would.'

She went on picking at the scab. 'We've all got secrets, Torak.'

'Not like this.'

'No,' she said in an odd voice. 'Not like this.'

Then she surprised him by asking which of the Soul-Eaters had put the mark on his chest.

' – It was Seshru. Why?'

She ripped off the scab and dug her fingernail into the rawness underneath. 'Where were the others?'

He swallowed. 'Thiazzi held me down. The Bat Mage watched. Eostra . . .' He shuddered as he recalled the ghastly wooden mask of the Eagle Owl Mage. 'I didn't see her. But there was an owl, watching from an ice hill . . .'

Suddenly he was back in the freezing dark of the Far North. He felt the powerful grip of the Oak Mage. He saw the hunched bulk of the Bat Mage standing guard, and caught the orange glare of the greatest of owls. Then Seshru the Viper Mage was blotting out the stars, and he was staring up into eyes the deep blue of the sky before middle-night. He watched her perfect mouth pronouncing his fate as she drove the bone needle again and again into his skin and smeared him with the blood of murdered hunters. *This mark will be like the harpoon head beneath the skin of the seal. One twitch and it will draw you . . .*

'Torak?' said Renn.

He was back in the shelter.

'What are you going to do?'

'What I should have done in the beginning. I'm going to cut it out. Tell me how to do the rite.'

'No,' she said without hesitation.

'Renn. You've got to.'

'No! You couldn't do it on your own, you don't know Magecraft.'

'I've got to try.'

'Yes, and I'll help you.'

'No. If you helped me, you'd be outcast too.'

'I don't care.'

'Well I do.'

Renn pressed her lips together. She could be incredibly stubborn.

So could he. 'Renn. Listen to me. Not long ago, they took Wolf – because of me. He was nearly killed – because of me. That's why I haven't howled for him now, because he'd only try to help, and get hurt. If you got hurt because of me . . . ' He stopped. 'You've got to swear – swear on your bow and your three souls – that if they cast me out, you won't try to help.'

A noise in the clearing. Torak saw the bent figure of the Raven Mage hobbling towards them.

'Renn!' he said in an urgent whisper. 'Do this for me! Swear!'

Renn raised her head, and in her dark eyes, two tiny flames leapt. 'No,' she said.

'The clans have gathered,' said Saeunn in her raven's croak. 'The elders have decided. Renn. Leave.'

Renn lifted her chin.

'Leave.'

Defiantly, Renn turned to Torak. 'I meant what I said.' Then she was gone.

The Raven Mage told Torak to gather his things, and waited at the mouth of the shelter, clutching her staff in one shrivelled claw. Her sunken eyes watched him without pity. A life spent peering into the world of the spirits had detached her from the feelings of the living.

'Not the sleeping-sack,' she rasped.

'Why not?' said Torak.

'The outcast shall be as one dead.'

Torak's belly turned over. Until now, he'd clung to a faint hope that Fin-Kedinn might be able to save him.

The rain came, pattering onto the hide roof and making the fire smoke. He picked up the last of his gear and glanced around. Often, he'd hated this shelter. He'd never got used to the Raven way of staying in the same camp for three or four moons, instead of moving on every few days, as he'd done with Fa. Now he couldn't imagine leaving it and never coming back.

'It is time,' said Saeunn.

He followed her into the clearing.

The clans were gathered about a huge long-fire. It was still light, but the rain clouds turned it to dusk. Torak was glad of the rain. People would think he was shivering with cold, not fear.

The crowd parted to let them through, and he took in a blur of firelit faces. Raven. Willow. Viper. Boar. But no Mountain or Ice clans, and none from the Deep Forest or the Sea. This was a matter for the Open Forest. He wondered when his kinsman in the Seal Clan would get to hear of what had happened. What would Bale think?

Aki had planted himself at the front of the throng. He'd scrubbed his skin clean of pine-pitch, but it had gone a blotchy red, and he'd had to cut his hair short, like boar bristles. He wore two throwing-axes in his belt, a birch-bark horn at his hip, and a triumphant expression. Clearly he would lose no time in hunting the outcast.

Rain hissed on the fire and dripped off the trees that watched at the edge of the clearing. Rain trickled down Renn's cheeks like tears. But it couldn't be tears, because Renn never cried.

Fin-Kedinn was waiting by the fire with the other clan elders. His face was impassive. He didn't look at Torak.

Saeunn hobbled to Fin-Kedinn's side, and addressed the clans. 'I am the oldest of the clans of the Open Forest,' she declared. 'I speak for them all.' She paused. 'The boy bears the mark of the Soul-Eater. The law is clear. He must be cast out.'

'Ah.' A sigh rose from the crowd.

Torak's knees sagged.

'Wait!' A man's voice called from the edge of the clearing.

All heads turned.

Torak saw a tall figure step into the firelight. Rain plastered his long dark hair to his skull, except for two shaven strips at the temples. His eyes had an odd yellow gleam, but his high-boned face seemed strangely familiar.

Then Torak saw the clan-tattoos, and the back of his neck prickled. Two dotted lines on the cheekbones. A strip of sodden grey fur on the left side of his parka.

Aki had seen it too. 'No!' he cried. 'You can't stop it now, the elders have spoken!'

The tall man stared at Aki – and the Boar Clan boy drew back, abashed.

'Who are you?' said Torak.

The tall man turned and fixed his gaze on him. 'I am Maheegun. Leader of the Wolf Clan.'

THREE

They emerged from the trees as soundlessly as a wolf pack.

Women, men and children: plainly clad in reindeer hide to blend into the Forest. An amulet of raw amber gleamed at every throat, and like Maheegun, their temples were shaven and stained with red ochre. As they moved into the firelight, Torak saw that the whites of their eyes were yellow. Like wolves.

The Leader seemed to recognize Fin-Kedinn, as he gave a distant nod; but he neither smiled, nor placed his fists on his breast in friendship. Torak was reminded of a lead wolf loftily assessing a stranger.

The rest of the Wolf Clan gave the same remote half-bow, except for a woman who smiled at Fin-Kedinn in a way that briefly made her young again. For answer, the

Raven Leader put his hand on his heart and bowed to her. Torak recalled that long ago, Fin-Kedinn had been fostered with the Wolf Clan.

'Your message stone was found,' Maheegun told the Raven Leader. 'Why did you summon us? And to such a gathering.'

'I needed you to come,' Fin-Kedinn calmly replied.

Maheegun drew himself up to his full height and they stared at each other. The Wolf Leader was the first to look away. His yellow gaze flicked to Torak's clan-creature skin, then back to Fin-Kedinn. 'Who is this?'

'The son of the Wolf Mage.'

The Wolves gasped. Some grasped their amulets, others made the sign of the hand at Torak, as if warding off evil.

'The one you speak of,' said Maheegun, 'was the greatest Mage we ever had. He alone – for a few heartbeats – managed to become wolf. But he turned Soul-Eater.' He touched his temple. 'Because of him, we bear the mark of shame.'

This was too much for Torak. 'What shame?' he cried. 'My father shattered the fire-opal! He broke up the Soul-Eaters! Wasn't that enough to make amends?'

Maheegun ignored him. 'Again, Fin-Kedinn, I say: why did you summon us?'

Swiftly, Fin-Kedinn told how Torak had come to live with the Ravens, and why he needed his clan to vouch for him now. As proof of Torak's identity, he held up Torak's mother's medicine horn and the blue slate knife which had belonged to his father.

The Wolf Leader listened in silence; but when Fin-Kedinn offered him the objects, he recoiled. 'Keep them away, they're unclean!'

'No they're not!' said Torak. 'Fa gave them to me when he was dying!'

'Torak, enough,' warned Fin-Kedinn.

The woman who'd smiled came forwards. 'Maheegun,' she said, 'we don't need proof. You have only to look at the boy's face. He is the son of the Wolf Mage.'

A shiver ran through her clan. At the corner of his vision, Torak saw Renn raise her fist in triumph.

'Yes,' said Maheegun. 'And yet – I cannot vouch for him.'

Torak's jaw dropped.

Even Fin-Kedinn seemed shaken. 'But you must. He's your kinsman.' When the Wolf Leader did not reply, he said, 'Maheegun, I know this boy. He was marked against his will, he's no Soul-Eater.'

Maheegun frowned. 'You misunderstand, this is not my choice. Did I say that I *will* not vouch for him? No. I said I *can* not. This boy is the son of the Wolf Mage, yes. But he is *not* Wolf Clan!'

For a moment, nobody spoke.

'Of course I'm Wolf Clan!' shouted Torak. 'My mother named my clan when I was born, just like everybody else. And Fa gave me my clan-tattoos when I was seven!'

'No,' said Maheegun.

Drawing close to Torak, he put out his hand and touched Torak's cheek with his forefinger.

Torak flinched. He caught the Leader's musty smell of wet reindeer hide. He felt the calloused finger trace the old scar that cut across the clan-tattoo on his left cheek.

'Not Wolf Clan,' murmured Maheegun, and his yellow eyes pierced Torak's. '*Clanless . . .*'

There was a stunned silence. Then everyone spoke at once.

'What are you talking about?' cried Torak. 'I'm Wolf Clan! I've been Wolf Clan since the night I was born!'

'It's only a scar,' protested Fin-Kedinn, 'it means nothing.'

'How could he be clanless?' exclaimed Renn. 'Nobody's clanless! It isn't possible!'

'Maheegun is right,' rasped Saeunn.

All heads turned to her.

'The scar is no accident,' she declared. 'The boy's father made it on purpose, to show that he is not truly Wolf.'

'That's not true!' Torak burst out. 'Besides, how could you even know?'

'He told me,' said the Raven Mage. 'He sought me out at the clan meet by the Sea.' Her flinty gaze caught his. 'You know this. You were there.'

'It isn't true,' whispered Torak. But in that instant, he knew it was.

He was seven summers old, and Fa had left him with a gaggle of jeering children while he went off to speak to someone, he wouldn't say who. Torak had never seen so many people. He'd been frightened and excited and proud of his new clan-tattoos, although it was annoying that Fa had covered them up with bearberry juice, saying they needed a disguise; making a game of it.

The rain had stopped, and the trees dripped sadly. *Clanless*, they murmured.

'How could this be?' said Fin-Kedinn.

'Only his mother knew the answer,' Saeunn replied. 'She declared him clanless before she died.' Suddenly, she struck the earth with her staff. 'But this is of no concern to us! It alters nothing! The boy has no clan to vouch for him. By law, he must be cast out.'

'*No!*' shouted Renn. 'I don't *care* if he's clanless! This isn't *fair!*'

23

She ran into the middle of the clearing. Her wet hair clung to her neck in little red snakes, and her face was fierce. Torak thought she looked older than her thirteen summers, and beautiful.

Saeunn opened her mouth to silence her, but Fin-Kedinn raised his palm to let her speak.

'You all know Torak,' began Renn, fixing them with her gaze. 'You do, Thull. And you, Luta, and Sialot and Poi and Etan . . . ' One by one, she named the Ravens. Then she named those in the other clans whom Torak had met over the past two summers. 'You all know what he's done for us. He destroyed the bear. He rid the Forest of the sickness. This winter we would have been overrun by demons if it hadn't been for him.'

She paused to make them think about that. 'Yes, he did wrong. He hid the Soul-Eater tattoo when he should have told us. But he doesn't deserve to be cast out! How can you stand by and let this happen? Where's the *justice* in it?'

Fin-Kedinn ran his hand over his dark-red beard. Doubt crept into the faces of some of the watchers. But there was no swaying Saeunn. Again she struck the earth with her staff. 'Clan law *must* be upheld! The wrongdoer *must* be cast out!' She rounded on Renn. 'And let there be no doubt, if anyone dares help him, they too will be cast out!'

Renn glared at Saeunn in silent rebellion, but Torak caught her eye and shook his head. *Don't. You'll only make it worse.*

Afterwards, he could never remember much of the rite of casting out, except for fragments, like flashes of lightning in a storm.

Renn looking on with her fists clenched and her shoulders up around her ears.

Aki stroking his axe.

Luta swallowing tears as she offered the basket of river clay, for all to mark their cheeks in mourning.

'*The outcast shall be as one dead,*' intoned Saeunn.

One by one, each of the Ravens took a piece of Torak's gear and destroyed it, then purified their hands with a spruce bough, which they threw on the fire – just as they would have done if he'd actually died.

Thull took Torak's fishing spear and buried it under the trees.

Luta laid his cooking-skin on the fire.

Dari did the same with his auroch-horn spoon.

Etan stamped on his birch-bark drinking cup.

Sialot and Poi took his arrows and snapped them in two.

Others took his waterskin and his seal-hide winter clothing – which he'd outgrown and had been saving for bedding – and burnt it.

Finally, Renn laid his medicine pouch gently on the embers. She was the only one to look him in the eye. Torak knew she would have said sorry if she could.

As the clearing filled with the bitter stink of burning hide, Saeunn made Torak lie on his back, and tattooed his forehead with the mark of the outcast: a small black ring, like a Death Mark.

At last he stood alone, with nothing but his bow, three arrows, his knife, medicine horn and tinder pouch. All had been daubed with red ochre. As one who is dead.

So far, Fin-Kedinn had taken no part in the rite, but now he walked towards Torak. His hand shook slightly as he took his knife from its sheath.

Torak braced himself.

It hurt more than he could have imagined. Without a word, the Raven Leader cut the clan-creature skin from Torak's jerkin, and placed the tattered wolf fur on the fire.

25

Torak bit his lower lip as he watched the fur blacken and smoke.

'The outcast has until dawn to get away,' said Fin-Kedinn. His voice was steady, but the glitter in his eyes betrayed what this was costing him. 'Until then, he may pass freely in the Forest. After that, anyone who sees him must kill him.' He paused. Then he made the sideways cut of the palm, which meant outcast. 'It is done.'

Torak stared at the fire, where the last trace of the boy he had been – Torak of the Wolf Clan – blazed, collapsed in a heap of glowing ash, and was blown to nothingness by the wind.

Behind him, a murmur ran through the crowd. He turned, and was startled to see the watchers parting to let someone through. He saw Maheegun place a hand on his breast and bow low to the newcomer. He saw the rest of the Wolf Clan do the same.

Then he realized why.

A great grey wolf padded into the clearing. Raindrops beaded his silver fur, and his eyes were amber, like sunlight in clear water.

Dogs fled. People drew back. All except Renn, who gave Torak a defiant nod.

Torak knelt as Wolf padded towards him.

There were times when Wolf would have leapt at Torak and given him an ecstatic welcome, waggling his paws and grunt-whining as he licked his nose and smothered him in wolf kisses. This wasn't one of them. Tonight Wolf was the guide, his eyes alight with the mysterious certainty which came to him at times.

They touched noses, and Torak's gaze briefly grazed Wolf's in greeting. *Pack-brother*, he said in wolf talk.

He saw Maheegun stiffen. *Yes*, he told the Wolf Leader

silently. *I may not be Wolf Clan, but I can do what you cannot. I can talk wolf.*

He rose to his feet, and together, he and Wolf passed through the crowd to the edge of the clearing. Then Torak turned for one last look at the people who had cast him out.

'I may be outcast,' he told them, 'and clanless, but I'm no Soul-Eater. And I will find a way to prove it!'

It was a dank, chill night, and Torak ran through the Forest with Wolf running tirelessly beside him. They didn't stop to rest: without a sleeping-sack, Torak would have frozen. Better to keep going. That way, too, it was harder to think.

The sky was beginning to turn grey when Wolf halted: ears pricked, hackles raised. 'Uff!' he barked softly. *Danger!*

Soon afterwards, Torak heard it too. Birch-bark horns in the distance. The baying of dogs.

His hand tightened on the hilt of his knife.

Aki hadn't wasted any time.

FOUR

Wolf heard the dogs baying, and flicked one ear in scorn. They couldn't catch him!

But they might catch Tall Tailless.

As always, his pack-brother ran on his hind legs, which made him piteously slow: Wolf had to keep stopping to let him catch up. And because he couldn't smell or hear very much, he would never get away from the dogs if it weren't for Wolf.

But he made up for it by being so clever. Sometimes he was even cleverer than a normal wolf. Earlier, he'd hidden his scent by swimming through a Fast Wet. Then he'd woken a Bright Beast-that-Bites Hot and smeared ash on his face, paws and overpelt. Wolf didn't like that because it made him sneeze, but he understood why it had to be done.

He just wished Tall Tailless were faster.

With the wind behind them, they wound through the trees, following the trails which wolves made long ago when the Forest was young. The baying faded, and Wolf raised his tail to tell his pack-brother that the pursuers were far behind.

They kept going.

The ground became stony. They climbed a rise where watchful pines whispered encouragement. Tall Tailless slipped, scattering pebbles which hit Wolf on the nose. Wolf moved past him – then realized he'd gone too far and fell behind, because Tall Tailless was the lead wolf.

Tall Tailless pulled off his beaver-hide overpaws and climbed on in his bare pads. Wolf had often seen him do this, but he still found it disturbing. And Tall Tailless had such strange paws! The toes of his hindpaws were stubby and useless, while his front toes were very long and good at gripping. Wolf watched in admiration as his pack-brother used them to grab juniper branches and haul himself up the slope.

Suddenly, Tall Tailless disappeared.

Wolf's pelt tightened with alarm.

Then he saw that his pack-brother had found a Den. It was hidden behind the junipers, and it smelt of pine marten and hawk. Wolf gave a disapproving bark. *Not here!* During the Great Cold, he'd been trapped by the bad taillesses in a Den like this one.

Tall Tailless stayed on all fours, panting. If he'd had a tail, it would have drooped. If only he didn't need so many rests!

Then Wolf remembered when he was a cub, and needed lots of rests himself, and Tall Tailless had carried him in his forepaws.

29

Feeling bad, Wolf rubbed against his pack-brother and licked his ear. Tall Tailless was shaking. Wolf smelt pain and anger, chewed up with loneliness and fear.

Why was this happening? Wolf didn't understand. Many lopes away, the dogs were angry because they couldn't find the scent. *Where! Where!* they yapped. The wind carried the smell of their anger, and that of the young male tailless from the pack which smelt of boar. But *why* were they hunting Tall Tailless? And why had he left the raven pack? Sometimes a young wolf leaves his pack to start one of his own, but this didn't feel like that. This felt wrong.

The lead wolf of the raven pack had spoken harshly in tailless talk. He'd taken his great claw and torn the wolf fur from Tall Tailless' overpelt: the wolf fur that had been part of Tall Tailless since Wolf first knew him. The lead wolf had done this terrible thing – but underneath, Wolf had sensed his biting sorrow.

The pack-sister puzzled Wolf even more. She hadn't tried to stop the pack leader, and she hadn't come with Tall Tailless.

What did it mean?

Down in the valley, the dogs were casting for the scent. His pack-brother couldn't hear them yet, but Wolf's fur prickled.

What is it? Tall Tailless asked with his eyes.

Wolf glanced at the beloved, furless face. Tall Tailless couldn't lope much further. Wolf had to make sure that the dogs didn't find him.

Grunt-whining softly, he nudged his pack-brother under the chin. *I'm sorry, I must leave. Don't follow.* Then he was out of the Den, racing down the slope.

He flew over the rocks and splashed through the Fast

Wet, thrusting it aside with his big paws. Scrambling up the bank, he shook himself dry and set off again. It was good to run freely, without waiting for Tall Tailless, and he felt no fear of the dogs. Compared to a wolf, dogs are like cubs.

As he ran, he noticed things in the Forest which troubled him. A viper gliding up-Wet with her head held high. An owl feather caught in bracken. An oak tree whispering secrets to its vast and ancient pack. It reminded him of the bad taillesses who'd kept him tied up in the tiny stone Den.

'*Where! Where!*' yelped the dogs.

Wolf forgot the bad taillesses and slowed to a walk.

He reached the valley bottom, and a tangle of scent trails. Through the trees, he saw the young male from the boar pack, clutching a great claw in his forepaw and stinking of blood-hunger. In the other paw he held a scrap of silver hide which smelt of fish-dog and Tall Tailless. Wolf recognized this as a scrap of Tall Tailless' old overpelt.

One of the dogs sniffed the silver pelt to remind herself of the scent.

Now Wolf understood. The pelt was helping the dogs find his pack-brother. He must take it. Then they would chase him, and he would lead them away from Tall Tailless.

Wolf's claws tightened with excitement. He felt the power in his shoulders and haunches, and knew with a fierce joy that he could lope faster than the fastest dog.

Placing his pads with care, he crept forwards.

FIVE

A smell of earth and decay clogged Torak's nostrils. The cramped little cave reminded him of the Raven bone-grounds.

Don't think about that. Think about staying alive.

The clamour of dogs had faded. Whatever Wolf had done, it seemed to have worked; but Torak wished he would return. He told himself that Wolf would find him when he was ready.

Forcing his stiff legs to move, he crawled out and started up the slope. The rocks were slippery with rain. He kept his boots off till his feet grew numb.

His plan had been to set a false trail north from the Raven camp, then double back and make for the valleys to the south, where he'd lived with Fa. Instead, Aki had forced him into a huge loop up and down the Green River.

He was now somewhere on Broken Ridge, not far from where he'd found the red deer antlers.

His sides ached, and on his forehead the new tattoo throbbed. He found a willow tree, muttered a quick apology, and peeled off a slip of bast. Having chewed it, he smeared the stinging pulp on the wound; then cut a strip of buckskin from his jerkin and tied it round as a headband. It would keep the medicine in place, and hide the outcast tattoo.

With a jolt, he remembered that he'd used the same medicine on the night Fa was killed. For a moment, it seemed as if everything that had happened since – finding Wolf, meeting Renn and Fin-Kedinn – as if none of that had been real. Here he was alone again, and on the run.

Before him the ground fell away into dense woods of oak, beech and pine. He caught the distant glint of the Axehandle. Many canoes plied its course, especially during the salmon run. He must stay well back from its banks.

Keeping to deep cover, he began the descent through willowherb and waist-high bracken. He was light-headed with hunger, but he had no food, no axe, and only three arrows. Somehow he had to eat before he got too weak to run. Somehow he had to find a hidden valley where he could survive on his own. Somehow he had to get rid of the mark of the Soul-Eater and force the clans to take him back . . .

The task was too huge. He'd never do it.

Then he remembered something Fin-Kedinn had said the previous moon, when they were gathering bark to make a fishing net. It had been a bitter day like this one, and Torak had stared at the slimy willow wands piled at his feet, wondering how he was ever going to turn them into a net.

'Don't think about the net,' Fin-Kedinn had told him. 'Take a single willow wand and strip it. You can do that, can't you?'

'Of course.' He'd learnt how to strip a stick before he was old enough to hold a knife.

'Then do it,' said the Raven Leader. 'Step by step. One branch at a time. Don't think about the net.'

Now, as Torak felt the rain soaking his buckskins, he nodded. Step by step. Food. Shelter. Yes. Leave the rest till tomorrow.

He found an elk trail which stayed concealed as it wound east along the valley flank. The rain stopped. The sun came out.

As he went, he became aware that although the Ravens were lost to him, the Forest was not. 'Forest,' he said softly. 'I've always honoured you. Help me survive.'

The Forest shook the raindrops from its boughs, and told him to look around.

By the trail he saw a sturdy birch tree with leaves still pleated from the bud. It would give him a quick, strengthening drink. Why hadn't he thought of that before?

Asking the tree's permission, he used his knife to cut a shallow hole in the bark at the base of the trunk. Tree-blood oozed. He stuck a hollow elder stem in the wound to funnel the drips, and tied on a birch-bark cone with honeysuckle, to catch them.

While the cone was filling, he found a digging stick and dug up some crow garlic. Sticking one bulb in a fork of the birch for the clan guardian, he ate the rest. They made his eyes water, but they warmed him up a bit.

After that he found some comfrey roots – very acrid and sticky – and, in a boggy hollow, the best of all: a clump of spotted orchid. The roots were so starchy it was like eating glue, but they were the most nourishing food in the Forest, if you couldn't get meat.

By now, the cone was brimming. After thanking the tree's spirit and pressing the bark over the wound to heal it, he drained the cone. The birch-blood tasted cool and dizzyingly sweet. The strength of the Forest became his.

Food made him feel a little better.

I can do this, he told himself. I can make dogwood arrows and harden the tips in a fire. I can make willowherb snares, and catch fish with bramble-thorn hooks. The Forest will help me.

Mid-afternoon was wearing on as he neared the valley bottom, where he had to wade through piles of last autumn's leaves. His confidence waned. His legs wouldn't carry him much further.

With no axe, building a shelter would be hard, but again, the Forest helped. He found a storm-toppled beech which had fallen onto a boulder. It gave him the perfect frame. All he had to do was pile branches on either side and leafmould on top of that. It was well placed, too: on the edge of a willow thicket where he could hide if he had to.

The air was turning sharp, but he couldn't risk a fire, so for warmth, he stuffed grass down his jerkin, boots and leggings. It was scratchy, and it tickled when beetles and spiders scuttled out, but it would stop him freezing.

Like a badger, he dragged armfuls of leaves into the shelter and snuggled under them, relishing the woody tang. After a prayer of thanks to the Forest, he shut his eyes. He was exhausted.

He was also wide awake.

Thoughts he'd been avoiding for a night and a day took hold. Like a burr in a wolf's fur, they wouldn't let go.

Outcast. Clanless.

How could he be clanless?

He thought of the garlic he'd put in the tree as an offering for the clan guardian. But if he had no clan, he had no guardian. No guardian. That made him feel breathless. How could anyone survive without a guardian?

His fingers touched the scar that cut through his 'clan-tattoo'. He couldn't remember getting it; scars weren't something you bothered about, everyone had them. He had one on his forearm from the night the bear attacked, and another on his calf from the boar's tusk. Renn had one on her hand from a tokoroth bite, and on her foot from stamping on a flint shard when she was three. Fin-Kedinn had lots from hunting accidents and fights when he was young, and the big, puckered scar on his thigh from the bear.

Scowling, Torak burrowed deeper into the leaves. *Don't think about the Ravens. Think about Fa, and why he never told you. Think about your mother, and why she declared you clanless.*

A gust of wind stirred the willows, and they moaned. In the distance, Torak heard the tuneless bellowing of an abandoned elk. In early summer, the Forest rang with their miserable cries. Their mothers, unable to look after last summer's young as well as a newborn calf, abruptly rejected the older ones, driving them away with savage kicks. For a moon or so, the young elk blundered about, seeking comfort from any large creature they met, until they were killed by hunters, or learned to fend for themselves.

I want my mother, bellowed the elk.

Torak squeezed his eyes shut.

He knew so little about his mother, and yet the thought of her had always been with him: a kernel of warmth, even through the bleakest times. He had loved her almost without thinking. He had believed that she had loved him. But to have declared him clanless . . .

It felt as if she'd abandoned him.

Where do I go now? he thought. Where do I belong?

Another gust, and the willows replied. *You belong here. In the Forest.*

Listening to them, he fell into sleep.

With a jolt, he fell out of it.

Voices. Above him on the slope.

He lay rigid, heart pounding.

Then he thought, if they were hunting, they wouldn't be talking.

Crawling out as quietly as he could, he shouldered his quiver and bow and dismantled his shelter, sweeping the area around it with crushed garlic leaves to mask his scent. He crept into the willows. Shadows were lengthening, but the first stars weren't yet out. He hadn't slept long.

The voices came nearer, then stopped fifty paces above him. Through the branches, he spotted a Viper hunting party on the elk trail he'd used earlier. No dogs. That was something. And he'd swept the trail clear of tracks. Hadn't he?

It wasn't only Viper Clan. A party of Ravens seemed to have met them on the trail. He saw Thull, Sialot, Fin-Kedinn. Renn.

It gave him a sick feeling to be peering at them like a stranger, to be unable to go to them.

He watched the younger Viper men wait respectfully for Fin-Kedinn to speak, then preen themselves as he admired their roe buck kill. He saw two Viper children shyly eyeing Renn, who pretended not to notice as she polished her bow with a handful of crushed hazelnuts.

Their voices reached him. They were talking about Aki.

'His wretched dogs nearly ruined our hunt!' complained a Viper man. 'If this goes on . . .'

'It won't,' said Fin-Kedinn. 'Aki won't catch Torak.'

'Still,' said the Viper. 'Those dogs are frightening the prey. The sooner the outcast is out of our range, the better.'

'Oh, he'll be long gone by now,' said Fin-Kedinn, his voice carrying in the still evening air. 'He wouldn't be such a fool as to stay around here, not with the clan meet coming up.'

The clan meet. Torak had forgotten all about the great gathering of the clans which took place every three summers, and which this summer would be held at the mouth of the Whitewater, not two daywalks from where he hid.

The hunters said their farewells and parted, the Vipers heading south for their camp on the Widewater, the Ravens west.

Don't go, Torak silently begged Fin-Kedinn. He felt hollow as he watched the broad-shouldered figure moving off into the trees with Renn. He watched till his eyes ached.

Long after they'd gone, he remained in the willows, while night deepened around him.

A twig cracked.

He froze.

Another twig. Loud. Deliberate.

'It's me!' whispered Renn. 'Where are you?'

Torak shut his eyes. He couldn't answer her. He'd only put her in danger.

'Torak!' Now she sounded angry as well as scared. 'I *know* you're in there! You left a scrap of chewed bast on the trail. It was all I could do to pick it up before the others spotted it!'

He *hated* staying silent.

'Oh, all right then!' she breathed. 'Maybe this will change your mind!' More rustling. 'I've brought what you'll need for getting rid of the Soul-Eater tattoo. That's why I'm here, to tell you how to do it.' Another pause. 'If you don't come out *right now*, I won't!'

SIX

'What do you think you're *doing*?' whispered Torak as he yanked Renn into the thicket. 'If anyone saw you!'

'They didn't,' she replied with more confidence than she felt. 'I've brought you some food and a sleeping-sack, but I didn't manage to steal an axe, so you'll – '

'Renn. No. You can't get mixed up in this!'

'I already am. Have a salmon cake.'

When he didn't move, she added, 'Well if you don't want it, I'll have to leave it for anyone to find!'

That worked, and he snatched it from her, demolishing it with fierce concentration. As she crouched beside him in the sour-smelling gloom, she wondered when he'd last eaten.

'There's lots more salmon cakes,' she told him. 'And

blood sausage and dried auroch tongue, and a bag of hazelnuts. Should be enough for half a moon, if you're careful.'

She was talking too much, she knew that. But he looked so different. That headband made him seem older, and there was a tautness in his face. He kept glancing about, as if at any moment a hunter might leap from the shadows.

This, she thought, is what it is to be prey.

Out loud, she asked where Wolf was, and Torak told her that he'd gone to lure Aki off the scent. Then he asked how she'd got away from Fin-Kedinn, and she told him about turning back to "check some snares", then picking up the supplies she'd hidden earlier, along with a woodpigeon which she would take to camp as proof of the "snares". She didn't mention the tightness in her chest as she'd deceived Fin-Kedinn, or the pain in his eyes when he'd realized what she was doing.

'He guessed I was here, didn't he?' said Torak. 'What he said about the clan meet. He was warning me.'

'I think so. Maybe.'

She passed him another salmon cake, and ate a couple of hazelnuts to keep him company. Then she said, 'I've been trying to understand how all this happened. Those red deer antlers, with Aki's mark rubbed out. Someone did that. Someone wanted you cast out.'

He glanced at her. 'The Soul-Eaters.'

She nodded. 'They'll have come south by now. And they know you're a spirit walker. They want your power.'

'They want the last piece of the fire-opal, too.'

'Wherever that is.'

In the deep blue night, young owls called to each other as they glided between the trees, and bats flitted over the bracken with a swift, light crackling of wings.

41

Torak wiped his mouth on the back of his hand. 'Renn,' he said. 'I'm sorry.'

'For what?'

'For all this. For not telling you about the mark. If only I'd told you. It just – it never seemed the right time.'

Her throat closed. 'I know how that can be. It's never easy to tell things. Secrets, I mean.'

'Well. I'm sorry.'

They finished eating, then Torak strapped the sleeping-sack to his back and shouldered his quiver and bow, and Renn re-packed the food pouch and placed a morsel of salmon cake in a willow for the clan guardian. As soon as she'd done it, she wished she'd waited till later, so that Torak hadn't seen. He told her he didn't mind, but she could see that he did.

'It's strange,' he said. 'All my life I've been doing that. And I haven't got a guardian.'

'It's still an offering. For the Forest.'

'I suppose.' He paused. 'But how is it possible, Renn? How can I not have a clan?'

'I don't know.'

'I've got a clan-soul, I can tell right from wrong. So how?'

She shook her head. 'Saeunn says no-one's ever been clanless before.'

He looked appalled – and she was furious with herself. Oh, very clever, Renn, that's really made him feel better. 'Anyway,' she went on quickly, 'I don't think I'd want to be part of that Wolf Clan. Those yellow eyes . . . ' She shuddered. 'I asked their Mage how they do it, and she said she puts something in the water. Once she got it wrong, and they turned pink instead.' She chewed her lip. 'I made that bit up. A joke.'

Torak forced a smile. She felt achingly sorry for him.

42

'But if I'm not Wolf Clan,' he said, 'what am I?'

She drew a breath. 'You're Wolf's pack-brother. You're my friend. And *that's* never going to change.'

Torak blinked. He rubbed a hand over his face and shouldered the food pouch, and coughed. 'Fin-Kedinn will be wondering where you are. You said you know how to do the rite?'

'– Yes,' said Renn.

He caught something in her tone. 'Are you sure?'

'Yes,' she repeated. In fact, she'd had to piece it together in snatches gleaned from Saeunn, so she wasn't *entirely* sure. But it wouldn't help Torak to know that.

The rite didn't take long to describe, but when Renn came to the part about cutting out the tattoo, they both felt sick.

'Here,' she said shakily, untying her swansfoot medicine pouch from her belt. 'It's got most of what you'll need.'

Torak took it and stared at it.

'You must wait till the moon is full,' she went on. 'Until then, you'll have to find somewhere safe to hide.'

'*Safe?*'

'Well. Safer. We'd better decide where to meet.'

'What do you mean?'

'At the full moon. For the rite.'

'Oh, no. No.' To her dismay, he wore his stubborn look: the one that reminded her of Wolf refusing to get into a skinboat.

'Torak,' she said, 'You can't do this on your own. I only told you what's involved so that you can prepare yourself, but I'll be there to help.'

'No.'

'Yes.'

'But you hate Magecraft.'

43

'That doesn't matter! At least I know how to do it!'

He stood up. 'Listen, Renn. This isn't like those other times, when you ran off and Fin-Kedinn was angry for a while and then forgave you. This could get you killed.'

'I do know the risks, but – '

'No. Coming here tonight was incredibly brave, but you cannot – you *must not* – do any more!'

Renn stood up. 'What I do or don't do is not for you to decide.' She turned to untangle her bow from a branch. 'And in case you've forgotten, on all those "other times", as you call them, I did actually . . . Torak? Torak!'

But he was gone, melting in the night as soundlessly as a ghost.

SEVEN

The full moon was riding high in the dark-blue sky, but Torak still wasn't ready. He'd put off gathering the rowan boughs for as long as he could, dreading the moment when he would have to begin the rite.

For half a moon he'd lain low, surviving on Renn's supplies and any hares, squirrels and birds he could catch. Day had merged into day: scrabbling for food, hiding in thickets; muttering to himself, just to hear the sound of a voice.

Aki and his dogs hadn't come again. The clans were labouring to get in the last of the salmon, and the Boar Leader worked his son hard.

'Find a place that feels as if it has power,' Renn had said as they'd huddled in the thicket. 'Do it there.'

Torak had found such a place – but it probably wasn't

what she'd had in mind. He stood on the south slope of the steep valley which the clans call the Twin Rivers, where the Axehandle and Green Rivers collide in a thunderous battle to make the Whitewater. A desolate place, perpetually misted in spray, where birch and rowan clung to life amid huge, tumbled boulders.

And dangerously close to people. From here the Whitewater crashed down to the Sea – where, not half a daywalk to the west, the clan meet was gathering. Torak was far too close – but that was the plan. No-one would look for him here. And the rapids would mask his cries if the pain got too bad.

Pushing the thought aside, he cut another rowan bough, and wished for the hundredth time that he had an axe.

Behind him, a branch snapped.

He spun round.

A shadow emerged from the trees.

He stumbled backwards.

The shadow lumbered into him – and elk and boy sprang apart with startled bellows.

'You again!' cried Torak. 'Go *away*! I told you, I'm not your mother!'

The elk put down its head and nuzzled him, and he felt the hot, fuzzy nubs where its antlers would grow. The elk was enormous, but it moved with awkward humility, as if apologizing for being so big. Torak saw the wound on its flank where its mother had kicked it, and felt a twinge of sympathy.

The elk didn't understand why its mother had rejected it. It didn't even know enough to be afraid of Wolf, who only left it alone because the hunting was good. Twice it had blundered into Torak and he'd chased it away. He couldn't kill it because he would take days to make use of the carcass, and he couldn't let it follow him, as then it would never learn to fear hunters. Now it seemed to think they were friends.

'Shoo!' he said, waving his arms.

The elk gazed at him with confused brown eyes.

'Go away!' He punched it on the nose.

The elk swung round and wandered off into the trees – and Torak was alone again. Dread flooded back. Now nothing stood between him and the rite.

The thought of cutting out the tattoo turned him sick with terror. The thought of what he might become if he didn't was worse. Over the past few days, the mark had begun to burn. He could feel it eating into his flesh.

The place he'd chosen was twenty paces above the river: a great, hunched boulder guarded by rowans. Moonlight gleamed faintly on the stone. Torak wished the dark were deeper than this eerie twilight; but in summer the sun never slept for long.

Leaving sleeping-sack, quiver and bow at the foot of the rock, he climbed. Moss crumbled beneath his boots, releasing a whiff of decay. The granite felt cold under his fingers. As he reached the top, the roar of the rapids pounded through him, drowning out the sounds of the Forest. To the west, red knife-pricks of campfires mocked his loneliness.

Wolf returned from the hunt, his muzzle black with blood. Rising effortlessly on his hind legs, he placed his forepaws on the rock, ready to leap up and join Torak.

No, Torak told him in wolf talk. *Stay down.*

Wolf sat on his haunches and gazed at him, puzzled.

Torak forced himself to ignore him. Wolf wouldn't understand what he was about to do, and there was no way of telling him.

For the first time in his life, he was going to do Magecraft. He was going to meddle with the forces that Mages use to see the future, heal the sick and find prey: forces he didn't understand and couldn't control.

'It's a way of getting deeper,' Renn had told him, trying to explain what came as naturally to her as tracking did to him. 'A way of touching the Nanuak itself. But you've got to be careful. It's like dipping your foot in a fast river. If you go too deep, you'll be swept away.'

The Nanuak.

Torak felt it inside him: the raw power which pulses through all living things – river, rock, tree, hunter, prey – which links them with the World Spirit itself.

Wiping the spray from his face, he untied the swansfoot pouch from his belt. The claws felt sharp, the hide scaly. Opening the pouch, he laid out the things Renn had given him.

'There are five kinds of Magecraft,' she had said. 'Sending. Summoning. Cleansing. Binding. Severing. The one for this rite will be cleansing. And – severing.' She'd swallowed. 'You'll need something from each of the four quarters of the clans: Forest, Ice, Mountain, Sea. For the Forest, your mother's medicine horn. Take earthblood from it and mix it with fat – any creature's will do, as long as it's not a water creature – then draw a line round the tattoo. That shows you where to – to cut.' She drew a breath. 'For Ice, the swansfoot pouch. It belonged to the White Fox Mage, so it's full of good power.'

'For the Mountain?' said Torak, feeling cold.

From the pouch she drew a wristband of dried rowan berries threaded on a willowherb cord. 'I met some Rowan Clan, they were going early to the clan meet to get the best camping spot. I swapped this for an arrow.'

'Won't they notice if you're not wearing it?'

'I thought of that, split it in two.' She held up her hand to show an identical band. Then she tied the other one round his wrist. She scowled, but he guessed that, like him, she felt better for sharing this between them.

'When the time comes,' she said, 'you must make a special drink to purify yourself. Root of hedge mustard, ground with alder bark, betony and elder leaves, steeped in strong water. Use Axehandle water, that's important, because it gets its power from the ice river in the Mountains. And leave it to stand in the moonlight for as long as you can.'

He'd prepared the drink at dusk, mixing it in a cup he'd made of squirrel rawhide, and leaving it on the rock to catch the first rays of the moon while he went off to gather rowan branches.

'I don't think there's anything in it that'll cause your souls to walk,' Renn had said, 'but you'd better mark your face with the sign of the hand and pass rowan leaves over yourself. And of course, I'll be with you, in case – anything happens.'

'What do I use for the Sea?'

'Your father's knife. It's Sea slate. And Torak – grind it *sharp*. It'll hurt less.'

In horror, he watched her take out a little horn needle-case, a coil of sinew thread and a slender bone fishing-hook.

'What's the hook for?' he asked.

Renn didn't meet his eyes. 'You mustn't cut too deep, or you'll cut into the muscle.'

Torak put his hand to his chest.

'I'll show you.' With her knife she scratched a cross on the knee of her legging. 'This is the tattoo. You – you cut round it in a sort of – willow-leaf shape. Then you – you hook the skin in the middle and lift.' Beads of sweat stood out on her forehead as she hooked the mark, tenting the buckskin. 'That way you can – c-cut under your skin, and lift off the tattoo. Then press the sides of the wound together and s-stitch it shut.'

They had both been shaking by the time she'd finished.

Spray from the Twin Rivers was icy on Torak's face as he knelt and drank the bitter herb drink. He purified himself with rowan, marked his face with the sign of the hand. Set out the needles and the hook. He felt as if he was going to be sick.

Below him, Wolf leapt to his feet: muzzle lifted, tail raised. He'd caught a scent.

What is it? Torak asked in wolf talk.

Other.

Other what?

Other. Wolf padded in circles, then gazed up at Torak, his eyes an alien silver in the moonlight.

Whatever Wolf meant, Torak couldn't let it distract him. If he didn't start now, he'd never have the courage.

He pulled his jerkin over his head. Spray chilled his skin. His teeth chattered. Shakily, he daubed an earthblood line around the three-pronged fork of the Soul-Eater.

He drew his knife. Fa's knife. The Sea slate felt icy, the hilt heavy and warm.

Wolf gave a low growl.

Torak warned him to stay down – and prepared to make the first cut.

It was nearly dawn, and he lay in the shadow of the rock, shivering uncontrollably in his sleeping-sack. It hurt to breathe. It hurt to *be*. Nothing existed except this blazing pain in his chest.

A sob escaped him. He clenched his teeth. Fa did this too, he told himself. Fa cut out the mark, he got through this. So can you.

The voice of the Twin Rivers boomed in his head, like the throbbing in his chest.

But Fa had his mate to help him. Not like you. You're all alone.

Snarling, he pressed his face into the reindeer hide.

Something tickled his nose. It was one of Renn's long red hairs, left behind in what had been her sleeping-sack. He clutched it in his fist. Not alone, he told himself.

Some time later, he woke to the click of claws on stone. A cold nose nudged his cheek, and Wolf settled against him with a 'humph'!

'Not alone,' whispered Torak, sinking his fingers into his pack-brother's fur. *Don't ever leave me*, he said in wolf talk.

Wolf gave him another nose-nudge and a reassuring lick.

Clutching his scruff, Torak slid into evil dreams.

He dreamt that an elk was attacking Renn. Not the young elk which wanted to make friends with him, but a full-grown male.

Torak tried to move, but the dream dragged at his limbs, and he could only watch as Renn backed against the stump of an oak tree, looking about wildly for something to climb. Nothing: the river behind her, knee-high willows in front.

The elk gave a bellow that shook the earth, then put down its head to charge. One kick from those enormous hooves would brain a boar, or snap a wolf's spine in two. Renn didn't stand a chance.

The elk crashed towards her, and Torak felt the ground tremble; he smelt its musky rage. Suddenly he felt a jolting pain in his belly – a pain that was horribly familiar . . .

. . . and now it was *his* rage which powered the great body forwards, *his* antlers thrusting aside the branches as he thundered towards Renn.

This isn't a dream, he thought. *This is really happening!*

EIGHT

The elk burst from the thicket, and Renn flung herself behind the oak. With terrifying agility the elk spun on one hoof. Renn dodged – and dodged again. The elk gallopped off, then swung round for another attack.

Breathless, sweating, she crouched behind the stump. Nothing climbable within reach – this slope had been cleared for a camp two summers before – and although the river was ten paces away, she'd never make it. Besides, elk can swim.

A root was digging into her knee, and as she shifted position, she nearly fell down a hole. Some kind of burrow. Muttering thanks to her guardian, she hugged her weapons and wriggled in backwards. The elk couldn't reach her down here, the hole was too narrow for those antlers. And elk didn't dig. At least, not normal ones.

But this was nothing like a normal elk.

She'd had no warning, nothing at all. After a sleepless night, she'd crawled blearily from the shelter and set off upriver. If anyone asked, she would tell them she was hunting, but the truth was, she was worried about Torak. She wanted to find some trace of him, even though he was probably long gone.

Then the elk had emerged from the waterlogged thicket.

Renn had been startled, but not alarmed. The elk had probably been browsing on sedge, or diving for water lily roots. She would give it space to show that she wasn't hunting, and it would wander off.

Then everything changed.

Earth trickled onto her face, and she shook it off. Peering up at a grey disc of sky, her hunter's eye spotted a few black and white hairs snagged on the edge. She hoped the badger whose sett she'd invaded was fast asleep and a lot further inside. Caught between a mad elk and an outraged badger. Not much of a choice.

What to do now? Her bow and arrows were mercifully unharmed, her axe still in her hand. She could either wait till help came along, or fight her way out.

Fighting would get her killed. The elk was so tall that she could have run under its belly without ducking, and its antlers were wider than her outstretched arms; one swipe would gut her like a fish. And those hooves . . . Once, she'd seen a cow elk kill a bear with just two kicks: one on the jaw to stun, and then – rearing on its hind legs – both front hooves hammering down to split the skull.

But this elk wasn't a cow protecting her calf. It was a bull; and the rut, when bulls become lethal, was four moons away.

So why had it attacked? Sickness? A wound gone bad? She'd seen no sign of either. Demons? No. It didn't feel like that. And yet – there was something.

More earth trickled onto her face, and she spat out gritty crumbs. With infinite care, she pushed herself up and peered over the edge.

Early sunlight speared the bracken. A breeze woke the willows. The river murmured on its way to the Sea. So peaceful . . .

There. Beside that clump of burdock: the edge of a huge, splayed hoof; a fetlock dark with sweat.

The blood roared in her ears.

The elk lowered its head and its long tongue curled out, moistening its nose to sharpen its sense of smell. Its large ears tilted towards her.

She froze.

It knew she was there. One eye was blind red jelly, punctured by a rival's antler the previous rut. The other was fixed on hers.

She caught her breath. She sensed the spirit behind that stare.

'It can't be,' she whispered.

The elk pawed the burdock.

It's an elk, she told herself. Nothing to do with Torak.

And yet, she knew – with the certainty which came to her at times and which Saeunn called her inner eye – she *knew* that Torak's souls were in that elk. He was spirit walking. He was attacking *her*.

'This can't be,' she whispered again. 'Why would he attack me?'

Feeling dizzy and sick, she gripped the handle of her axe. There was no way out. Whatever happened next, one of them would die.

Wolf stood guard while Tall Tailless huddled in the reindeer pelt, twitching and moaning in his sleep.

The scent of the Otherness which Wolf had caught in the Dark was gone, but he sensed that it hadn't gone far. It was a new smell, but it reminded him of something. Something bad.

Ordinarily he would have raced off to find it, but Tall Tailless had said never to leave him. This puzzled Wolf a lot. He left Tall Tailless all the time. To hunt, to roll in scat, to gobble up delicious rotten carcasses which his pack-brother unaccountably disliked. But it didn't matter how long Wolf was away, because he always came back.

Wolf hated not understanding. But he couldn't get his jaws around the answer.

Then he heard howling.

Wolves. Many lopes off, although he couldn't tell exactly where, because they were howling with their muzzles all pointing different ways. Wolf understood this. It was the time when the Lights get longer, eating up the Darks: the time when wolf cubs are born. This pack had cubs. It didn't want others to find its Den. The pack that Wolf had run with on the Mountain had used the same trick.

Wait! He sprang to his feet. This *was* the Mountain pack! He knew the leader's howl!

Lashing his tail, he howled an answer. *I'm here! Here!* In his head he saw the pack standing close together, muzzles lifted to the Up, eyes slitted in the joy of the howl. He was seized with longing to go to them.

The pack fell silent.

Wolf's tail stilled.

He wished Tall Tailless would wake up. But he went on twitching and moaning in his sleep.

A little later, Wolf heard a frantic yip-and-yowling in tailless talk. It was the pack-sister. He didn't understand what she was saying, but he could hear that she was in trouble.

Wolf pawed Tall Tailless to wake him.

His pack-brother didn't stir.

Wolf snapped at his overpelt and tugged at the long dark fur on his head. When that didn't work, he barked in his ears. That never failed.

It did now.

Wolf's pelt tightened as he realized that what lay here, curled in the reindeer hide, was only the *meat* of Tall Tailless. The bit inside – the breath that walked – was gone.

Wolf knew because it had happened before. Sometimes he would see the walking breath leave his pack-brother's body. It was the same size and shape and smell as Tall Tailless, but Wolf knew not to get too close.

Wolf ran in circles. The scent trail told him that the walking breath of Tall Tailless had gone to find the pack-sister. That was what Wolf must do, too.

He flew through the Forest. He startled a mare and her foals, and nearly trod on a sleeping piglet, annoying its mother, but he was gone before she'd lumbered to her feet. Weaving between the alders at the edge of the Fast Wet, he loped towards the pack-sister's howls. He smelt her fierce resolve. He smelt fresh blood and angry elk.

In mid-yowl, the pack-sister's voice broke off.

Wolf quickened his pace.

Suddenly the wind swung round, carrying a new scent to his nose: the scent of Otherness.

57

Wolf slewed to a halt. The Otherness was heading for Tall Tailless' defenceless body.

Wolf hesitated.

What should he do?

NINE

Torak woke with a struggle, as if fighting his way up from the bottom of a lake. Something had happened in the night – something terrible – but he couldn't remember what.

He was lying in his sleeping-sack with the early sun in his eyes. His mouth tasted as if he'd been eating ash, and the wound in his chest hurt savagely.

Then he saw the strand of dark-red hair in his hand, and everything flooded back. Bracken whipping past his antlers, mud squelching beneath his hooves. Flint flashing, red hair flying. Then – nothing.

What had he done?

In a heartbeat he was out of the sleeping-sack, startling Wolf.

The pack-sister! Torak said in wolf talk. *Is she all right?*

Don't know, came the reply. A lick on the muzzle. *Are you?*

Torak didn't answer. He never spirit walked in his sleep. And it couldn't have been the drink he'd made for the rite, Renn had told him it wouldn't make his souls wander. Besides, he'd daubed the sign of the hand on his cheek, like she'd said. With his fingers he searched his face, but the earthblood was gone. He must have rubbed it off while he slept.

How could this have happened? He glanced at the crusted scab on his chest. The mark was gone – but the power of the Soul-Eaters was great. Maybe while he slept, they had forced him to do this: to attack the person he cared about most.

It took him the whole morning to reach the clearing. He had some idea of where it lay, having noticed the badger sett and the stump on previous hunts; and Wolf helped, too. But when they got there, Torak didn't recognize it. The bracken and willowherb had been flattened as if by a hailstorm, the oak kicked to splinters. Here and there he saw scarlet spatters on green leaves.

The world tilted. He tasted bile. He fought to stay calm, to piece together what had happened.

In the churned mud near the stump he found a print of Renn's boot; a red hair snagged at one of the entrances to the sett. On the riverbank he found drag-marks where canoes had been drawn up. A mess of men's footprints, deeper on their way back to the boats. They'd been carrying something heavy.

Maybe they had arrived in time, killed the elk and taken it with them in the boats.

Maybe it was Renn they'd carried away.

Torak's mind refused to work. His tracker's skill deserted him.

I did this, he thought. There is something inside me that I can't control.

Wolf nudged his thigh, asking when they were going. Torak asked him if he'd tried to help the pack-sister, and Wolf replied that he'd wanted to, but then he'd smelt "Other".

What do you mean? said Torak, but Wolf's answer was unclear. Wolves don't only talk with grunts and whines and howls, but with subtle movements of the body: a tilt of the head, a flick of the ears or tail, the fluffing up or sleeking down of fur. Not even Torak knew every sign. All he could gather was that Wolf had caught a bad scent making for his pack-brother, and raced to his defence, but whatever it was had gone by the time he'd arrived.

Torak stared at the desolation around him. He should get under cover; at any moment a canoe might slide into view. He didn't care. He had to go to the clan meet and find out what had happened to Renn.

Dusk was coming on by the time he reached the river mouth where the clans were gathered. At this time of summer, the night wouldn't get any darker. Which made what he was doing even more dangerous.

Apart from the headband, he hadn't stopped to disguise himself, simply smearing wood-ash on his skin to put off the dogs. For the rest, he would rely on his hunter's ability to stay out of sight, and the fact that he'd persuaded Wolf – with some difficulty – not to come too.

He found a stand of juniper and pine well back from the camp, hid his sleeping-sack in some brambles to retrieve later, and crouched down to plot his next move.

Around the mouth of the Whitewater, fires glowed orange

in the deep blue dusk. Before them, black figures reached stick-limbs towards the sky, like paintings on a rock. So many people! For a moment Torak was small again, just short of his eighth birthnight, and proud to be going with Fa to the clan meet by the Sea.

The Mountain Hare Clan had built their reindeer-hide shelters on the rocks above the shore, perhaps because this reminded them of home. The Rowan Clan's turf domes squatted in the meadows, while the Salmon Clan had pitched their fish-skin tents on the foreshore, and the Sea-eagles, who didn't seem to care, had made their untidy stick piles wherever they'd found space. The Open Forest clans had camped nearest the trees, but Torak couldn't see the Ravens' open-fronted shelters.

'They say the Wolf Clan's headed south,' said a man's voice, startlingly close.

Torak froze.

'Good riddance,' snorted another man. 'I never feel easy with them around.'

A muffled curse as one of them tripped over a root.

'Still, they should've stayed,' said the first man. 'It's a clan meet, that's what it's for.'

'What about the Deep Forest clans?' said his companion. 'No sign of them, either.'

'I hear there's trouble between the Aurochs and the Forest Horses . . .'

Their voices faded as they headed towards the river – and Torak breathed again.

It was some time before he dared move. Keeping to the edge of the Forest, he came to a pine-ringed hollow where a throng of people crowded round a large fire. Smells of baked salmon and roasting meat mingled with the music of voice, pipe and drum.

The fire was made of three pine logs burning along their length. A Raven long-fire. He'd found them.

Dry-mouthed, he hid in a clump of yews beyond the light.

He saw Fin-Kedinn deep in talk with the Salmon Clan Leader as they cut hunks off a glistening side of red deer and filled peoples' bowls.

He saw Saeunn and two other Mages a little way off, by a smaller blaze which gave off a heady scent of juniper. One Mage cast handfuls of bones and watched how they fell, while a second read the smoke snaking into the sky. Saeunn rocked back and forth, spitting spells.

Above Torak's head, a branch creaked – and a raven peered down at him with bright, unforgiving eyes. He begged it not to betray him.

The guardian spread its wings and flew, swooping low over the Mages' fire. Saeunn raised her head to follow it. Then she turned and looked straight at Torak.

She can't see you, he told himself. But in the firelight, the stare of the Raven Mage was red with secret knowledge. Who knew what she could see?

Just when Torak couldn't bear it any longer, Saeunn turned back to her spells.

Shaky with relief, he scanned the firelit faces. He saw the Boar Clan Leader jabbing his finger at the Whale Leader to emphasize a point, Aki sitting nearby, watching his father with an odd mix of fear and longing.

Then Torak saw her.

Renn sat cross-legged at the front of the throng, scowling into the flames. She was pale, and her right forearm was bound in soft buckskin, but apart from that, she appeared unhurt.

The tightness in his chest loosened as if a rawhide strap had snapped.

She's all right.

A dog padded over to him; luckily, one he knew. He shooed it away.

Next time, he might not be so lucky. He had to get away before they found him.

He stayed where he was.

Maybe it was seeing Renn again. Maybe it was the wild hope that with the mark of the Soul-Eater cut out, he could simply step into the light, and everyone would welcome him back.

He stayed.

And that changed everything.

The moon made its way across the sky, and still Torak watched.

He saw men, women and children dipping beakers in pails of brewed birch-blood. He saw them stepping into the space around the long-fire to offer a story, a song.

A Willow man sang of the salmon run to the music of deer-hoof rattles and duck-bone pipes.

A Rowan woman created a prowling shadow bear by moving her hands behind a firelit hide.

So it went on through the brief summer night. Torak found himself drawn into the stories: the ancient memories which the clans had told on nights such as this since the Beginning.

It was a while before he noticed that Renn had gone as white as chalk.

Two masked figures were now dancing round the fire: a midge with a long, pointed wooden beak, and an irascible elk. The midge – with a Viper woman behind the mask –

zoomed about, whining and poking with her beak, to delighted squeals from children and laughter from their parents. But Renn had eyes only for the elk. Her mouth was a tense line as she watched it sweep the shadows with its antlers. Torak could see that she was re-living the attack.

By chance, the elk moved to the other side of the fire, and it was the midge who now targeted her. Distractedly she batted it away, but it came whining back, as midges do.

Leave her alone, urged Torak.

Just as the midge zoomed in for another attack, a young man rose, grasped the midge's beak lightly in one hand, and pretended to swat it with the other. He did it with such good humour that the Viper woman played along with him, buzzing away with an aggrieved whine which made everybody laugh.

Renn threw the young man a grateful glance, and he shrugged and sat down again. Then Torak noticed the wavy blue tattoos on his arms: the mark of the Seal Clan. He nearly cried out.

It was Bale. His kinsman.

Bale had put on muscle since the previous summer, and firelight glinted in the beginnings of a beard, but apart from that he hadn't changed. The same long fair hair beaded with shells and capelin bones, the same intelligent face. The same blue eyes that seemed to hold the light of sun on Sea.

The last time they'd seen each other, they'd talked about hunting together, and Torak had made a joke about a Seal in a Forest. It hurt to think of that now.

Suddenly, a horn boomed into the night.

Ravens exploded from the trees.

Dancers, watchers, all went still.

Leaning on her staff, Saeunn hobbled into the light. 'A Soul-Eater!' she cried. 'A Soul-Eater is come among us!'

Fear rippled through the throng.

'I read it in the bones,' croaked the Raven Mage, circling the fire, searching their faces. 'I see it in the smoke. A Soul-Eater is among us – a Soul-Eater to the marrow!'

People clutched their children and gripped amulets and weapons. Fin-Kedinn's features never moved as he watched his Mage seek the evil one.

As Torak hid in the dark beneath the yews, the meaning of what Saeunn had sensed crashed upon him. A Soul-Eater to the marrow . . .

He had carried the mark on his chest for too long. It had gnawed its way into his bones, and he was one of them. He would never be free.

The rite hadn't worked.

TEN

There was uproar around the long-fire. Dogs barking, a hornet buzz of voices. Mouths turned ugly with fear, eyes became shadowy hollows.

Fin-Kedinn called for calm – and the uproar diminished.

'But we've got to go after him now!' shouted Aki. 'If we don't –'

'If you go now,' said the Raven Leader, 'you'll be setting off blind. Remember, it's not just an outcast out there. What about the Oak Mage? The Viper Mage. The Eagle Owl Mage. Three Soul-Eaters of enormous power – and they could be anywhere. Are you strong enough to fight them alone, Aki? Are any of you?'

Aki made to reply, but his father snarled at him, and Aki cringed as if to ward off a blow.

Torak had seen enough. He fled. What a fool he'd been

to believe they would take him back. They would never take him back.

As he ran, the scab on his chest cracked open. He gasped in pain. *One twitch and it will draw you*, hissed the Viper Mage.

Having retrieved his sleeping-sack, he took a different path to disperse his scent, and now through the trees he glimpsed the Ravens' shelters. They were deserted.

With every moment the danger grew – and yet he couldn't drag himself away. He was leaving them for ever, he knew that now, but he had to be close to them one last time. He had to say goodbye.

He found the Raven Leader's shelter and peered in. There was Fin-Kedinn's axe propped against the doorpost; his bow, his fishing spear. But nothing of Renn's, which was odd.

His axe.

It was beautiful, a blade of polished greenstone mounted on a sturdy ash handle. It fitted Torak's grip perfectly. As his fingers closed around it, he felt the Raven Leader's strength, his force of will. Torak had lost his own axe in the Far North; Fin-Kedinn had been going to help him make a new one. There was much that Fin-Kedinn had been going to teach him.

His grip tightened. To steal a man's axe is one of the worst things you can do. To steal Fin-Kedinnn's . . .

But he needed it.

Scarcely believing what he was doing, he stuck the axe in his belt and moved on, seeking the shelter where Renn slept. It was madness to stay any longer, but he couldn't leave till he'd found it.

He was astonished to discover that she was now sharing a shelter with Saeunn: he recognized it by its stale, old-woman smell. How Renn would hate that.

It hurt to see her gear, piled untidily in the corner. Her beloved bow hung from a cross-beam. As he touched it, he seemed to hear her voice: mocking, kind. The first day they'd met, when the Ravens were enemies and he had to fight for his life, she had given him a beaker of elderberry juice. *'It's only fair,'* she'd said.

On her willow-branch mat lay a new medicine pouch he hadn't seen before; she must have made it when she'd given him hers. He upended it, and among the dried mushrooms and tangles of hair, he was surprised to see the white pebble on which he'd daubed his clan-tattoo last summer. She had kept it all this time.

His hand closed over it. This would tell her better than anything that he was never coming back.

He ran fast and low, heading upstream, keeping to the thickets by the river. He hadn't gone far when he heard slight, furtive sounds of pursuit.

It couldn't be Aki, he would've made more noise. And whoever it was, they were good, moving almost noiselessly, and staying in the shadows.

They were good, but he was better.

The river flowed deep and slow between half-drowned alders. Torak took off his boots and tied them round his neck. Then, balancing quiver, bow and sleeping-sack roll on his head, he waded in. The cold took his breath away, but he gritted his teeth and kept going till he was up to his chest.

Bracing his legs against the current, he waited. He heard the slap and suck of water around the trees. Then stealthy footsteps.

From the bank, someone softly called his name.

He tensed.

'Torak!' Renn whispered again. 'Where are you?'

He made no answer.

Then another voice. 'Kinsman, it's me!'

Torak flinched.

'We're alone, I swear it!' Bale said in a hoarse whisper. 'Come out! I mean you no harm! Renn's told me everything. I know you're outcast, but we're still kin! I want to help!'

Torak clenched his jaw. Renn had already risked her life to help him, and it had come to nothing. He couldn't put her or Bale in any more danger.

Like all hunters, Renn and Bale knew how to wait. So did Torak.

At last, he heard Bale sigh. 'Let's go,' he told Renn.

'No!' she protested. Torak heard a stirring of branches as she moved closer – and suddenly there she was at the water's edge.

'Torak!' Her voice was recklessly loud. 'I know you're there, I can feel you listening! Please. *Please*! You've got to let us help you!'

Not answering Bale had been hard, but ignoring Renn was one of the hardest things Torak had ever done. The urge to cry out – to give some sign that only she would understand – was almost overwhelming. Go back to camp, he begged her. I can't bear it.

Bale put his hand on Renn's shoulder. 'Come on. Either he's not here, or he doesn't want to be found.'

Angrily, she shook him off. But when he started for camp, she followed.

Torak waited till he was sure they were gone, then waded back to dry ground. Frozen, numb, he pulled on his boots. The scab on his chest was open, he felt warmth seeping out. Good. Let it bleed.

He followed the river upstream, running punishingly fast so that he wouldn't have to think, but at last he had to stop. He slumped against a whitebeam tree at the edge of a clearing. It would be dawn soon. Far in the distance, he heard dogs.

He found that he was still clutching the pebble he'd taken from Renn's medicine pouch. He stared at the dotted lines which he'd used to think were his clan-tattoo, but were now meaningless smudges.

That's the old Torak, he thought.

He realized that for the past half-moon, he'd merely been playing at being outcast, finding any excuse to stay near the Ravens. He'd been like that young elk, bleating for its mother. If it didn't learn to survive on its own, it would get killed. He wasn't going to make the same mistake.

His fist closed over the pebble. Leave it. Leave it all behind.

He tucked the pebble in a cleft of the whitebeam tree and ran.

丰丰

Mist beaded the bracken and lent the leaves of the whitebeam a frosty glitter. Torak's pebble nestled safe in its smooth brown arms.

A roe buck entered the clearing and began to browse. A robin started to sing. A blackbird awoke. The rising sun burned off the mist.

Suddenly the buck jerked up its head and fled. Robin and blackbird flew off with shrill calls of alarm.

A shadow fell across the whitebeam.

The Forest held its breath.

A green hand reached out and took the pebble from the tree.

ELEVEN

'He's here,' said Aki. 'I can feel it.'

'Well I can't,' panted the Willow girl, battling the current to keep abreast of him. 'Won't he have headed south instead of east? That's where he came from.'

'Which is why the others have gone south to cut him off,' growled Aki.

'We're too far upstream,' Raut said uneasily. 'We should go back.'

'No,' snapped Aki.

'Then let's put in for a rest,' protested another boy. 'If I paddle much longer, my arms will fall off!'

'Me too,' puffed the girl. 'There was an inlet back there. Let's go.'

A murmur of assent – to which Aki grudgingly agreed – and they brought their dugouts about.

Perched in a willow, Torak breathed out. When he was sure it wasn't a bluff, he slipped into the water and waded for the bank.

Wolf was waiting. He watched with interest as Torak stuffed his boots with grass to warm up his feet; then they headed upstream.

All day the hunters had tracked them: east of Twin Rivers and up the Axehandle. Whenever Torak tried heading south, the second group of hunters drove him back. It was only by staying in the thickets near the river that he'd kept them off the scent.

He was cold, wet, and he hadn't slept since the night before last. He was beginning to miss things. A while back, he'd almost tripped over a boar enjoying a wallow. Why hadn't he seen its tracks? A child of five summers would have spotted them.

Because of Aki, he'd given up all thought of going south. His only hope was to cross the Axehandle and make for the gullies leading off it to the north. It was rough country without much prey, and few people ventured in except for the odd lonely wanderer. That was the point.

The river turned angrier, and he caught the distant roar of rapids. Around mid-morning, Wolf tensed. Then Torak heard it too: paddles slicing the water; dogs panting, keeping level with the dugouts. Aki and his friends hadn't rested for long.

Torak made his way across the willow bog, squelching through hare-grass, avoiding the pale-green moss which was so delicate that a footprint would remain stamped on it for days. Wolf managed better, his big, slightly webbed paws letting him run lightly over the surface.

To his dismay, Torak saw that his pursuers weren't continuing upriver, but crossing it, as if they'd guessed his plan. In their dugouts they made it with ease. He watched them hoist the boats on their shoulders and climb the bank. They meant to carry them round the rapids and lie in wait for him above.

He had no choice but to go on.

The river turned rougher, crashing over rocks and soaking him in spray. As he clambered past the rapids, he watched for his pursuers on the other side. From memory, he guessed he was nearing the place where – on the opposite bank – two gullies led off from the Axehandle valley. The autumn before last, he and Renn had found a fallen oak and used it to get across. Maybe . . .

The oak was gone, washed away by floods.

For a moment, Torak didn't know what to do. His head felt tight. A buzzing in his ears made it hard to think. There had to be some way of crossing.

There was. Ahead, the valley narrowed, drowned thickets giving way to boulders and straggling trees. A pine had fallen and now spanned the river, ten paces above it. As a walkway, it wasn't promising: the bark was slimy, branches stuck out, and when Torak put his hand on the trunk, it wobbled.

Good enough, he told himself.

Part of him knew this was a mistake – but strangely, he kept going.

Wolf raced lightly along the trunk, leaping the branches. When he reached the other side, he turned to Torak, wagging his tail. *Easy!*

No it's not, Torak wanted to say. Not on your hands and knees in slippery wet buckskin, with a sleeping-sack, bow and quiver on your back – and no claws.

He was nearly across when he heard voices. He glanced down – and nearly fell off in alarm.

Blue water and white foam swirled around moss-green boulders. On one, directly beneath him, stood Aki and Raut.

Torak held his breath. If one of them looked up . . .

'I've had enough,' said Raut. 'I'm going back.'

'Well I'm not!' snarled Aki.

Torak tried to move forwards, but Renn's rowanberry wristband snagged on a branch. He tried to unsnag it. The tree shook.

'The others have gone back,' said Raut, 'and so should we. We're out of our range.'

Again Torak tugged the wristband. It snapped. Rowanberries bounced onto the rocks.

Luckily, Aki was too incensed to notice. 'If you go now, you'll be going on foot! I'm keeping the boat!'

'You do that!' retorted Raut. Then more quietly, 'Aki, this isn't right! Why do you hate him so much?

'I don't,' snapped Aki.

'Then why all this?'

'I said I'd get him! I told Fa. I can't go back if I fail.'

'Well you'll have to do it without me. We'll split the provisions, then you're on your own!'

Weak with relief, Torak watched them head off downstream.

He'd just begun to move when Aki's voice rang out. 'I know you're out there, Soul-Eater! I'll find you, I swear it on my souls! I'll find you and I'll hunt you down!'

Wolf was waiting for him on the other side, but Torak barely greeted him. Huddled in his wet clothes, he thought about Aki's threat. Such determination.

He glanced at Wolf. Every moment they spent together put him at risk. Clan law forbids the killing of a hunter, *except* in self-defence. What if it came to a fight and Wolf tried to defend his pack-brother and Aki shot him?

A moment of pure panic. He couldn't be without Wolf.

It's the only way, he told himself. *And it isn't for ever.*

Split up, Torak told his pack-brother in wolf talk.

Wolf threw him a puzzled glance.

Impossible to get across that this wasn't for good, but only while Aki was close. With an effort, Torak hardened his heart and repeated the command. *Split up!*

Wolf looked offended. Then he shook himself and trotted off into the bracken.

Torak hadn't heard Aki or his dogs for a while, or seen any sign of Wolf.

The buzzing in his ears came and went, and the wound in his chest throbbed. Belatedly, he'd smeared it with chewed willow bast, but it refused to heal. The pain was a constant reminder that it wasn't only Aki who hunted him. The Soul-Eaters had hooked him with an unseen harpoon, and were drawing him in.

The ground became stonier. From where he stood, the riverbank dropped steeply to the Axehandle. He'd passed the rapids some time ago, but their thunder still filled his ears.

Leaning against a birch tree, he gulped the last of Renn's blood sausage. He didn't bother with an offering; he needed it all for himself.

He was thirsty, but it was a tough climb down to the river, so instead he slashed the birch trunk and drank. He left the bark oozing tree-blood and stumbled on. He knew that was wrong, but he did it anyway. Something was getting between him and the Forest. He was too tired to fight it.

Below him the river ran swift and deep. Should he stay this close, or get under cover? He decided to stay close.

Wrong choice. The boulders were treacherous with moss and he fell, bumping and rolling down the slope.

He ended up sprawled on a rock by the water's edge. The trees grew sparsely here, and as he struggled to his feet he got a clear view downstream – and saw a dugout nosing round the bend.

Aki saw him, and yelled in triumph.

Desperately, Torak looked about. No time to climb the slope. Up ahead, a rockfall blocked his way. He was trapped.

And Aki had a quiverful of arrows.

TWELVE

Torak threw off his gear and jumped in the river.

The cold was a punch in the chest, and the current tugged off his boots and blinded him with his hair. Spluttering, he surfaced among willows. He clung to one. It didn't give much cover. He took a deep breath and pulled himself under.

The river was murky, eager to carry him to Aki. His numb fingers lost their grip, and as the current spun him, he caught a flash of the log he was about to crash into.

He tried to dive, couldn't get deep enough, took a blow on the temple. Kicking water, he burst free – to a blaze of sunlight and a fishing spear aimed at his chest. It wasn't a log he'd crashed into, it was Aki's dugout.

Frantically, Torak twisted, then dived under the boat. He bobbed up on the other side. Aki was waiting. Again the spear jabbed. Again Torak dived beneath the boat.

His legs were stone, his chest bursting. An image flared in his mind of the elder-branch pipe he'd used for tapping birch-blood. Should've kept it, should've thought . . .

Once more he surfaced – but this time as Aki lunged, Torak grabbed the spear-shaft and yanked with all his might. Aki howled and pitched over the side.

Locked together, they fought, each battling to wrench the spear from the other. Aki jerked the shaft beneath Torak's chin and slammed him against the boat. Choking, Torak drove his knee into Aki's groin. Aki roared and let go of the spear. Torak went for it, but the river carried it away.

That lunge nearly cost him his life. As he reached for the spear, Aki seized his hair and pushed him under. Flailing, Torak clutched Aki's jerkin, leggings – anything. Couldn't catch hold of the slippery buckskin, couldn't claw loose from the grip on his hair. His sight darkened, his mouth gaped to scream – and the river took the bubbles of his breath. In the last moment he twisted round and sank his teeth into Aki's thigh.

A muffled bellow, and Aki released him. Torak exploded from the water, gulping air like a landed salmon.

Forcing himself under again, he surfaced in a clump of alders, upstream of the dugout. Aki was downstream, his bristly scalp just visible as he clung to a tree and fought for breath. The boat was between them, wedged among willows. That gave Torak an idea.

Sinking beneath the surface, he let the river carry him, emerging without a ripple closer to the dugout, but still upstream. He heard Aki's laboured breathing on the other side of the boat, but couldn't see him. The Boar Clan boy sounded spent, and Torak hesitated. Then a hardness like a splinter of bone seemed to enter his heart.

Bracing his shoulders against a willow, he kicked the dugout with both feet. It bucked like a forest horse. He kicked again – it jolted loose – and the river took hold.

The moment before the dugout struck Aki, Torak grabbed a tree and pulled himself high enough to see. He saw the boy's head jerk up, his eyes widen in fear. He saw the heavy oak smack into him and bear him down, down towards the rapids. Aki didn't even have time to scream.

Grimly, Torak clung to the tree. The lapping water was gentle. From downstream came no sound except the roar of the rapids.

Torak turned and swam upriver to where he'd left his gear. He hauled himself out and collapsed. The muddy taste of the river was in his mouth, the sour smell of moss in his nostrils. The wound in his chest ached.

Retrieving his things, he spotted a way up the rocks which he hadn't noticed before, and started to climb. Granite scratched his bare feet, and he remembered that the river had taken his boots. He shrugged.

When he reached the top, he retraced his steps till the rapids were in sight. To make sure.

The dugout had slammed into a boulder above them. Between boulder and boat, Torak glimpsed a hand. It wasn't moving. Maybe Aki was unconscious and drowning. Maybe he was already dead. Torak couldn't bring himself to care.

Drawing his knife, he cut a switch from an elder tree and trimmed it to make a breathing tube. Then he jammed it in his belt and started upstream, leaving Aki to his fate.

There was something wrong with Tall Tailless.

Wolf had sensed this in his pack-brother for a while. Tall

Tailless no longer listened to Wolf, or even to the Forest, and he was beginning to do bad things.

It was getting worse. A badness was gnawing him on the inside, like the badness that had gnawed the tip of Wolf's tail in the Great Cold.

Anxiously, Wolf followed his pack-brother, staying out of sight because Tall Tailless had told him to go away, but watching nevertheless.

Wolf kept level with him now as they followed the Fast Wet towards the Mountains. As he wove between the trees, Wolf smelt otter and beaver, and a whiff of the Otherness which hid its true scent. He didn't know what to do about that, so he chewed a juniper branch, that made him feel better.

Suddenly, he smelt wolf.

The scent drove all else from his mind. Yes, fresh wolf scat, and the strong, sweet scent-markings of the lead wolf.

His heart gave a bound. He *knew* this scent! The Mountain pack!

Wild with joy, Wolf gave two short barks: *Where are you?*

The wind carried an answering howl – and Wolf flew towards it. Now he could be among wolves again, *and* help Tall Tailless! This was what Tall Tailless needed: to be among his own kind, to be among wolves!

It didn't take long to find them, because they'd paused to wash the blood from their muzzles at a little Fast Wet. As Wolf sped towards them, he took in everything in a snap. The hunt had been good: he smelt deer blood on their fur, saw their bellies sagging with meat they were carrying back to the Den.

The lead pair were the same, but there had been changes, as there always are in a wolf pack. The old wolf was gone, and the one who loved digging for mice was lame and had become underwolf, while the cubs who'd played with Wolf on the Mountain were young full-growns like himself, although smaller.

One of these was a beautiful, dark-furred female who'd been extremely good at hunt-the-lemming. She caught Wolf's scent and gave an excited twitch of her tail – but she didn't come to greet him, because it was up to the leaders to decide if he was allowed back.

Skittering to a halt, Wolf approached the lead male in the proper way for a young full-grown to greet his elder. Sleeking back his ears, Wolf belly-crawled towards him, apologizing for being gone so long.

The leader looked proudly away. With fearsome speed, he grabbed Wolf's muzzle in his jaws, threw him onto his back, and stood over him, growling.

Wolf thumped his tail and whined.

The pack watched.

The leader released Wolf and raised his head, narrowing his eyes. Wolf took the hint and licked the leader's muzzle, whining respectfully and waggling his hindquarters to thank him for being allowed back.

Now the lead female shouldered her mate aside to get her share of the greeting, and after that, everyone followed in a frenzy of nibble-greeting and rubbing of flanks.

Darkfur playfully pawed Wolf's shoulder, but was body-slammed away by a male with a black ear: the leader of the young full-growns. Blackear tried to muzzle-grab Wolf, but Wolf wriggled out of Blackear's grip, muzzle-grabbed him back and flipped him onto his flank, straddling him and growling till Blackear thumped his tail in apology. Wolf released him and licked his nose to show that this was accepted. *So. Now I am above you in the pack.* And that was decided.

At the same time, Wolf was breathing in the wonderful, sweet smell of cubs on everyone's fur. The fierce love of wolf cubs flared in his chest. Oh, to race to the Den and meet them! To snuffle them and let them clamber over him!

Why did you leave? Darkfur asked with a glance and a twitch of her tail.

Why did you leave the Mountain? Wolf replied.

The others crowded round, and he got as many answers as there were wolves. *Thunderer. Great Soft Cold. Cubs. Ancient Den. Big Wet. Wrong Smell. Needed. Sent . . .*

Suddenly, the lead female raised her muzzle and tasted the air. Then she flicked an ear at Wolf. *You hunt with us now.*

Wolf wagged his tail. *I bring my pack-brother.*

A ripple of tension ran through her. *You are of this pack. No other.*

Anxiously, Wolf dipped his head. *He is my pack-brother. He is – he has no tail. He runs on hind legs.*

The lead male gave an irritable twitch. *He is not-wolf!*

Wolf whined and dropped his ears to show – as politely as he could – that this wasn't so.

A glance passed between the lead pair. Darkfur threw Wolf a puzzled look.

The lead male moved off, then turned his grizzled head. *A wolf cannot be of two packs.*

Wolf's tail drooped.

The Up darkened, and the Wet began to fall.

Wolf stood in the Wet and watched the Mountain pack trotting away into the trees.

THIRTEEN

It was raining, and Torak was chilled to the bone, but he was too scared to wake up a fire. The rockfall had crushed his shelter. He'd only just escaped.

For half a moon he'd survived in the gulley off the Axehandle. At least, he *thought* it was half a moon, although he was losing track of time, as he was losing his skill at tracking prey. When Wolf was with him, things were better; but then he would start worrying that Wolf was in danger, and send him away again – and things would turn bad.

Now the rocks had forced him from the gully. Or maybe it was the Hidden People. They were everywhere: in tree and rock and stream. Maybe they were watching him right now.

Shouldering his bow, he headed off. 'Step by step,' he muttered, 'that's the way.'

He twitched. Fin-Kedinn had told him that. But Fin-Kedinn had cast him out. Thinking of him hurt.

It hurt to think about Renn, too. She had Bale now. He'd seen that. She didn't need him any more.

At the Axehandle he stooped to drink, and his name-soul stared back. He recoiled. He looked like the Walker. Filthy. Mad. Was that how he was going to end up?

He stumbled upriver, talking to himself, fingering the wound on his chest. He'd yanked out the stitches, but it still refused to heal.

He walked for a long time, till he reached the very edge of the Forest. He found himself on a hillside, with the east wind cold on his face, like icy breath. Before him, stretching all the way to the High Mountains, lay a vast inland sea: an endless expanse of misty, shimmering grey. Lake, mist, rain. He couldn't tell where one ended and the other began. The world had turned to water.

Lake Axehead, he thought muzzily. This must be Lake Axehead.

A strange, shivering cry split the air.

Torak gave a start.

The cry fell away. Its echo lingered in his mind.

'Lake Axehead is – different,' Renn had told him once. 'So are the Otters.' Torak had seen some at last winter's feast, but he didn't know what kind of people they were; except that the Walker had been Otter Clan, and they'd cast him out.

Below him, the Axehandle seeped from the Lake through a marshy bed of reeds. To the south, needle-pricks of watery green light glimmered in the haze. That must be the Otters' camp. He remembered hearing that they only camped on the south shore. He didn't know why.

Better avoid the south shore, then, and keep to the north.

Wolf appeared and gave him a subdued greeting, rubbing his wet flank against Torak's thigh. Together they descended the slope.

The ground turned boggy. They leapt from tussock to tussock, sending up silver darts of water. The reeds – which had appeared knee-high – now loomed taller than the tallest man.

Torak hated them. He hated the murky, rotten-smelling water lapping their stems; their menacing, knife-sharp leaves; their bent brown heads that slyly watched him pass.

He came to a tussock like a hunched man about to rise. Beyond it, a walkway disappeared into the reeds. It was only logs lashed together with wovenbark rope, but Torak felt its power, and caught a faint hum at the edge of hearing.

Nothing would make him go in there.

With the reed-bed on his right, he squelched north. To his relief, Wolf found firmer ground: an elk trail skirting the shore. But shortly afterwards, the mist closed in, and his spirits sank.

Wolf, too, seemed cowed as he padded forwards. Then the mist swallowed him, leaving Torak on his own. He didn't dare howl. He dreaded to think what might answer. Putting out his hands, he groped forwards.

Suddenly, Wolf hurtled towards him, eyes bulging with terror. He sped past Torak and vanished the way they'd come. At the same moment, Torak's fingers sank into a clammy, stinking softness. With a gasp he sprang back. Something red flapped wetly in his face. He tore it off. The mist thinned. His heart jerked. The trail was barred:

strung across with a nightmare tangle of fleshy, glistening coils. He breathed the stench of blood, saw plump, wriggling maggots. He'd stumbled into a web. A web of entrails.

Whimpering, he fled, rubbing his face where the web had touched it. Splashing back into the marsh, he sank to his knees, and the reeds rippled with laughter.

He was back at the walkway.

'No,' he whispered. 'Not in there.'

He ran south. The marshy Axehandle was easily crossed, and Wolf joined him, his big paws scarcely sinking.

They hadn't gone far when they heard voices, saw lights bobbing up and down. Otter Clan hunters.

Then there they were: small, lithe people with spears and fierce green faces, paddling swift craft of yellow reeds.

'There!' shouted one. 'Near the reeds!'

Reeds to his left. To his right, a hillside of crowberry scrub, giving no cover. He barked a command to Wolf to split up – Wolf obeyed – Torak waded into the reeds.

Grimacing as his feet sank into slime, he forced himself deeper, up to his neck. They wouldn't find him here.

The mist parted, and ahead there were no more reeds. He'd reached open water.

He spotted a floating beech bough, probably ripped off in a storm. He ducked behind it.

Something slithered over his foot. He cried out.

More shouts from the Otters – they'd heard him. Now they were coming through the mist: three reed boats curved at prow and stern, like water birds. Two hunters in each, one with a paddle, the other a rushlight and a greenstone fishing spear.

Dipping behind the branch, Torak peered through the leaves.

Somewhere behind him rose the eerie, shivering cry he'd heard before.

The Otters froze. Then the woman in the middle boat dug in her paddle and slid forwards, coming to a smooth halt not two paces from Torak's branch.

He didn't dare duck, in case the movement caught her eye.

As she steadied the craft, her companion scanned the reeds, unaware that the quarry lay under his nose.

Like his mate, he wore a sleeveless tunic of golden wovengrass. His long brown hair flowed free, except for a band of silver fish skin at his brow, and another that braided his beard into a fish tail. His earlobes were pierced by bone fish-hooks, carved to look like leaping trout, and from one hung a tuft of dark-brown otter fur. The man's face was covered in green clay – Torak saw the fine cracks around his eyes and mouth – and his clan-tattoos were blue-green waves undulating up his throat, so that his head resembled an outlandish pod emerging from reeds.

A pod with eyes. Restless with waterlight, they flickered past Torak's branch – then returned for another look.

In the distance, a wolf howled.

The Otter man hissed, and his mate touched her clan-creature fur.

More howls. Torak knew it was Wolf, but he couldn't understand what he was saying. He could only hear the urgency.

The howling unnerved the Otters. The woman steered her craft away from the branch, and Torak sent Wolf silent thanks.

There was a splash behind him, and he turned to see a large grey bird staring at him with a vivid scarlet eye. It flew off, swooping over the Otters.

The woman followed its flight, and nodded as if it had spoken. Raising her hand, she made an undulating signal to her companions in the other boats, and Torak saw them spreading out.

If he left the shelter of the branch, they would see him. If he stayed, they would surround him.

Unless . . .

He still had that elder-stem pipe. It was less than a forearm long, and he couldn't remember checking if it was hollow all the way through. He'd soon find out.

Taking one end between his lips, he sank.

Water filled his nostrils, but he forced himself to breathe through his mouth, praying they wouldn't hear him. Slowly he swam sideways into the reeds, hoping to slip past their cordon.

Staying at the right depth was harder than he'd expected. His gear weighed him down, and to keep the stem upright, he had to tread water and tilt his head back. With aching neck, he stared through a forest of reeds. Above him the skin of the Lake was bright and hard as ice, flecked with drifting constellations of dust.

He heard the nibbles of feeding fish, caught a red flash as a shoal of char sped past. Glancing down, he saw that the bottom of the Lake was within reach. Bars of light slid over boulders and tree-trunks furred with weeds. His feet sank into mud which eddied like green smoke. His free hand touched a lattice of reeds which sagged, then sprang back.

It wasn't reeds, it was a net, a wovenbark net, hanging from wooden floats and weighted with stones: too tough to cut, and so big that he couldn't see the ends.

Whipping round, he glimpsed another. The Otters were surrounding him.

He threw away the elder stem and dived.

Shouts above: they'd spotted him.

He swam deeper, under the nets, dreading the stab of a fishing spear between his shoulder blades.

Lights flashed in his head, and the shouts faded to a dull boom as he swam down.

Suddenly he became aware of a distant shrilling. Faster than thought it sped towards him, louder and louder, a needle of ice piercing his mind.

A dizzying trail of bubbles swept past him. Then another criss-crossed the first, and another. He caught a flicker of fins, a ripple of watery laughter. Dread seized him. He'd heard it before, when he'd been swept over the Thunder Falls. The Hidden People of the Lake had come for him.

They swarmed around him, boneless fingers trailing over his eyes and mouth. *You are for us,* they gurgled, *boy with the drifting souls! Give us the silver bubbles of your breath, and we will draw you into the deep!*

His chest was caught in a rib-crushing grip. Darkness bled across his sight. Wriggling like an eel, he shrugged off his sleeping-sack, and the Hidden People whirled it away.

His bow went next, but his quiver-strap snagged in his belt. He drew his knife and cut it; felt the tug of hands dragging it into the murk. Grabbing his chance, he kicked for the glimmer of the world above.

Heedless of spears and hunters, he burst from the surface.

The reeds were all around him; silent and still. Then he recognized the humped tussock. He was back at the walkway. Narrow as a hand, it beckoned him into the dripping green tunnel.

In the distance, he heard voices. Hushed, frightened.

'Arrin found a bow,' said a man. 'A little west of south.'

'The Hidden Ones have taken him,' said a woman.

'Or the Lake,' put in another man, older than the first.

'Quiet, they'll hear!' said the younger man. 'Let's go, or they'll take us too!'

'If we go now,' said the woman, 'we go empty-handed. The bow of a drowned outcast isn't what Ananda sent us to fetch.'

'If Ananda wants healing water,' growled the older man, 'she can fetch it herself. I'm not going near that spring now.'

Their voices became less distinct as they paddled away. ' . . . keep watch here, in case he tries to come south . . . '

Wretchedly, Torak hauled himself onto firmer ground and stared at the walkway. To the south were the Otters. To the north that terrible, stinking web. He had no choice.

Wolf emerged from the mist and stood beside him. He didn't seem frightened – but then, it was getting harder to read his moods.

Torak knew now that it was to this place that he'd been driven ever since he'd been cast out. East, always east – till he'd ended up here.

The wound in his chest throbbed. Through the hissing of the reeds, he seemed to hear the voice of Seshru the Viper Mage. ' . . . *like the harpoon head beneath the skin of the seal. One twitch and it will draw you, no matter how hard you struggle . . .* '

He no longer had the will to resist. He stumbled past Wolf and onto the walkway.

High above the north shore of the Lake, on a stony headland which rose clear of the mist, a stream bubbled.

Beside the stream burned a ring of green fire.

Within the ring of fire lay a pebble marked with the tattoo of the Wolf Clan.

Upon the pebble lay the shrivelled scrap of Torak's skin which bore the mark of the Soul-Eater.

Around pebble and skin wound the coils of a green clay serpent.

Slowly, the clay dried. Inexorably, the serpent tightened its grip upon skin and stone.

A green hand passed over the pebble: once, twice, three times.

A voice began to murmur, mingling with the hissing of the flames, like a demon slipping in and out of evil dreams.

When reed quakes, when storm breaks, remember me
When thunder growls, when wind howls, remember me
I am the reed and the storm, the thunder and the wind
I summon you, I bind your souls to mine
You can never be free
You belong to me

FOURTEEN

The walkway lurched, nearly tipping Torak into the
Lake. He dropped to all fours and clung on with both
hands.

Behind him Wolf stood, his claws digging into the
wood. He hated this.

There was no room for Torak to turn, so he cast an
encouraging glance over his shoulder. Wolf dropped his
ears and gave an unhappy twitch of his tail.

The walkway stopped rocking, and Torak rose. The logs
were treacherous, the reeds so thick he had to push them
aside. He shrank from the touch of their long, clammy
fingers.

The mist closed in. The walkway dwindled to a line of
single logs lashed end to end, secured by posts sunk in the
reedbed. There were so many turns that Torak lost his

bearings. He didn't know if he was heading out into the Lake, or skirting the shore.

At times, sour brown water slopped over his feet. At others, he found himself crossing a stinking swamp. And the reeds kept changing: from ashen spears with feathery purple plumes, to creaking canes with brown club heads that tapped him furtively on the shoulder. They didn't want him here. If he fell in, they would hold him under till he drowned, or the Hidden People dragged him into the slime.

He'd seen it happen. Once, he and Fa had found a red deer stag trapped up to its neck in a swamp. It was half dead of exhaustion, but they couldn't end its misery. It's bad luck to interfere with those the Hidden People have claimed. Instead, Fa had knelt and stroked its cheek, murmuring a prayer to help it on its way. Afterwards, Torak had been haunted by the look in those dull brown eyes. He'd wondered how long the stag had taken to die.

Wolf's warning 'uff' dragged him back to the present.

Ahead, something crouched on the walkway.

Torak's hand went to his shoulder – but of course he had no clan-creature skin. Nothing to protect him from demon or tokoroth.

As he drew nearer, he saw that it wasn't a creature but a post, planted by the walkway and rising to chest height. It had been limed a sickly grey, and painted with a dizzying fish-bone pattern of tiny green dots. It was topped by a small, misshapen head of green clay into which were pressed two white snail-shell eyes.

The shimmering dots made Torak giddy, but he couldn't look away. The power of the thing filled his mind, like the silent boom after thunder.

Wolf felt it too, and set back his ears. Even the reeds leaned away, fearing to touch.

Torak remembered that he still had Renn's swansfoot pouch, with his medicine horn inside, and the strand of her hair. What would she have done?

The mark of the hand. Maybe that would help.

The ochre in the horn was clogged with damp, and he had to spit in it to make it runny; nothing would have made him use Lake water. Pouring the red liquid into his palm, he daubed the mark on his cheek. He tried to do the same for Wolf – on his forehead, so he couldn't lick it off – but only managed a crude smear. As he finished, the humming in his head grew worse. Someone didn't like him using earthblood.

Holding his breath, he edged past the post. Wolf followed, hackles raised. As they passed it, the reeds stirred angrily, and the humming grew stronger.

Torak reached a turn in the walkway – and there, guarded by club-headed reeds, stood *three* posts, their white eyes staring from mouthless faces of green clay.

Something slithered across his cheek. He dashed it away, and the walkway rocked wildly. Too late, he saw that its far end had been untied and was floating free. He lurched – righted himself – and backed into Wolf, who yelped and nearly fell in.

Trembling, they stood together, while around them the reeds rustled.

'What do you want?' cried Torak.

The reeds fell silent. That was worse. He shouldn't have shouted.

He made to go on – and caught his breath.

The posts were gone.

The reeds were different, too. Those surrounding the posts had had brown club heads, but these were a feathery purple.

With a shiver, Torak realized what this meant. It wasn't the posts which had moved, it was the walkway. While he'd been fighting for balance, someone had rearranged the logs.

For the first time since entering the reed-bed, it occurred to him to turn back. But he couldn't, and that frightened him more than anything. His thoughts were no longer his own. The mist had seeped inside his head. Here, in this nebulous half-world which was neither land nor lake, he was losing his very self.

Wolf nose-nudged his thigh and gave an anxious whine. Torak glanced down – and frowned. Wolf was trying to tell him something, but he couldn't understand. He, Torak, who had learned wolf talk as a baby – *he couldn't understand*.

He stumbled on, with Wolf padding after him.

They hadn't gone far when the walkway forked. Both ways were marked by a post. The left-hand post had been beheaded; the right-hand one bore a green clay head, but the eyes had been plucked out, leaving blind hollows. Tied around the brow was a viper's shed skin. Skewered to it by a bone needle was a tiny, shrivelled heart.

Seshru the Viper Mage.

Torak wiped icy sweat from his face.

Behind him he caught a flash of movement vanishing into the reeds. There, among the leaves. White eyes.

'Who's there?' he said.

The eyes blinked – then reappeared on the other side of the walkway: blue-white, flickering like flame.

'Who's there?' Torak whispered.

Eyes glowed all around him. The humming rose to an ear-splitting whine.

Whimpering, Torak ran for the nearest walkway, the one with the viper skin. The log shuddered – tipped – and threw him off. The murky waters of the Lake closed over his head.

Down he went, groping for reeds, walkway, anything. Couldn't find it, couldn't tell up from down.

A splash and a flurry of bubbles as Wolf leapt in after him. Desperately Torak swam for the flailing paws – but Wolf had disappeared.

Wolf! he screamed in his mind. But his pack-brother was gone.

Frantically, he swam through a slippery mass of reeds.

Suddenly there were no more reeds and the water was freezing and he was swimming over bottomless dark.

FIFTEEN

Torak was woken by something slithering over his face.

With a shudder he started up – and glimpsed a scaly tail vanishing into the undergrowth.

He was lying on a pile of rotting pine-needles at the edge of a silent forest. Below him, a beach of charcoal-coloured pebbles sloped down to the flinty waters of the Lake.

How had he got here? He couldn't remember.

The east wind whistled over the stones, making him shiver. His clothes felt gritty and damp, and there was a humming in his ears. He was hungry and he missed Wolf, but he didn't dare howl. He wasn't even sure if he could.

The mist had cleared, but an ashen haze robbed the sun of warmth. At the south end of the beach, the reeds stood sentinel. Below him the Lake stretched to the edge of sight, opaque and forbidding.

He got to his feet. The pine-needles were strewn along the shore in broad swathes, as if washed up by a great flood. And the trees, he noticed uneasily, leaned back from the Lake.

He ran into the Forest.

There was no birdsong, and the trees watched him sullenly. He found a stream of muddy water and drank; spotted a few shrivelled lingonberries left over from last autumn, and gobbled them up. In the mud he saw tracks: webbed, with a tail drag. He scowled. He knew this creature, but he couldn't bring it to mind. That frightened him. Once, he had known every sign of every creature in the Forest.

He wondered how he was going to survive. He had no sleeping-sack, no bow, no arrows, no food. Only an axe, a knife, a half-empty medicine horn and a pouch of sodden tinder. And he'd forgotten how to hunt.

The ground climbed, and he reached a small, windy lake where the sun stabbed his eyes and the clamour of frogs hurt his head. He stumbled back into the trees, but they tripped him and scratched his face. Even the Forest had turned against him.

The trees ended. He was back at the reed-bed. He staggered north along the edge of the Forest, till he came to a place where the reeds narrowed to a stretch an arrowshot across.

Beyond them rose a granite rockface. It looked strangely enticing. Rowans and juniper clung to cracks, while ferns and orchids trembled in the spray from a waterfall. Above it swallows swooped and ravens wheeled, and on either side, Torak saw carvings of fish, elk, people:

hammer-etched into the rock and painted green. He guessed that the water flowed from the Otters' healing spring. If only he could reach it.

The reeds rattled, warning him back.

The sun began to sink, the trail veered south, and he found himself by the Lake, wading through pine-needles on a charcoal-coloured beach.

He halted. He recognized this beach. He was back where he'd started.

A horrible thought occurred to him.

To test it, he headed back into the Forest and re-traced his steps till he reached the reed-bed – except this time he turned south instead of north. Dusk was coming on when he finally stumbled onto the beach. Same beach. Same tracks. His own.

An island. The Lake had spewed him onto an island, where even the Otters feared to come. He was trapped: his escape cut off by the Lake to the east, the reeds to the west.

The wind stirred the trees. He stared at them. What were their names? 'Pine,' he said haltingly. 'Birch. Juniper?'

Listen to what the Forest is telling you, Fa used to say. But the Forest no longer spoke to him.

Gathering sticks and tinder, he blundered onto the beach and laid them in the lee of a boulder, so the Otters wouldn't see. At first his strike-fire refused to make sparks, but at last he managed it. Muttering, he hunched over the fire.

On the Lake, a lonely cry echoed. The red-eyed bird that had betrayed him in the reeds.

More voices joined in. Not birds. Wolves.

Leaping to his feet, Torak drew his knife. He'd always loved wolf song. But it struck terror in him now.

Another wolf called to the pack. Torak knew that howl. It was Wolf, his Wolf – and yet he couldn't make out what Wolf was saying. The familiar voice had become as incomprehensible as the yowl of a lynx.

'Wolf!' cried Torak. 'Come back!'

But Wolf didn't come.

Wolf had forsaken him.

Torak's fists clenched at his sides. So be it.

Wolf raced through the Forest. *Where was Tall Tailless?*

One moment they'd been together, fighting the Big Wet, and then he was gone! Wolf had tried to howl, but the Wet had come roaring into his gullet and he'd panicked. He'd forgotten Tall Tailless, forgotten everything except lashing out with his paws – until at last he'd struck land.

Now he ran this way and that, snuffing for scents. He smelt bracken and beaver, otter and lingonberry; he heard the taillesses on their floating reeds, and the Hidden Ones slithering in and out of the Wet. Worry gnawed him. Maybe Tall Tailless had become Not-Breath.

A cry rang through the trees: a desperate tailless yowl.

Wolf halted, swivelling his ears, lifting his muzzle. He caught the scent. Tall Tailless!

Wolf flew along the scent trail. He wove between trees, leapt over bracken – and there at last was his pack-brother, crouching behind a boulder at the edge of the Big Wet, by a small Bright Beast-that-Bites-Hot.

Wolf burst from the trees, and Tall Tailless turned and stared.

Wolf loped over the black stones and threw himself at

his pack-brother, pawing his chest and snuffle-licking his muzzle.

Tall Tailless pushed him away. Then he waved his great claw at Wolf.

Wolf jumped back.

Again Tall Tailless lashed out, yowling in tailless talk.

Wolf heard the terror in his yowl, he saw it in the beautiful silver eyes. How could this be? Tall Tailless couldn't be *scared* of him?

Bewildered, Wolf sat down. He felt a whine beginning in his chest.

Suddenly, Tall Tailless grabbed a limb of the Bright Beast and lunged at Wolf – *lunged at him with the Bright Beast!* Wolf leapt sideways, but the Bright Beast bit him on the muzzle and he yelped.

Tall Tailless bared his teeth in a snarl and attacked again. Wolf couldn't understand the yowls, but he knew what they meant. *Go away! You're no longer my pack-brother! Go away!*

Wild with pain and terror, Wolf fled.

After Wolf had gone, Torak stayed shivering on the beach.

He was exhausted but he didn't dare sleep. If he slept, they would come for him. The wolves. The Otter Clan. The Hidden People. The Soul-Eaters. All, all were against him.

Clutching axe and knife, he rocked back and forth, staring at the flames. He was hungry. He ought to set snares and fishing lines, but he couldn't remember how.

He began to nod.

Red eyes came at him. He woke with a cry. The eyes were real. Not red, but yellow. Wolf eyes.

Seizing a burning branch, he lashed out, etching the shadows with a glittering trail of sparks.

The wolves drew back. Their eyes were blank and terrible. They made no sound.

Wolf was among them. Wolf who had been his pack-brother, but had forsaken him.

With head lowered and tail lashing, Wolf moved menacingly forwards.

Torak's heart twisted. Wolf had come to taunt him. *See, I have a new pack! I don't need you!*

'Get away from me,' whispered Torak.

Wolf's ears twitched. His tail went still.

'Get back!' snarled Torak. He swung the branch at Wolf, who leapt out of the way.

The wolves watched in unblinking silence. Then, one by one, they trotted into the Forest.

Wolf was the last to go. For a moment he glanced back at Torak. Then he too vanished like mist.

It was very quiet after he'd gone.

A large black bird flew overhead with a scornful cark! Torak tried to remember its name. Raven. Raven Clan . . . Renn. She'd been his friend. Hadn't she? He couldn't remember her face.

He touched the oozing wound on his breastbone. There had been something he had to do . . .

The Soul-Eaters. He'd been going to prove that he wasn't one of them. Make the clans take him back.

It all seemed very long ago.

The sun dipped below the trees, and shadows crept down the beach as he sat by the dying fire. The buzzing in his head got worse. He sensed the Hidden People all around: watching, waiting. Feverishly, he fed the fire.

The faint moon rose in the blue sky, and it occurred to

him that tonight was Midsummer Night. His birthnight.

'Fourteen,' he muttered. His voice sound harsh and unfamiliar. 'You're fourteen summers old. Happy birthnight, Torak.'

He started to laugh.

Once he'd started, he couldn't stop.

SIXTEEN

Fin-Kedinn plunged the spear into the fire, and a blizzard of sparks engulfed the antlers mounted on its head.

The Ravens gave a joyful shout and the proud, happy trees rustled approval. It was Midsummer night, the night when the clans honoured the Forest by walking sunwise round the fire, garlanding the trees with necklaces of bone and berries.

All except Renn.

To have taken part would have felt as if she were betraying Torak. Tonight was his birthnight. How could she sit here enjoying salmon-liver stew and flame-blackened boar?

It was nearly a moon since the clan meet; nearly two since he'd been cast out. She missed him all the time. The misery was always with her, like a stone in her chest.

'What if something happens to him?' she'd said to Fin-Kedinn that morning. 'If he fell and broke his leg and couldn't hunt.'

'He's tough,' her uncle had said. 'He's survived on his own before, he can do it again.'

'For how long?'

To that, Fin-Kedinn had no answer.

Since the clan meet, the Ravens had moved east up the Axehandle, and whenever she could, Renn had secretly combed the Forest for any trace of Torak. In vain. Sometimes she woke in the night and thought, what if he never comes back?

She had no idea whether he'd done the rite, but she sensed that something was terribly wrong. The signs were bad. If only she knew what they meant.

She fingered the scar where the elk's antler had gashed her forearm. The wound had healed, but the memory was still raw. If that hunting party hadn't heard her cries . . .

Then, shortly after the clan meet, Aki had gone missing. His friends had found nothing but the remains of his boat. Renn had a dreadful feeling that Torak had been involved.

And nobody seemed to care. Everyone seemed to be pretending he didn't exist.

On the other side of the fire, Bale was twisting bramble twine for more garlands. He'd tied back his hair with a strip of seal hide, and he looked very handsome. Renn resented him. He'd stayed with the Ravens when the rest of his clan had returned to the islands, but instead of trying to find Torak, he'd gone hunting on the coast in his precious skinboat. She was disappointed. She'd expected more of him.

'May the World Spirit walk beneath your boughs,' Fin-

107

Kedinn told the Forest. 'May you grow strong, and seed many saplings!'

Suddenly, Renn couldn't bear it. Leaping to her feet, she ran from the camp.

The Raven Mage squatted on the riverbank like a toad. She'd left the celebrations to cast the bones. Now she regarded Renn without emotion. 'So. You seek my help at last.'

'No,' said Renn. 'I've never wanted your help.'

'You seek it all the same.'

Renn set her teeth. Throwing herself down in the bracken, she shredded a burdock leaf. 'I've been seeing signs. I don't know what they mean. Teach me how to read them.'

'No,' said Saeunn. 'You're not ready.'

Renn stared at her. 'You're the one who's always forcing me to learn Magecraft!'

'If you tried to read the signs now, you could do great harm.'

'Why,' said Renn.

With her staff, the Raven Mage drew a circle in the mud, and placed within it three dull white pebbles. 'Your talent lies in linking signs to make a pattern. Until now, your dreams have done this for you. To do it at will, in your waking life, you would have to open your mind completely.'

Renn raised her chin. 'I could do that.'

'Fool of a girl!' Saeunn struck the earth with her staff. 'Have you learned nothing? Your first moon bleed has brought a fearsome increase in your power – but it is raw, untried! To open your mind now could be fatal – to you and to others!'

For a moment they glared at each other, the crone and

108

the girl, linked only by the unforgiving bond of Magecraft.

Renn was the first to look away. 'Why didn't you tell him he was clanless?'

'The time wasn't right.'

'How could you keep that from him?'

'You've kept things from him too.'

Renn flinched.

'He has a destiny,' declared the Raven Mage. 'This is part of it. So is being cast out.'

Renn was about to ask more when Bale came into view on the path. She told him to go away. He ignored her.

'If this is about Torak,' he said to Saeunn, 'I've a right to hear. I'm his kin.'

'Then why don't you act like it,' said Renn, 'and try to help him?'

'Why don't you?' he shot back.

'No-one may help the outcast,' Saeunn reminded them.

'And squabbling won't help anyone,' said Fin-Kedinn, appearing behind Bale.

Saeunn indicated Renn. 'She says she sees signs.'

Renn bridled. She wasn't ready to speak of this to Fin-Kedinn, let alone Bale.

'What signs?' said Fin-Kedinn, sitting on the bank and motioning Bale to do the same.

Renn picked at a hole in the knee of her legging. 'He took your axe. He went into my medicine pouch and took a pebble he'd left me last summer. He spirit walked in the elk and he – he attacked me.'

'I'll never believe that was Torak,' said Bale.

'Well I'm not making it up!' snapped Renn.

'The pebble,' Saeunn cut in. 'Why wasn't I told?'

'Why should I tell you?' muttered Renn.

'Tell me now,' said the Raven Mage.

Renn swallowed. 'He'd put his mark on it. In alder juice.'

'His mark?' said Saeunn. 'His clan-tattoo?'

'Right down to the scar on his cheek.'

'Ah,' breathed the Raven Mage.

Renn felt a prickle of unease. 'I – I kept it safe. But at the clan meet, he took it.' And I know why, she thought miserably. He took it to tell me that he isn't coming back.

'Ah.' Saeunn picked up one of the white stones and turned it in her fingers. 'Now it becomes clear.'

'What does?' said Renn.

The Raven Mage leaned close, and Renn saw the threads of spittle webbing her toothless gums. 'The outcast,' said the Raven Mage, 'has fallen prey to the soul-sickness.'

For a moment there was silence. Then both Renn and Bale spoke at once.

'What's that?' said Bale.

'Is it because of the Soul-Eater tattoo?' said Renn. 'Did he try to cut it out and it didn't work and it made him sick?'

'Tattoos?' Saeunn spat. 'No! Even without tattoos, souls get sick, as well as bodies! They fall prey to demons. Spells.'

From her medicine pouch she shook three small, mottled bones and set them on the black earth. She touched the first with her knotted forefinger. 'If your name-soul falls sick, you forget who you are. You become like a ghost.' She touched the second. 'If the canker attacks your clan-soul, you lose your sense of good and evil. You become as a demon.' Her horny talon moved to the last bone. 'If your world-soul becomes palsied, you lose your link with other living things – hunter, prey, Forest. You become as a Lost One.' Tilting her palm, she dropped the stone, and it struck the world-soul bone, which jumped as if it were alive. 'If his name-pebble fell into the wrong hands . . .'

Renn shut her eyes.

Bale said, 'I don't believe this. Torak isn't sick, he's furious. I would be too, if I'd been cast out for something that wasn't my fault.'

Saeunn bristled like an angry raven, but Fin-Kedinn said, 'I think Saeunn's right, Torak is soul-sick. But who did this to him? Which of the three?'

'You mean the Soul-Eaters,' said Renn.

'Three survived the battle on the ice,' said Fin-Kedinn. 'Thiazzi. Eostra. Seshru. At the clan meet I spoke to people from all over the Forest and beyond, seeking clues as to where they might have gone. No-one's seen any trace of them.' He paused. 'And yet it seems to me that the manner in which Torak's tattoo was revealed, and his spirit walking in the elk – these bear the print of a single mind, working alone.'

Saeunn nodded. 'One mind, but which? For days I've fasted and read the bones. The Oak Mage and the Eagle Owl Mage feel far away. The one who haunts the Forest – who draws the outcast to her – is Seshru the Viper Mage.'

Fin-Kedinn bowed his head.

Renn dug her fingernails into her palms.

Bale was puzzled. 'But – she's only one woman. How much harm can she do?'

'More than you could possibly imagine,' said Fin-Kedinn.

Saeunn turned to Renn. 'You were the last to have seen her. Tell him what she is.'

Renn couldn't speak. She was back in the forest of stone, in the flickering torchlight and the stink of slaughter, watching the snake-haired mask of the Viper Mage whirling, hissing as she sought the Otherworld with dead gutskin eyes . . .

'Renn,' Fin-Kedinn said softly.

She drew a breath. 'She – she does everything sideways, like a snake. She lies all the time. She makes you see things that aren't there. She makes you do things.'

'I don't understand,' said Bale. 'I spoke to some Vipers at the clan meet, and they told me they've never *had* a Mage who turned Soul-Eater. So how can this Seshru be – '

'Like a snake,' said Fin-Kedinn, 'she sheds one self and becomes another.'

Bale was aghast. 'She changed her name? But no-one would do that, it's a kind of death!'

'That's what it means to be a Soul-Eater,' said Renn. 'You sacrifice all that you were. You live only for power.'

Bale stared at her as if seeing her for the first time.

Fin-Kedinn picked up the bones and poured them slowly from palm to palm. 'So now we know. Torak is soul-sick – and at the mercy of the Viper Mage.'

'The Viper Mage has no mercy,' said Saeunn.

丰丰

Next morning, Renn woke early, and went to see Fin-Kedinn.

She found him fishing for pike in the shallows where a brook flowed into the Axehandle. When he saw her, he drew in his line. The hook was empty.

'What is it, Renn?' His face was grave. He had guessed why she'd come.

'I don't want to lie to you,' she said. 'I don't want to sneak away. But I have to try to find – '

'No, don't say it,' he warned. 'Don't tell me anything you couldn't tell the Leader of any other clan.'

She bit her lip. 'He's out there. Alone. Soul-sick.'

'I know.'

'Then why don't you come with me?'

'I can't be seen to break clan law.' He met her eyes. 'You of all people mustn't do this. What if he's already in her power? A spirit walker in the hands of a Soul-Eater. I can't think of anything more dangerous.'

'He's my friend. I've got to try. You understand, don't you?'

Fin-Kedinn did not reply.

'Fin-Kedinn? You do understand?'

Suddenly he looked tired. 'You're no longer a child, Renn. You're old enough to make your own choices.'

No I'm not! she wanted to say. I need you to help me! Tell me what to do!

That night, Renn sat by a smoky little fire on the banks of the Axehandle, feeling lonely and scared.

Breaking clan law had been even worse than she'd feared. By doing so, she'd cut herself off from her clan and from Fin-Kedinn.

Huddling closer to the flames, she blew on her grouse-bone whistle, but got no answer. Torak and Wolf were far away.

She could feel her power churning inside her; the secrets rising to the surface, like splinters working their way through her flesh. She didn't want to do Magecraft, she hated it, but she had a feeling that to help Torak, she might be forced to try. Because Seshru was out here somewhere.

Hatred flared in her heart, and she perceived the Soul-Eater's plan so clearly that it could have been her own.

Seshru was hunting Torak in the same way that her clan-creature hunted its quarry. The viper sinks its poisoned fangs into its prey, then follows it through the Forest as it wanders, slowly weakening. The viper is patient. It waits till the prey falls. Only then does it feed.

Renn was woken by the sizzle of water on fire.

Bale stood over her, his dripping skinboat balanced on his shoulder.

She sat up, annoyed that he'd caught her dozing. 'I thought you went back to your island,' she said crossly.

He ignored that. 'I was wrong and you were right. Torak is soul-sick. But it's worse than we thought.'

SEVENTEEN

'A ki was barely alive,' said Bale. 'Somehow he'd crawled out of the water and collapsed in a thicket. The Wolf Clan found him a couple of days later.'

'A couple of days?' said Renn. 'He's been missing nearly a moon.'

'No. The Boar Clan just didn't bother to send us word.'

'Typical,' she said in disgust. 'But what were the Wolf Clan doing so far east?'

Bale looked grim. 'Tracking Torak. To "wipe out the dishonour once and for all".'

Renn shook her head. 'Did they say where his trail led?'

'East. They lost him in the reedbeds on Lake Axehead.'

She went cold. 'Lake Axehead? Why?'

Bale brushed that aside. 'Don't you see what this means? Torak left Aki to die!'

'Maybe he didn't know Aki was there.'

'Oh, he knew. Aki says he saw Torak looking down at him from the ridge. Then he turned and walked away.' He rubbed his face. 'I know Aki was hunting him, but to leave him to die . . . That's not Torak!'

Renn stared at the fire. Bale was right. But why Lake Axehead? There was a pattern to this, but she couldn't fathom it. She only knew that of all places, the Lake was the one she was least eager to see. Her father had died on the ice river at its eastern edge. She'd promised herself she would never go back.

Bale set down his skinboat and pulled off his gutskin parka. 'You're trying to find him too, aren't you?'

She didn't reply.

'Why now, when you weren't before?'

'I was.' She told him about her searches in the Forest.

'Me too,' he said, surprising her.

'You? I thought you were hunting with the Sea-eagles.'

He was affronted. 'With Torak an outcast?'

She thought for a moment. Then she said, 'You do know that we're breaking clan law? If you tell *anyone* . . .'

'Of course I know! But that goes for you too.'

Warily they studied each other. Then Bale said, 'I caught a fish. Can I cook it on your fire?'

Renn shrugged.

It was an impressively large bream, and Bale offered her a piece which she refused, then changed her mind when she smelt it cooking. In return she gave him some dried deer meat, and showed him how to spread it with juniper-berry and marrowfat paste.

While they ate, they talked guardedly. Bale told her how he'd prepared his skinboat for its freshwater "ordeal" by coating it with seal blubber and burnt seaweed, and

Renn showed him the seal-hide bow case she'd been given in the Far North. But she didn't mention what she'd guessed of Seshru's plans. Bale was Torak's kin, but she didn't know him very well, and if it came to a battle of wills between her and the Viper Mage, he would get in the way.

On the other hand, he was strong, and he had a skinboat.

She was pondering this when Bale rose to his feet, picked up his pack, and hoisted his boat on his shoulder.

She asked him where he was going.

'Lake Axehead. You go back to your clan. I'll find Torak.'

'*What?*'

'Well you're not coming in my skinboat.'

'I wouldn't want to,' she lied.

'And if you went overland, you'd never keep up.' Seeing her expression, he sighed. 'Where I come from, women stay on land. The men do the hunting and the fighting.'

Renn snorted. 'Not in the Forest.'

'Maybe. But I'm Seal Clan and that's my way. Go back to camp, Renn. You're not coming with me.'

In disbelief she watched him make for the shallows. 'Even if you do reach the Lake,' she called after him, 'what are you going to do? You don't know anything about it, or the Otters!'

'I'll take my chances,' he replied.

'Fine! But I'll tell you this. You're not going to beat the Soul-Eaters by being good with a paddle!'

'We'll see about that!'

'We shall indeed,' snarled Renn as she battled through the brambles.

117

There was no trail along this part of the Axehandle – at least, not that she could find – and she was hot, scratched and furious. It didn't help that she kept picturing Bale speeding serenely upriver.

Above the rapids she rested, then struggled through a stand of soggy alders. The river here formed pools where many clans came to fish. Renn noticed that someone had set lines and fish traps in several of the pools. She was wondering who it was when she caught a flash of fair hair by the water's edge.

Bale hadn't seen her. He was kneeling by his overturned skinboat, patching a small tear in its hull.

'Having problems?' she called.

'Snagged on a fish trap,' he said without looking round.

'Oh dear,' said Renn unfeelingly.

'It's not right!' he burst out. 'Leaving them there for anyone to run into! They should've put some kind of marker!'

'They did. Those strips of willow bark tied to the branches? That's what Forest people leave as a warning when they're fishing.'

Bale set his jaw.

'Well, good luck,' said Renn with a cheery smile. 'Hope it doesn't slow you down too much!'

Bale threw her a thunderous look.

She was still grinning as she left the pools.

Her grin didn't last. Across the river, she saw the mouth of the gully where she and Torak had first encountered the Walker, the autumn before last. Wolf had been a cub. When his pads got sore, Torak had carried him in his arms.

A fierce longing for them swept over her.

The pines gave way to towering oaks, and the Forest turned watchful. Renn wished Bale would sweep by in his skinboat. Surely it couldn't have taken this long to sew on a patch?

A little further on, two red deer fawns peeped from the bracken, then wobbled towards her on tiny hooves. They were almost within reach before they took fright and fled.

Renn put her hand to her raven feathers. When a creature goes out of its way to attract your attention, it's often a sign. What did this mean?

It was late afternoon when she climbed the ridge the clans call the Hogback, and stood gazing over the Lake.

The low sun turned the water a dazzling gold. She saw islands scattered across it, fragile as leaves, and below her, the great reed-bed which guarded the western shore. Far to the south, she made out the black dots of the Otter camp, and to the east, the cruel white slash of the ice river.

She'd been eight summers old when she last stood here: bewildered, unable to understand why her fa was never coming back. The Otters had found his body, and Fin-Kedinn and Saeunn had gone to rescue his scattered souls. Fin-Kedinn had insisted that Renn should come too. They'd stood on the Hogback, staring at this vast inland Sea.

'Why did he go all that way?' Renn asks her uncle. 'There isn't any prey on the ice river.'

'He wasn't hunting prey,' murmurs Fin-Kedinn.

'Then why?'

'I'll tell you when you're older.' He takes her hand in his warm, strong grip, and she clings on fiercely.

Now she was back on the Hogback; but there was no Fin-Kedinn to cling to.

By the time she had made her way down the ridge, she'd begun to see the hopelessness of her task. She had no idea where Torak had gone, and there was no-one to ask. No trail led along the shore – the Otters didn't need one, they always travelled by water – and even if she reached their camp on foot, what then?

She'd started picking her way south when she heard a stirring in the reeds.

'Bale?' she said uncertainly.

No answer. Only the creak and crunch of reeds, as if something were pushing its way towards her.

She stumbled backwards over the tussocky ground. 'Bale!' she whispered. 'If that's you, come out now, it isn't funny!'

The wind veered round, engulfing her in a stink that made her gag.

The reeds trembled – parted – and a boat slid towards her. From it stared a green man made of mouldy reeds.

Renn sprang back – and collided with something solid.

'What *is* that?' said Bale, behind her.

'What *was* that?' he said again, when they'd retreated a safe distance to a bay at the southern edge of the reeds.

'I think the Otters made it,' said Renn, 'to honour the Lake. They put food in it and leave it to go where it will. It's sacred. We shouldn't even have seen it.'

Bale bit his lip. 'I'm glad I found you. This place. I don't know its ways.'

Renn shrugged. 'Well, I need a boat, so I'm glad you found me, too.' That didn't sound as friendly as she'd intended, so she went on quickly, 'Before we do anything, we must honour the Lake. The Otters ask its permission for everything.'

Bale nodded. 'What do we do?'

Feeling a bit self-conscious, Renn left an offering of salmon cakes near the reeds. Then she made a paste of earthblood and Lake water and daubed a little on her forehead and her bow, asking the Lake to let them go in peace. Bale let her daub some on his forehead, and – after some persuasion – on his skinboat. After that they had a meal of dried deer meat, and he made a fish trap out of willow withes, and set it in the water.

The sun sank lower and the wind dropped. The Lake turned as smooth as polished basalt.

'The Viper Mage,' Bale said quietly. 'She's after Torak because he's a spirit walker. Isn't she?'

' – Yes,' said Renn. She wished he hadn't mentioned Seshru.

'And she's after the fire-opal, too.'

'Yes,' she said again. Lowering her voice, she added, 'It's the last piece left. One piece was lost in the black ice with the Bat Mage. One when the Seal Mage was taken by the Sea.'

'The Seal Mage?' Bale was startled. 'He had a piece of the fire-opal?'

'How else could he have made the tokoroths?'

He frowned. Renn guessed that he was remembering the bad times on his island, when the Seal Mage had created the sickness. Bale's little brother had been one of its victims.

A lonely, wavering cry echoed over the Lake.

Bale sprang to his feet. 'What was that?'

'A diverbird,' said Renn. 'They're the best swimmers in the Lake. The Otters make offerings to them, too.' She paused. 'Fin-Kedinn says the Otters are like their clan-creature. Always leaving little piles of half-chewed fish at the water's edge.'

Somewhere a trout leapt, and they jumped.
Bale shook himself, and went off to check his fish trap.
Renn stayed, brooding, on the shore.
'Renn,' called Bale in an altered voice.
'What?'
'You'd better come and see.'

EIGHTEEN

The big bream wriggled and gasped in the trap. It was a fine catch – except that it had two heads. Mouthless, misshapen, the second bulged like a canker, fighting its twin with horrible vigour.

'What did this?' said Bale with a grimace.

'Kill it,' said Renn.

'No!' ordered a voice behind them. 'Throw it back. Don't touch!'

They turned to face a cluster of sharp green faces and sharper spears.

Bale moved in front of Renn, but she stepped aside. With her fists on her heart, she addressed the woman who – to judge from her armlet of otter fur – was the Leader.

'I'm Raven Clan,' she said, 'my friend is Seal. We mean no harm.'

'No talk!' admonished the woman. Then to the others, 'Return that accursed thing to the Lake. We're taking the strangers to camp.'

'But Ananda, why?' protested a man. 'At a time like this –'

'At a time like this, Yolun,' cut in the Leader, 'we can't let them go free, they'd only make it worse.'

The man called Yolun lapsed into tight-lipped silence, while two others broke up the trap and set the monster free.

After that, things happened fast. Renn and Bale were seized and bundled into a reed boat with Yolun and another man. When they tried to resist, knives were pressed against their spines. They could only watch as their gear was tossed in the skinboat, which was lashed to the stern of another craft and towed.

They headed south. Beside her, Renn felt Bale shaking with rage. She threw him an urgent glance and shook her head. Fighting was useless. The Otters bristled with greenstone spears and arrows tipped with the beaks of diverbirds. Trying to escape would be futile. The only reason they hadn't been tied up was because there was no need.

Renn studied Yolun as he sat hunched in the prow, stabbing the water with his paddle. His fish-skin jerkin was fringed at neck and hem, evoking the reeds. His eyes were outlined with earthblood to imitate the red glare of the diverbird. He kept glancing resentfully over his shoulder; but beneath his hostility, Renn sensed something else.

Bale bent and whispered in her ear. 'Their craft are heavy and slow. If we could reach my skinboat, we could outrun them.'

'And go where?' she whispered back. 'They know the

Lake, we don't. Besides, I don't think they're angry so much as frightened.'

'That makes them even more dangerous.'

He was right.

The reed craft might not have the speed of a skinboat, but the Otters made steady progress, weaving unnerringly between the islands which dotted the Lake. As the light summer night wore on, their camp rose into view.

Like Bale, Renn was seeing it for the first time. Like him, she gasped.

'Why do they live like this?' he murmured.

'To be close to the Lake,' said Yolun. He stopped paddling, and for a moment his austere features glowed with fervour. 'The Lake is Mother and Father to us. From it comes all life. To it all life must return.' The resentment returned. 'We don't expect strangers to understand.'

'I'm no stranger,' said Renn. 'I'm Open Forest, like you.'

'You're not Otter Clan!' he snapped. 'No more talk.'

Wreathed in greenish smoke, the camp of the Otters floated above the Lake, linked to land by a single narrow walkway.

'It's built on stilts,' said Bale, amazed.

A forest of logs had been planted in the Lake, and on these lay wooden platforms bearing many squat reed domes. A bitter tang of smoke wafted towards them, with a powerful smell of fish. They saw smouldering brands mounted on posts; men and women gazing down at them, their eyes wide in their green-painted faces.

Renn was perplexed. The Otters were known as happy, playful people, like their clan-creature. Something had changed.

And all wore the green clay. Until now, Renn had never seen it, although she knew it was sacred to the Otters, who took it from a secret place on the north shore, and mixed it with fish oil. But they only ever used it to protect the sick and the dying. She wondered why the whole clan needed it now.

Yolun's companion moored the craft to one of the outer piles, and a hatch opened overhead. A rope ladder dropped down, and Yolun ordered them to climb.

They emerged into an acrid haze. Renn saw that what she'd taken for brands were chunks of horsehoof mushroom – burnt, she guessed, to keep away midges. And still the Otters stared.

She and Bale were pushed towards the largest shelter: a smoky hut lit by rushlights. Inside, she was assailed by a stink of rotting fish. The Otters seemed unconcerned, and even Bale merely wrinkled his nose. Out of politeness, Renn pretended not to notice.

When everyone had crawled inside, Ananda called for food. Seeing Renn's surprise, she said, 'We have a saying on the Lake. A stranger is my guest until proven my enemy.'

Yolun snorted, as if he'd had proof enough.

'We're not enemies,' said Bale.

'So you say,' said Ananda. 'Eat.'

There was silence while a boy and a young woman brought fish-shaped bowls of tight-woven sedge filled with reed-pollen gruel, and a basket piled with baked reed stems: charred on the outside, white and starchy when peeled.

Renn recognized the young woman as a Raven who'd mated with an Otter the previous summer. 'Dyrati?'

Dyrati avoided her eyes. 'Eat,' she said, ladling a grey sludge over Renn's gruel. It looked like thick honey, but the stench of rotten fish made Renn's eyes water.

'Stickleback grease,' said Dyrati. 'Eat!'

'Eat!' commanded Yolun. 'Or do you scorn our food?'

They were all watching her.

She prodded the stinking mess, and felt her gorge rise.

Bale came to her rescue. 'She isn't used to boats, it's turned her stomach.' Emptying her bowl into his, he started eating with every appearence of relish – and the Otters relaxed.

'How *can* you?' whispered Renn.

'I like it,' he mumbled with a shrug. 'We make the same thing in the islands, but with cod.'

'You'll be wondering why we have no fish to give you,' said Ananda. 'Even this grease is from last spring.' She searched their faces. 'Someone is making the Lake sick.'

The Otters began rocking and moaning, and many touched the tufts of clan-creature fur hanging from their ears.

'A while ago,' Ananda went on, 'a child fell ill, and our Mage sent us to fetch the sacred clay. We found the healing spring plundered. A stranger had stolen what only an Otter may touch. That's when the troubles began.' She shuddered. 'People would fall into a death-like sleep and wake screaming, bitten by slithering demons in their dreams. Then the catch failed.'

Yolun shook his head. 'There used to be times when the fish were so plentiful that you could step from your boat and run across their backs, all the way to the shore. But this spring – hardly any. And what we do take is twisted. Cursed.'

'Every spring,' said Ananda, 'the ice river in the east sends much water to the Lake. It's a time of great blessing, when the water rises so high that its voice beneath our shelters laps us to sleep. Not this spring. The Lake sinks lower and lower.'

'Trouble always comes from the west!' cried Yolun, fixing his red-rimmed eyes on the strangers. 'We heard tell of an outcast, heading for the Lake. Then we saw him. *He* stole the sacred clay, *he* brought the troubles! And now these strangers have come to make it worse!'

At the mention of Torak, Renn and Bale stiffened. Neither dared meet the other's glance.

The Leader was on it at once. 'You know the outcast. Who are you?'

'I'm Bale of the Seal Clan,' Bale said proudly.

'And I'm Renn of the Raven Clan. I'm Fin-Kedinn's brother's daughter. Dyrati knows me.'

Dyrati folded her arms and said not a word.

Renn showed them her wrist-guard. 'See this? It's greenstone. Fin-Kedinn made it for me in the Otter way, which he learnt when he lived with your clan.'

An old man lifted rheumy eyes from his bowl. 'I remember. An angry young man, but he honoured the Lake.'

'Even if the girl is who she says,' said Yolun, 'what of the boy? A Seal on the Lake? How can that be right?'

'He has the waterskill,' Renn said quickly. 'And look at the reeds tattooed on his arms.'

Bale's tattoos were of seaweed, but he had the sense to keep quiet.

'None of this matters!' exclaimed Yolun. 'You all saw how they started when I mentioned the outcast!'

The Leader searched Bale's face. 'Do you know the outcast?'

Bale lifted his chin. 'Yes. But that's no crime.'

'Helping him is,' snarled Yolun.

Bale tensed.

'You see that?' cried Yolun. 'They're in league with him,

that makes them outcast too! Ananda, we must kill them, or the troubles will get worse!'

'No!' protested Renn. 'We have nothing to do with your troubles. But – but I do know who's causing them.'

'How can you know? Why are you here?' Ananda leaned closer. She had strange, grey-green eyes which seemed to hold the light of the Lake.

Renn's heart began to race. If she lied, the Leader would know it. If she admitted their purpose . . .

'The evils you speak of,' Renn said carefully, 'the failed catch, the biting demons – these will spread to the Forest if they're not stopped.' She paused. 'There's a Soul-Eater on the Lake. That's why this is happening. That's why we've come.'

There was stillness in the shelter. The only sounds were the sputter of rushlights and the splash of water far below.

'She's lying,' said Yolun. 'A Soul-Eater? Where's the proof?'

The Leader never took her eyes off Renn. 'She speaks the truth,' she said at last. 'But not the whole truth.' She gave a curt nod. 'The Mage will uncover the rest.'

NINETEEN

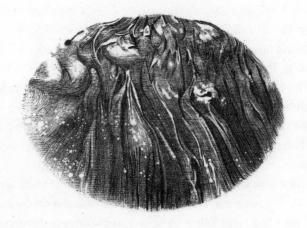

'Say nothing,' Renn whispered to Bale as Yolun pushed them along a walkway wreathed in smoke.

Bale bent his head to hers. 'You heard Ananda. Their Mage will find out the truth. How do we stop him?'

'Keep your thoughts away from Torak,' she replied. 'Fix your mind on the strongest feeling you know. Anger. Hatred. Grief.'

He frowned. 'Those are all bad.'

The smoke parted, and they found themselves on a round platform on which stood a small reed shelter. The doorway was edged with the teeth of an enormous pike. Above it swam an otter, beautifully carved in gleaming alder wood.

Yolun forced them to their knees, and Ananda motioned them to enter. Filled with misgiving, they crawled inside.

Renn caught the dank smell of reeds; the splash and gurgle of the Lake. Through gaps in the floor, its restless glimmer rippled over the walls. She heard Bale's sharp intake of breath. Then she saw why.

Two children sat cross-legged in the gloom. Their heads were bowed, their pale hair pooled on the floor. Both wore sleeveless tunics of silver fish-skin, sewn with strips of green-stained hide in a pattern of waving reeds.

Twins, thought Renn. Dread stole through her. First the twin fawns, then the two-headed fish. Now this. What did it mean?

Ananda and Yolun forced her and Bale lower, then touched their own foreheads to the floor. 'Mage,' they said.

As one, the twins raised their heads.

Their hair was the greenish gold of mildewed reeds, and their skin had the glistening pallor of the newly drowned. The boy's eyes were bright with waterlight, but the girl's were a misty, sightless white.

'She sees the world of the spirit,' said Yolun with reverence.

'How can this be?' said Bale. 'They can't be more than ten summers old.'

The boy's lips drew back from pointed grey teeth. 'Age has no meaning,' he said in a thin, piping voice. 'We are the spirit reborn. We are the Mage.'

Renn felt a shiver run down her spine.

'We were here at the Beginning,' said the boy. 'We saw the Great Flood wash the land clean. We saw the Lake become.'

The blind girl moaned. The boy's face tightened in distress. 'But now evil dishonours the Lake! The terror comes in the night!'

Ananda spoke. 'Mage, these strangers admit to knowing the outcast who took the sacred clay.'

'The outcast didn't take it,' said the boy. 'He caused it to be taken.'

'But Mage,' said Yolun, 'it's the same thing.'

'No,' said the boy.

'Then tell us,' said Ananda. 'Why have they come? What should we do with them?'

The blind girl put her hand on her twin's knee, and he nodded as if she'd spoken. 'We will make them tell.' He gave a sharp grey smile. 'We will ride with the spirits on the voice of diverbird and reed. We will draw out the truth.' Then to Yolun, 'Shut in the dark.'

Yolun untied a rolled-up mat, covering the doorway.

Renn felt trapped. If these weird children discovered that they wanted to help Torak – if they really *could* see her thoughts . . .

In the gloom, she saw the boy take a pouch made from the skin of a whole salmon. From its jaws he drew a segment of reed, which he slit with his thumbnail. Softly he blew through the slit, and the shelter filled with the wavering cry of the diverbird.

Now the girl withdrew a long loop of twisted sedge and wove it between her fingers. Renn saw patterns form: a fishing net, a boat, a tiny Death Platform. Her thoughts began to unravel.

She shook herself awake.

'Soft, soft,' whispered the boy. '*It comes.*'

First they heard it, swooshing and gurgling into the shelter. Then they felt it: water swirling round their legs.

Renn gave a start. Bale shifted in alarm.

'Don't move,' warned the boy.

Now Renn felt the slippery coldness of waterweed

winding about her. She glanced down. The shelter was dry. And yet – *she felt it*: waterweed coiling about her legs, her waist, her arms. She struggled. She couldn't move.

She could only watch as the blind girl reached both hands towards Bale. He tried to pull away, but the unseen waterweed held him fast.

The tips of the girl's fingers were white and puckered, as if they'd been too long in the water. Like minnows they flickered over his face, tracing the line of his jaw, the muscles of his throat.

The blind girl opened her mouth, and her voice was as the rushing of waves drawing back over shingle. 'Your brother is better now,' she murmured. 'Death healed his pain.'

Bale gasped.

The white fingers darted to the nape of his neck – and she drew back with a moan. 'Ah! You must use your time well!'

She released him – and Bale bowed his head, breathing hard.

Renn braced herself as the blind girl turned to her. Shutting her eyes, Renn felt a fluttering on her face, soft and chill as the touch of a frog. She tried to turn her mind from Torak, but the thin fingers reached into her thoughts and pulled him to the surface, so that he was *all* she could think of.

She saw him not as she'd seen him last, huddled in the willow thicket, but on a day in spring when they'd been hunting. He was down on one knee, examining the bitten-off end of a hazel twig. His dark hair flopped in his eyes, and his face wore the rapt expression it always did when he was tracking. He caught her watching, and flashed one of his rare, wolfish grins.

The blind child reached for the image.

With all her strength, Renn thrust the memory down deep.

'Ah,' said the blind girl, 'this one is strong!'

Her fingers flitted to Renn's wrists, lingering on the zigzag tattoos. 'A battle rages within her,' she whispered. 'She must take care, or it will tear her apart.'

Again an image of Torak rose in Renn's mind, but this time he stood on a black shore, and his face was so savage that she hardly knew him.

Again the cold fingers groped for the image.

With a huge effort of will, Renn pushed Torak away and fixed her thoughts on the Viper Mage. She breathed on the spark of hatred which slept in her heart, and it flared into life: a hot, bright flame. She fixed her mind on that.

The blind child sighed.

Renn shuddered and opened her eyes.

Ananda spoke in hushed tones. 'What of the outcast? Are they in league with him?'

'No,' murmured the blind girl. 'But they are bound to him. He by the bone, she by the heart.'

Ananda frowned. 'There's no crime in that. We'll have to send them back to the Forest.'

'No!' cried the twins together. 'The Lake has need of them! The boy's strength, the girl's power! They are needed to fight the terror which comes in the night!'

The girl turned her misty eyes on Renn. 'You know this terror. You have power to fight it, yet you're afraid. Why? Why do you fear your power?'

Yolun stared at Renn. 'Are you a Mage, too?'

She shook her head.

'Tell. Tell,' urged the twins.

For a third time, Renn felt the girl probing her thoughts,

delving even deeper, seeking her most closely guarded secrets.

No! she screamed in her head. She fought, but the waterweed held her fast.

In desperation, she breathed life once again into that tiny flame of hatred. It brightened – engulfed the shelter in fire . . .

The blind girl cried out.

The boy fell back.

Renn felt the waterweed snap and slither away.

Wearily, the boy sat up. 'They may pass freely. Give them clothes and food fit for the Lake and send them east.'

Yolun sprang to his feet. 'No! This can't be!'

'But Mage!' cried Ananda. 'Are you sure?'

'We see them travelling east,' panted the boy. 'East to the ice river. She will use her power. He will help her. They will find what they seek.'

'No!' protested Yolun.

'Let them go,' ordered the boy. 'If they do wrong, the Lake will take them, and you will find their bones rolling in the Bay of Lost Things.'

Yolun looked thunderous; Ananda bewildered.

Trembling, Renn crawled for the mouth of the shelter. Suddenly, the blind girl seized her wrists. Renn tried to pull away, but the bony fingers were strong.

'Beware the cold red fire,' breathed the girl. 'Beware the Lake that kills!'

Renn wrenched herself free and stumbled from the shelter.

TWENTY

'Why are they letting us go?' said Bale. 'It's too easy, I don't like it.'

Renn didn't answer. The encounter with the twins had left her drained, and terrified of what they might have seen in her thoughts.

She and Bale were back in the main shelter, where Ananda had left them. Yolun peered in, and jerked his head at Bale. 'Out,' he growled. 'I'm to give you supplies and Lake-worthy clothes.'

Renn made to follow, but he stopped her. 'Not you! A woman will see to you!'

Renn soon discovered that Yolun wasn't the only one who hated seeing them freed. When Dyrati brought her new clothes, she refused to meet her eyes, and dumped the clothes on the mat. 'You won't be needing your buckskins,' she said sullenly. 'Too heavy when wet, too stiff when dry. Put these on.' She indicated a pair of calf-length leggings of soft elk hide and a sleeveless jerkin of finely woven sedge. 'You'll have to sew on your clan-creature feathers yourself.'

In uncomfortable silence, Renn changed her clothes and cut off her clan-creature feathers to sew on later. When she tried to thank Dyrati, the older girl made for the door.

'Dyrati?' said Renn. 'What have I done?'

Dyrati's mouth tightened. 'As if you didn't know. You might have fooled our Mage, but you can't fool me.'

'What do you mean?'

Dyrati turned on her and made the sign of the hand. 'Stay away! I've told them what you are! I've told them what we used to whisper behind your back. You with your black, black eyes and your dreams that come true! You're bad luck. Everyone knows it. Everyone knows that whoever gets close to you comes to harm!'

Renn felt sick. 'That's not true.'

'You know it is! Your brother. Your father. Torak. Someone should warn that Seal boy before it's too late!' Then she was gone, leaving Renn on her own.

She was shaken. What if Dyrati was right?

Oh, nonsense! she told herself. Dyrati's just a spiteful girl who's never liked you.

The trouble was, nobody did like her much. They tolerated her because she was Fin-Kedinn's bone kin, but they were scared of her talent for Magecraft.

Misery welled up inside her, and she longed for Torak. Only Torak had ever been her friend.

On the walkway she found Bale, who now wore elk-hide leggings and a jerkin of silvery fish-skin. 'Are you all right?' he asked when he saw her face.

'No,' she snapped.

He raised an eyebrow, but made no comment.

Watched by Ananda and a cluster of silent Otters, they made their way towards the hatch, then climbed down the rope ladder and into the skinboat.

'Our gear's all stowed,' said Bale as he untied the moorings and pushed off. 'Let's go before they change their minds.'

The Lake was treacherous with hidden currents, and the skinboat bucked wildly. Several times, Renn nearly fell out.

'It doesn't like fresh water,' said Bale, excusing his beloved craft's poor performance. 'It's my fault. It sits much lower than in the Sea, I'm not used to that.'

Huddled behind him, Renn was soon soaked, despite the beaver-hide mantle she'd found in one of the packs. She felt like a burden. Bale was much stronger and better at skinboating, and when she did try to help, she ended up clashing paddles with his.

Every so often, she made herself feel useful by taking out her grouse-bone whistle and calling for Wolf. But she never got an answer, and that only made things worse.

Dread settled inside her when she thought of what lay ahead. *She will use her power*, the Otter Mage had said. But Renn didn't want to use her power, not ever.

They pitched camp for the night in a sheltered bay. Their Forest food had run out, but the Otters had provisioned them with salmonskins of roasted reed pollen, so they made a cheerless gruel.

Bale seemed preoccupied. When they'd eaten he said,

'What did the Otter Mage mean when she said you're afraid of your power?'

Renn braced herself.

'She meant Magecraft, didn't she?' When she didn't answer, he said, 'If we can't find Torak, it might be the only way. You have the skill. Why not use it?'

'That's easy for you to say,' she muttered.

'But for Torak. You'd do it for Torak?'

She made no reply.

'What are you afraid of?'

'I'm not afraid!'

After that, they didn't speak. Bale upended the skinboat on shoresticks and covered it with pine boughs for a shelter, then rolled himself in his beaver-fur mantle and turned his back on her. It was a long time before Renn got to sleep.

They paddled east throughout the next day, but saw no sign of Torak. Renn had no sense that they were getting closer to him – but they were getting closer to something. The dread inside her grew worse.

As the sun began to sink, they were buffeted by a strong east wind, and Bale had to work hard to keep them moving forwards. Then, as they rounded an island, Renn felt a chill on her face, and there it was: the relentless glare of the ice river.

The dread in her belly hardened to stone. Somewhere out there, her father had found his death.

Bale twisted to face her. 'This doesn't feel right. Why would he go there? There's no prey, nothing!'

'The Otter Mage said we would find what we sought in the east.' But Renn knew better than most that the prophesies of Mages are tricky things, and can have many different meanings.

As they paddled nearer, the chill became a freezing blast, and the ice turned blue. Renn craned her neck at the shining cliffs which towered overhead. She heard the trickle of meltwater, but she couldn't see it. No falls tumbling from the cliffs; just that dazzling blue ice.

'We're too close,' said Bale. 'We'd better turn back, make camp at that bay we passed. We've come as far east as we can.'

In her sleep that night, Renn saw Torak.

He crouched on a beach of black sand, his clothes in tatters, his face wild and hopeless as he lashed out with a flaming brand – *lashed out at Wolf.*

Renn gasped – and woke.

Bale was gone.

Emerging from the shelter, she saw him watching two reed boats putting out from their bay.

'I had a dream,' she told him. 'Torak's worse, he can't last much longer.'

Bale nodded grimly. 'Trouble is, he's a long way away.'

'How do you know?'

He pointed to the boats. 'They've been out here looking for fish for the past five days, so they didn't know who we were. They were helpful. Told me what the others kept from us. Someone found Torak's bow in the reed-bed.'

'The reed-bed?' Renn was aghast.

'Near the Island of the Hidden People. The Otter Mage sent us the wrong way.' He punched his palm. 'Ah, Renn, we were so close! If only we'd known, we might have found him by now!'

'But to send us the wrong way! Why?'

'What does that matter? We're further away than ever. And if you're right, he's running out of time.'

She thought quickly. 'How long will it take us to get there?'

'As the raven flies, maybe a day. By skinboat, with all these islands in between? Two days, maybe three.'

'Let's get going!'

'Not yet.' He pointed east. Above the ice river, purple-grey clouds were massing. The World Spirit was restless.

'But we can still try!' she said desperately.

'If I knew the Lake, yes. But out here, with a storm coming? No. We'd be no use to Torak drowned.'

She ran to the water's edge. Now she saw that everything had conspired to bring her here. Maybe this was why the Otter Mage had sent them east: to force her into doing what she'd resolved she never would.

Turning her back on the ice river, she stared west. Spiky black islands floated on the amber Lake. Somewhere beyond them, Torak was dying of soul-sickness.

'Then I've got no choice.' She faced Bale. 'We'll have to send help from here.'

'What do you mean?'

She took a deep breath. 'I'll have to do Magecraft.'

'Renn, this is madness!' yelled Bale as he fought to keep the skinboat afloat in the teeth of the storm. 'We've got to get back to shore!'

'Not yet!' shouted Renn. 'We have to get past that last island! I *must* have a clear view to the west, or the help won't reach him!'

'But we're taking water!'

'If you care about Torak, *keep going*!'

The sky turned black, the wind screamed in her ears, tugging at her clothes and whipping her hair about her face, churning the Lake to a frenzy of white water. The skinboat reared and plunged, and only Bale's skill kept them from going under.

Somehow, she managed to stay kneeling on the crossbar, gripping the boat with one hand as she thrust the other into her medicine pouch. She'd done all she could on the shore. Only the final charm remained.

As she pulled out what she needed and held it up, she felt a thrill of grim satisfaction. The Viper Mage might have Torak's name-pebble, but she, Renn, possessed something just as potent.

'What's that?' cried Bale.

'His hair,' she shouted. 'Last winter he needed a disguise, and I cut it off and kept it!'

Staggering to her feet, she raised her fist, and Torak's long dark locks streamed in the wind.

Bale grabbed her belt to hold her steady. 'For the last time, we've got to get back to shore! That's hail on the way! If it holes the boat, we're sunk!'

'Not yet!'

Throwing back her head, Renn howled the charm to the storm – she summoned the power of the guardian of all Ravens, who flies over ice and mountain, Forest and Sea – she summoned it and sent it to seek Torak – and the wind wrenched the charm from her lips and bore it west across the Lake.

But in the midst of the charm, as she braced her legs on the frame of the pitching boat and clutched Bale's shoulder to steady herself, she felt a powerful will confronting hers.

I feel your purpose . . . You shall not succeed.

Renn's knees buckled. She nearly went down.

You shall not succeed.

She tried to shut it from her mind – but it was too strong. Stronger than the Otter Mage, stronger even than

Saeunn – it had the awesome power of the Soul-Eater – and it was not to be outdone by the puny spell of some untried girl.

The World Spirit hammered open the clouds, and down came the hail, pummelling their faces with arrows of ice.

Bale swung the skinboat about. 'Rocks! Rocks ahead!'

Renn raised her fist one final time. 'Fly!' she screamed. 'Fly to the aid of the soul-sick!' The wind ripped Torak's hair from her fingers and scattered it over the Lake, and Renn was flung backwards as the skinboat gave a terrific heave and reared out of the water.

'We've hit a rock!' yelled Bale. 'Grab hold of the boat! *Don't let go!*'

The hailstorm thundered west, carrying Renn's charm with it. It swept across the Lake, flattening the reeds, pounding the Island of the Hidden People.

At the edge of the black beach, the pine trees thrashed, and beneath them Torak's miserable shelter shook. Pine cones and branches rained down upon it. Then something heavy dropped out of a tree and thudded onto the roof . . .

. . . and Torak woke up.

TWENTY-ONE

Torak cowered on his scratchy bed of pine-needles, listening to the World Spirit punishing the trees.

He was terrified of the hail, and of whatever had fallen onto the roof. He was terrified of everything: the Lake, the Hidden People, but most of all, the wolves. They were waiting for him in the Forest. Sometimes he glimpsed the big grey one sneaking about just out of stone-shot, waiting to pounce.

Because of the wolves, he hadn't dared go into the Forest. Instead, he eked out an existence on frost-shrivelled berries and blackened mushrooms, with the occasional slimy green hopping thing when he could catch one.

The world no longer made sense. The sky screamed at him, and from the trees, little red scuttling things pelted him with wooden fruit. Darts of green lightning shot past, laughing at him, and slithery brown creatures bobbed about in the water, scolding him. While he slept, a monster came and gnawed his shelter, and when he woke up, he saw branches swimming upstream.

Again something thudded onto the roof. This time, it squawked.

Torak shut his eyes tight.

At last the storm blew over and the hail stopped. Shaking with fear, he grabbed his axe and crawled out.

The ice had flattened undergrowth and ripped off branches; it had covered the beach in hard, translucent pebbles which crunched under his bare feet. In a patch of crushed bracken, something stirred.

No. Two somethings. A pair of big black birds.

Gripping his axe, Torak edged closer.

The larger one gave a terrified squawk and flapped its wings, while the smaller one tucked its head into its shoulders and pretended it wasn't there.

Torak saw the wreck of a nest, high in a tree. The birds must have fallen out, bounced off his shelter, and into the bracken.

He took a step closer – which sent them into a frenzy of wing-flapping and high-pitched squeaks.

He blinked. *They* were frightened of *him*.

He saw that the corners of their mouths were a crinkly pink, and although the span of their wings was almost as wide as his outstretched arms, all that flapping wasn't achieving anything.

'You can't fly,' he said out loud.

That put an end to the flapping. They huddled together and stared up at him, shivering with terror.

His belly tightened. So much meat. And as they couldn't fly, it would be easy.

To his dismay, he couldn't do it. They reminded him of something. Or someone. He didn't remember what.

A rapid 'quork quork quork' split the sky, and he dropped to all fours.

High overhead, another big black bird wheeled – only this one could fly. Alighting on the remains of the nest, it glared down at him. Its head-feathers were fluffed up like ears, its wings spread.

Angrily it snapped off a twig and threw it at him. Then it threw down several of the wooden fruit. 'Quork quork quork'!

'Leave me alone!' he shouted. Greatly daring, he picked up a wooden fruit and threw it back.

The bird hitched itself into the sky and flew away.

When he was sure it wasn't coming back, Torak left the young ones on their own and went to forage on the shore. If he couldn't eat them, they were no use to him.

He found a grubby mushroom which tasted all right, except for the bits that wriggled and crunched because he'd forgotten to shake out the woodlice. Then he caught two of the slimy green hopping things, which he killed with a stone. He ate one raw and tied the other to his belt for later.

Returning to the shelter, he found the young ones where he'd left them. When they saw the green thing at his belt, they flapped their wings and made squeaky begging noises.

'No!' he said. 'It's mine!'

The squeaks became outraged squawks. They didn't stop.

Maybe if he made them a shelter, they'd shut up.

Piling an armful of twigs in the fork of a tree, he grabbed the bigger bird and shoved it on top.

It pecked his sleeve and tugged.

'Let go!' he protested.

The powerful beak was bigger than Torak's middle finger, and it easily ripped off the sleeve. Gripping the buckskin in its formidable talons, the bird settled down to shred it, eyeing Torak as if to say, *I wouldn't have to do this if you'd fed me like I asked*.

In the bracken, the smaller one laughed.

Torak scooped her up and chucked her in the nest. She thanked him by waggling her hindquarters and spurting him with white droppings.

'Hey! Stop it!' he shouted.

'Hey top it!' she croaked.

Torak blinked. Birds didn't talk.

Did they?

If they could talk, maybe he shouldn't let them starve.

Foraging in the undergrowth, he caught some spiders and squashed them in his fist. The birds gobbled them up, and would've started on his fingers if he'd let them.

He fed them a leg of the green thing. And another. He decided enough was enough. The larger bird stared at him reproachfully, then tucked its head into its back feathers and went to sleep. Then the smaller one did the same.

Torak wanted to sleep too, but first he cut a scrap of skin from the green hopping thing and put it on the roof. He had no idea why he did this, but it felt important.

Yawning, he ate the rest of the green hopping thing, then crawled into the shelter and burrowed into the pine-needles.

Just before he slept, he said out loud, '*Frog*. The slimy green hopping thing is a *frog*.'

The young black birds ruled his days.

They were noisy and hungry, and if he didn't feed them often, they got noisier. But they had keen eyes and ears, and they scared off the biting monster which came in the night, and the red scuttling things in the trees.

After a few days, he took to letting them out of the nest. They hopped and waddled after him, and he found himself showing them things, and remembering as he did so.

'This is a pine cone. Hard to eat. And this is lingonberry, very good – ow! And this is willowherb. If you peel it, you can wind it into twine. See?'

The birds watched with their intense black gaze, and prodded everything with their beaks, to see if they could eat it.

Mostly, they could. They ate berries, crickets, frogs, scat, his clothes if he let them. But although they got quite adept with their large beaks, they preferred stealing food to catching it themselves.

They were good at it, too. When Torak caught his first tiny fish with a bramble-thorn hook on a line, he was so proud that he rashly showed it to them. Next day, he found the bigger one pulling in the line with its beak, while the smaller one looked on hopefully.

To deter them, Torak planted his knife by the line; but although they left the line alone, they picked at the sinew binding on the hilt. He swapped his axe for the knife, and that worked better.

Next day, as he emerged from the shelter, the bigger one cawed a greeting from the nest – and flew down to him.

'You flew!' said Torak, amazed.

Startled by its achievement, the bird sat trembling at his feet. Then it spread its wings and flew to the top of a tree –

where it lost courage and begged forlornly to be rescued. Torak eventually tempted it down with a handful of chopped frog and a couple of fish eyes, and from then on, it sat and laughed at its sister, who was still flapping furiously in the nest. It was mid-afternoon by the time she made her first flight.

After that, they learned rapidly, and soon the sky rang with their raucous cries as they wheeled and somersaulted overhead. Their feathers were a glossy black, with beautiful rainbow glints of violet and green, and when they flew, their wings made a strong, dry rustling, like the wind in the reeds. It made Torak wistful, as if he too had once been able to fly, but never would again.

One morning, they lifted into the sky, and didn't come back.

Torak told himself it didn't matter. He set a snare – one of his newly regained skills – and ate a few berries, taking care to leave some on a boulder, as an offering.

But he missed the ravens. He'd got to like them. And they reminded him of something – he couldn't remember what – except that he knew the memory was a good one.

When dusk fell, he checked the snares he'd set the previous night. He was in luck: a water bird. He woke up a fire and roasted it, but didn't have the heart to eat much.

Suddenly he heard a familiar cawing; then strong, rhythmic wingbeats – and down they came, alighting with a thud, one on each shoulder.

He yelped – their claws were sharp – and lifted them off. But he was glad they'd come back.

That night, all three of them had a feast. The ravens – whom he'd named Rip and Rek – ate so much that they got too fat to fly, and he had to carry them to their roost.

After they'd gone to sleep, he sat by the Lake, watching

the young swifts screaming overhead, while a woodpecker flashed past like green lightning, and a red squirrel dangled from one foot to reach an unripe hazelnut on another branch. As the moon rose, a beaver waddled out of the Forest, cast Torak a wary look, and settled down to gnaw on a willow sapling. The tree toppled, the beaver chewed off a branch, then swam upstream, dragging it behind him.

For the first time in many days, Torak felt almost at peace. The wound on his chest seemed finally to be healing, and he was no longer afraid. He knew that a lot was still missing from his memory, but the world was beginning to make sense.

The Lake stilled, and the Forest settled down for the brief summer night.

Torak felt eyes on him, and glanced over his shoulder.

From the trees, an amber gaze met his.

He started to his feet.

A grey shadow turned and disappeared into the trees.

TWENTY-TWO

A wolf cannot be of two packs.

Wolf was tasting the bitterness of this to the full. He couldn't eat or sleep or enjoy a good howl with the others. Since that terrible moment when Tall Tailless had bitten his muzzle with the Bright Beast, misery ran with him wherever he went.

And now, as he made his way through the Forest, jealousy ran with him too. *What was Tall Tailless doing with those ravens?* Wolves and ravens sometimes play together and help each other in the hunt, but they are not pack-brothers.

When Wolf reached the denning place, the rest of the pack had already returned from the kill, and the cubs had fed and gone into the Den to sleep. Wolf ran to touch noses with the lead pair, followed by the others; then everyone padded back to their sleeping places to snooze. Whitepaw, who'd stayed at the Den with the cubs, went off to check that the Forest was clear of lynx and bear and the Otherness which stalked the Big Wet, and Wolf slumped down to guard the cubs.

Tall Tailless no longer wanted him for a pack-brother. He never howled for him or came to seek him in the Forest.

And now those ravens.

The cubs burst from the Den and came racing over to Wolf, barking furiously – and for a while the misery was chased away. Leaping to his feet, he gave the high cub-greeting, and they nudged him with their stubby muzzles, and he lashed his tail as he heaved up the reindeer meat he carried in his belly. The cubs were growing fast, and soon the pack would move from the Den to a place many lopes away, where they would learn to hunt.

As Wolf thought about this, the misery slunk back. Leaving the Den would take him even further from Tall Tailless.

He lay down and put his muzzle between his paws.

As he was cub-watcher, though, he kept one ear on the cubs, and he soon became aware that they were stalking him like prey.

Growler, the cleverest, was innocently pawing a stick, but edging closer all the time; Snap, the smallest but fiercest, was down on her belly, sneaking up on Wolf from behind; and the more timid Digger was waiting to pounce when the others broke cover.

Suddenly, Snap charged – and sank her sharp little teeth into Wolf's flank. Growler sprang at Wolf's muzzle, and Digger attacked his tail. Wolf obligingly lay on his side, and they clambered on top of him. They chewed his ears, so he covered them with his paws, so they chewed his paws instead. And he let them, because they were cubs.

Digger bounded off and dug up a new plaything: the foreleg of a fawn, with the hoof still on. Snap advanced with a snarl – *That's mine, I'm the lead cub!* – and while she was standing over Digger to punish him, Growler sneaked between them and made off with the prize.

As Wolf watched Growler trying to get his jaws around the hoof, he was suddenly a cub again, back with Tall Tailless at their first kill, chewing a hoof that his pack-brother had given him. Misery grabbed him by the throat. The hurt was so bad that he whined.

Darkfur woke, and came to lick his muzzle, careful to avoid the Bright Beast-bitten side. Wolf was grateful, but the hurt didn't go away.

Whitepaw returned and took over watching the cubs, and Wolf went off and tried to sleep. But the thought of those ravens pecking kept him awake.

He sprang up. This was no good. He had to know for sure.

It didn't take long to reach the Den of Tall Tailless. Wolf sank into the bracken and belly-crawled closer.

Before long, Tall Tailless came out, stretching and talking to himself. His voice was deeper and rougher than before, but his scent was the same.

It hurt, being so near, yet unable to greet him. Wolf's tail ached to wag. He longed to feel those blunt claws scratching his flank.

He was wondering whether to risk the faintest of whines, when the matter was taken out of his jaws.

The ravens lit onto the ground, and Tall Tailless greeted them in tailless talk.

Wolf froze.

Tall Tailless squatted and stroked the ravens' wings. Gently, he took the bigger one's beak in his forepaw and gave it an affectionate shake, and the raven gurgled.

Jealousy sank its teeth into Wolf's heart. Tall Tailless used to muzzle-grab *him*, and they would roll together, growling and play-biting.

Now Tall Tailless was walking off along the Big Wet to hunt, and the ravens were with him, wheeling in the Up – just as Wolf used to trot beside him, proud and happy to be his pack-brother.

And still Wolf stayed in the bracken. When he smelt that they were truly gone, he raced into the Den and snuffled about, torturing himself with that beloved, now painful scent.

Suddenly he heard wingbeats – then a rasping 'quork quork quork'! As he left the Den, a pine cone hit him on the nose. The ravens were back. They sat on a branch, *laughing at him*!

Wolf sprang at them – and they lifted into the Up, then swooped low, but just out of reach, *taunting* him.

He waited till they came again – he leapt – snapped a tail feather, tore it to pieces. With furious caws the ravens soared into the Up. Down they came in a flurry of angry wings, diving, pecking. Again and again Wolf leapt – twisting, snapping – until he forced them to seek refuge in a tree, where they sat, cawing and pelting him with sticks. *This is our Den! Go away!*

Wolf's snarls shook him from nose to tail. They didn't dare make another attack.

Bristling with fury, Wolf bit off a willow branch and savaged it to shreds. Then he turned and raced into the Forest. His limbs itched with the blood-urge, his pelt prickled with rage.

So. This was how it ended.

Don't ever leave me, Tall Tailless had said. Then he'd chased Wolf away with the Bright Beast-that-Bites-Hot, and made a new pack – *with ravens*.

Well, let him! Wolf had another pack too.

TWENTY-THREE

When Torak returned to the shelter, he knew at once that something was wrong.

The ravens sat in their pine tree looking ruffled and aggrieved, and the bigger one was missing a tail feather.

'What happened?' he said. But they were too upset to come down.

In the shelter, he found his pine-needle bedding pocked with odd, fist-sized hollows. He sensed that this ought to mean something, but it didn't. His mind was still healing, his tracking powers only slowly coming back; and over the last few days, a fever and a cough had crept up on him, which didn't help.

Outside, he found the remains of a branch, savaged to pieces. A shred of chewed raven feather. A paw-print.

Frowning, he squatted to examine it.

The sun sank below the trees, and the Lake turned a dark wolf grey. Wolf grey . . .

Slowly, Torak rose to his feet. 'Wolf,' he said out loud.

For the first time in days, he saw clearly. He saw Wolf coming to watch over him, as he had done since they'd parted – and finding the ravens. He saw Wolf leaping at them, snapping a feather; taking out his rage and hurt on a branch.

The truth crashed over Torak. It wasn't Wolf who had forsaken him. It was he who had forsaken Wolf. Wolf, his faithful pack-brother, who had hunted by his side and guarded him from danger. And how had he repaid him? He had chased him away with burning brands; he had replaced him with ravens!

The guilt was almost more than he could bear. 'I've got to find him!' he cried. 'I've got to make it all right!'

He hadn't been in the Forest since his madness, and it felt unnervingly dark and still. He wondered if, like Wolf, it was angry with him for having forsaken it.

But trees live longer than people, and are slower to anger. The Forest welcomed him back. It gave him juicy strawberries which soothed his sore throat, and when the midges became annoying, it provided yarrow leaves to rub on his skin. For tinder it offered horsehoof mushroom; and best of all, it showed him Wolf's trail: a hair snagged on brambles, moss scuffed off a log.

The trail led uphill, past the little lake he'd found before, now ablaze with golden water lilies in the evening sun.

The wolves had chosen their denning place well: on a slope just west of the little lake, guarded by watchful pines.

The Den was at the foot of a red boulder almost as tall as Torak, and around it the ground was hard-packed by the padding of many feet, and littered with shards of bone.

But no wolves. And no cubs either, although he saw plenty of tiny paw-prints. Then he realized his mistake. The cubs would be asleep in the Den, and the pack was out hunting, it wouldn't be back before dawn. He had a long wait ahead.

As he breathed in the rich, sweet scent of wolves, he was overcome by longing and remorse. Wolves had saved him when he was a baby; and yet for days, he had feared them as ravening monsters.

With shocking suddenness, a large wolf emerged from behind the boulder. Its muzzle wrinkled in a snarl as it stalked towards him.

Hardly daring to breathe, Torak edged back. The pack had left someone to guard the cubs. He should have thought.

The cub-watcher advanced on him.

Torak averted his gaze and whined distressfully. *Sorry! Don't attack!*

The cub-watcher growled. *Go away!*

Slowly, Torak withdrew to the far side of the water lily lake. To be threatened by a wolf! He was still far from full recovery.

The short summer night descended as he waited. Frogs piped in the reeds. An otter surfaced and stared at him, then flipped under, leaving the lily pads gently rocking.

He nodded off.

His dreams were troubled by strange yowls, and he woke with a start. He felt hot and thick-headed, and his throat was so sore that it hurt to swallow.

The night was unusually quiet.

Too quiet.

Vaguely troubled, he decided to check the Den – even though it wasn't yet dawn, and the pack wouldn't be back.

As before, the denning place seemed deserted, but mindful of the cub-watcher, Torak approached with caution. In the gloom, he made out a birch tree whose bark was badly scratched down one side. Too high for badger, too low for bear.

He felt a prickling between his shoulder blades. He knew that feeling; everyone does, who lives in a Forest. It's the feeling of being watched.

Drawing his knife, he moved as silently as his laboured breathing would allow.

Something lay at the foot of the boulder.

The cub-watcher. Its flank had been ripped open, its throat chewed to pulp. It had put up a desperate fight to save the cubs.

Torak knelt and placed his hand above one white paw. 'Go in peace. May you find the First Tree, and hunt for ever beneath its boughs.'

In the earth around the carcass he found tracks: rounder than a wolf's, their outline blurred by fur.

Lynx.

Rising, Torak looked about him.

Couldn't see anything. He must've scared it away.

But it was odd for a lynx to attack a full-grown wolf. Mostly they take hares and squirrels, and wolf cubs if they can get them. The lynx must have gone after the cubs, and the cub-watcher had leapt to their defence.

A whine from the Den told him that the wolf had done its job well. Sheathing his knife, Torak crawled inside.

The tunnel was just big enough to admit him. As he breathed its earthy wolf tang, he was back in the Den where Fa had put him as a baby. His pack-brothers mewed as they clambered over him, and the breath of the Mother heated his skin as she nose-nudged him to suckle. He snuggled into her furry flank, and her milk tasted rich and warm.

He was through the tunnel and into the birthing place. As his eyes adjusted to the dark, he saw that it was about the size of a Raven shelter, but only high enough for a wolf to stand in. He caught a gleam of eyes. A fluffy huddle shrank from him.

He whined to reassure the cubs, but they were terrified. He was a stranger, and they'd just lost their uncle.

Backing out, he emerged from the Den – to see a large shadow bound away from the slaughtered wolf.

'Be off!' he shouted, waving his arms. His shouts ended in a coughing fit which bent him double.

The lynx leapt into a tree and sat, lashing its tail.

Drawing his knife, Torak took his place by the dead wolf at the foot of the boulder. He would guard the cubs till the pack returned.

It was strange, though, that his arrival hadn't frightened the lynx away. Lynx rarely attack people, and when they hunt, they target the young and the sick.

More coughing seized him. When it was over, he was sweating. His breath sounded like the crisping of dry leaves.

Then it came to him. The lynx knew he was sick. It heard it in his voice and smelt it on his skin.

Like the cubs, he was simply prey.

TWENTY-FOUR

The lynx dropped soundlessly from the branch and began to prowl.

Torak tried howling for Wolf, but only managed a croak.

The night was warm, the stink of the slaughtered cub-watcher thick in his throat. The carcass lay so close that he could touch it.

Too close. He should drag it further off, so the lynx could feed in peace. Let it take the dead, and leave the living.

But while he was doing that, it might come for the cubs. He pictured the small souls padding about, nosing their corpses. He tightened his grip on his knife.

A noise behind him. He spun round. Saw only the boulder. But lynx are superb climbers: they leap on their prey from above.

If only he had his axe. Why had he left it at the shelter? To have left without food, axe or tinder . . .

No tinder.

Fire would have scared it away. He should have taken some of that horsehoof mushroom when he'd the chance. The old Torak – the one before the madness – would never have made that mistake.

Another spasm of coughing gripped. When it was over, his ribs ached, and black spots darted before his eyes.

The lynx crouched in the shadows, just out of reach. He saw its blank silver eyes, smelt its rank cat smell.

Then he saw something which made his belly turn over. At the mouth of the Den, directly behind the lynx, two stubby muzzles were emerging.

Torak barked a warning. *Uff!* Danger!

The muzzles edged back inside.

The lynx caught the movement and turned its head.

'Here! Here!' shouted Torak to distract it. Yelling, throwing stones, he edged away from the Den.

The lynx bared its teeth and hissed at him. But suddenly it twisted, snarling at a bolt of black lighting plummeting from the sky. Rip gave a deafening caw and soared out of reach, as Rek swept in to attack. Now both were mobbing the marauder: wheeling, swooping to peck. The lynx leapt for them – and they took refuge in a pine tree, raucously cawing.

Lashing its tail, the lynx slunk back to the carcass.

Torak stood with legs braced, shaking with fever. The scab on his breastbone had reopened, and warmth seeped down his chest.

He could see no sign of the cubs. But he knew that soon they would be nosing their way out again.

When they did, the lynx would be on them.

Wolf loped through the trees. He recognized those caws! What were the ravens doing at the Den?

The wind turned, carrying scents of lynx and wolf flesh and Tall Tailless. He quickened his pace, and the pack ran with him.

The females were fastest, and reached the Den before him. He saw the lead female leap at the lynx and chase it into the Forest, with Darkfur and the others in pursuit.

Wolf skittered to a halt. He saw Whitepaw lying Not-Breath by the Den. He saw Tall Tailless clutching his great claw in his forepaw. He knew at once what had happened. Anger, joy and sorrow fought within him.

The ravens cawed from the trees, but Wolf ignored them. At the edge of the denning place, he saw the misty shape of a wolf. He cast it a reassuring glance, and what was left of Whitepaw – the breath that walked – lingered for a moment; then, satisfied that the cubs were safe, trotted into the Forest.

Blackear, Prowler and the lead wolf were staring at Tall Tailless, hackles raised.

Wolf trembled with longing to go to him; but it was for the lead wolf to decide if Tall Tailless was a friend of the pack.

The lead wolf went to the meat which had been Whitepaw, then walked stiffly towards Tall Tailless.

Tall Tailless stood quietly, with eyes averted, as a stranger should. Wolf was troubled to see that he swayed.

Still with hackles raised, the lead wolf sniffed Tall Tailless.

The cubs appeared at the jaws of the Den, whining, but

they didn't come out. They were waiting to see what would happen.

The hackles of the lead wolf went down, and he rubbed his flank against Tall Tailless' leg. Then he ran to greet the cubs.

Prowler and Blackear bounded past Tall Tailless to do the same, and he sank to the ground – ignoring the ravens, Wolf noticed happily.

Dropping his ears, Wolf wagged his tail.

Pack-brother, said Tall Tailless.

Wolf gave a whine and raced towards him.

TWENTY-FIVE

Safe with the pack, Torak had his first good sleep in two moons.

He woke in the afternoon, curled up at the edge of the denning place. The wound on his chest hurt, but his cough was almost gone, and he felt much better.

The lead wolf started a howl, and the others joined in. Torak shut his eyes as the wolf-song surged through him. He heard grief for their dead pack-brother and delight in the cubs; gratitude for the friend who had saved them. He gave himself up to the joy of being back with Wolf.

Sensing Torak was awake, Wolf bounded over to him, and they licked muzzles in a playful, everyday way, as if all the bitterness had never happened.

I'm sorry, Torak said in wolf talk – although it was only a tiny part of what he felt.

I know, said Wolf.

And that was that.

The howl ended, and a young female – a beautiful black wolf with eyes like green amber – trotted up to Torak with a rotten fish head in her jaws, and set it before him as a present. He thanked her and they touched noses. Then she and Wolf raced off to play with the cubs.

Once he was sure that Wolf was deep in a game of tag, Torak stuck the fish head in the fork of a birch for Rip and Rek. He'd been careful not to make a fuss of them in front of his pack-brother, and they'd been sulking in a pine tree. Food changed that, and soon they were squabbling over the prize.

It was a hot afternoon and the dead wolf stank, so Torak dragged it into the Forest. Let the ravens peck it undisturbed; and if the lynx returned for its kill, let it feed.

Then he went to find food for himself. After cutting a spear from a hazel tree, he woke up a fire and hardened the tip, then went to try his luck in the water lily lake.

It wasn't long before he speared a pike. Watched by a clutch of curious wolves, he roasted it and ate all except the tail, which he tied to the reeds as an offering. Then he ate a few handfuls of crunchy watercress and some early cloudberries, which burst on his tongue like honey.

Feeling full for the first time in days, he sat under an alder to mend his clothes. Without needles and thread, this was easy. He simply cut off his leggings at the knee, and as his jerkin was already in shreds, he gave up on it and went bare-chested, using the scraps to make a new headband.

When that was done, he leaned back and did nothing at all.

On the lake, a mallard floated on its side, preening its belly feathers. A pair of teal flipped bottoms-up to feed.

An otter taught her cubs to swim, and they paddled furiously, too fluffy to sink.

The ravens were splashing in the shallows, and the cubs were playing hunt-the-cloudberry. In the boggy channels draining the lake, Wolf and three young full-growns were trying unsuccessfully to wade-herd fish.

Torak felt a thrill of pure happiness. Wolves, ravens, otters, trees, rocks, lake: he was at peace with them all. For a moment he felt his world-soul reaching out to the world-soul of every living creature, like threads of golden gossamer floating on the wind. Wolf's amber gaze sought his, and Torak knew that he felt it too: that everything was just *right*.

On the other side of the lake, the reeds parted, as if for an unseen presence, and the lead wolf turned his head to watch. Idly, Torak wondered what he saw.

The leader of the pack was a large slate-grey wolf with a white blaze on his chest. Torak admired the way he asserted his leadership firmly but without bluster, never demeaning himself by bullying, and always watching out for his pack. Like Fin-Kedinn, thought Torak with a twinge of longing.

The young wolves were romping about in the shallows. Wolf bounded over to Torak and went down on his forepaws, lashing his tail. *Come and play!*

Torak pulled off his knife, belt and leggings and jumped in.

After the heat of the afternoon, the water was deliciously cold. Down he swam through spears of sunlight and rippling green weeds. Golden roach flickered past, and blue-black tench. On the underside of a water lily leaf, a bubble hung like a pearl, and he popped it with his finger.

Wolf's paws flashed by, and Torak yanked his tail. Wolf gave a startled yelp – Torak burst into the sunshine in a glitter of droplets – and they wrestled: Wolf play-growling, Torak shouting with laughter.

He was happy. He could live like this for ever.

Wolf gave a great twisting leap and splashed down on Tall Tailless. His pack-brother slipped under the Wet, then burst out again with his yip-and-yowling laugh.

That prompted the lead female to start a howl, and Wolf joined in. The badness in Tall Tailless had been chased away, the ravens knew their place, and he, Wolf, could be with Tall Tailless *and* the pack!

The howl ended. Tall Tailless waded out and threw himself down to dry off, and Wolf trotted up the rise to catch the scents.

He smelt many good smells, but to his dismay, he also caught the scent of the Otherness. It was floating on the Big Wet, much closer than before. It was getting bolder.

The ravens picked up the scent, and lifted into the sky.

Wolf watched them go – but decided not to follow. If there was trouble, they would alert the pack. That was what ravens were for.

Watching Rip and Rek flying east reminded Torak that he had things to do: he needed to build a shelter and set some snares.

Wolf knew before he did that he was heading into the Forest. Wagging his tail to show that he understood, he bounded off to play with the cubs.

Torak pulled on his leggings and started for the spot by the stream where the beavers were busy. He heard the crack of a tail-slam. *Beware! Intruder!* But they weren't really scared, as they knew he would only take the wood which they couldn't use themselves.

He chose three saplings which they'd gnawed through but hadn't been able to drag away, because they'd got stuck halfway down. Back at the denning place, he built a lean-to, filling in the sides with branches and bracken. Then he made his way through the Forest, and at the black beach he dismantled his old shelter and wiped out all trace of his presence.

The wound on his chest was painful and hot, so he dressed it with chewed willow bast and bandaged it with buckskin from his jerkin. By the time he'd finished, he was shaking with fatigue. He'd done too much. He must be weaker than he thought. Curling up at the edge of the trees, he fell asleep.

He dreamed of Renn. He felt her presence, but couldn't see her. He could hear her, though, as plainly as if she stood behind him.

'Better look after that wound, Torak,' she said in her wry, gentle way, 'or it'll go bad.'

'I put some willow leaves on it,' he said.

'It still hurts, doesn't it? Remember that healing spring on the north shore? You go up there and bathe it, right now.'

'If you come too,' he said, desperate to keep her with him.

'Maybe,' she replied, and he heard the smile in her voice. She was getting fainter.

'Come back!' he called. 'Renn, don't go! I miss you!'

'Do you?' She sounded amused. 'Well, I miss you too.'

He didn't want her to go. He was frantic to stay in the dream.

Mewing in distress, he woke up.

Clouds covered the sun, and the beach was desolate. Trudging down to the Lake, Torak stared at his name-soul in the water. He saw the mark of the outcast on his forehead; on his chest, the ragged wound from the Soul-Eater tattoo.

For an afternoon, he had been happy on the island. Ravens, beavers, otters, wolves: all had accepted him. But he missed Fin-Kedinn and he missed Renn.

He wondered if he would ever see them again.

TWENTY-SIX

The morning after the hailstorm, Renn stared at the stony little islet where the Lake had thrown them, and wondered how in the name of the Spirit they were going to get off.

The day before, as she'd huddled on the rocks, she'd simply been glad to be alive. Now she gazed about her in dismay.

There were plenty of trees, so at least they had fire and shelter; but she could have circled the whole islet in less time than it takes to skin a squirrel. And squirrels were doubtless what they'd be eating, because there wasn't room for anything bigger, and all the other islands were too far away to swim to.

She watched Bale walk to the water's edge, scuffing through the pine-needles festooning the rocks. He'd hardly spoken since they'd woken up.

'We've still got our axes and knives,' she said. 'And my quiver and bow.'

'Just as well,' he said without turning round. 'We've lost everything else. Food. The beaver-hide capes. Both paddles.' He couldn't bring himself to mention the skinboat, which lay between them. Its whalebone spine was intact, but the ribs on the left flank were smashed, and the seal-hide covering badly ripped.

'I don't think we can repair it,' said Renn.

'We'll have to,' he snapped.

'There are trees. We could make a dugout.'

He turned on her. 'Do you know how long that would take? To hollow out a tree? Have you ever *made* a dugout?'

She hadn't. The Ravens built their canoes of deer hide and willow, lashed together with spruce root.

'Neither have I,' growled Bale. 'I'm Seal Clan, we take what the Sea Mother gives us. So unless you want to make a raft with a bunch of reeds, we're repairing my boat!'

Renn didn't argue. He hadn't blamed her for the mess they were in, and he could have, because it was her fault.

The worst of it was, she didn't know if her Magecraft had worked. She only knew that she felt more exhausted than ever before in her life. She'd ignored all the warnings, she'd hurled herself against that overpowering will – and achieved what? As much good as a sparrow flying into a rockface.

The wind whispered over the pine-needles, and she seemed to catch a ripple of mocking laughter. How Seshru must be sneering at her!

Bale knelt by his skinboat, stroking its flank as if it were a faithful old dog in need of reassurance.

'Bale,' she said. 'I'm sorry.'

He shrugged. 'It was to help Torak. It was worth it.'

I hope so, thought Renn.

Bale stood up and squared his shoulders. 'Right. I'll make a start on the repairs.'

She nodded. 'I'll build a shelter. And find us something to eat.'

It took them four long days to mend the boat.

Bale had to cut down an ash tree to make the new ribs. Thinning them with an axe would have been impossible, so he had to make an adze, and as there wasn't any flint, he had to fashion one from a lump of granite, chipping and pecking it with a rock. When the ribs were finally shaped, he had to steam them and bend them to fit the hull, then smooth any rough edges which might have pierced the seal hide.

To patch the hide, he and Renn pooled every scrap they could spare: his fish-skin jerkin, her salmonskin tinder pouch, and – with regret – her sealskin bow case. It was barely enough, but when Bale tried to increase their supply by trapping fish, what he caught was too horrifying to use.

Luckily, he still had his repair kit of bone needles and seal-gullet thread, but sewing the stiff hide was painfully slow. 'No, no, you do *double* seams,' he scolded her, 'and don't pierce the outside, it'll leak.' He was much better at it, so she left him to it. But even with his bone thimble, his fingers were raw by the time he'd finished.

While he worked on the boat, Renn built a shelter, tying bundles of reeds with cords of twisted sedge, and lashing these to a bent willow frame. She gathered burdock, mussels and water lily roots to eat – after mistakenly digging up iris, which tasted disgusting.

She also straightened her arrows and shot a goldeneye duck as it flew in to land. That gave much-needed meat, and she used the skin to make a new tinder pouch, and the

173

feathers for fletching. She sneaked a gobbet of fat to oil her bow, although it made her feel guilty, as Bale needed every morsel to waterproof the boat.

For that they heated a paste of pine-blood, charcoal and duck fat in a birchbark pail and daubed it on the hull with sticks wrapped in bark. Renn liked the smell of pine, but Bale wrinkled his nose. 'If only we had seal blubber,' he muttered.

'Surely it's ready now,' she said when they'd finished. She hadn't dreamt of Torak since the storm, but the memory was with her constantly.

'Tomorrow,' said Bale.

Her heart sank. 'Another day?'

'If we don't let it dry completely, we'll sink.'

'But –'

'Renn. I know what I'm talking about. We'll set off in the morning.'

She blew out a long breath. 'It's been so long. Anything could have happened to Torak.'

'I know,' said Bale. 'I do know.'

To work off her frustration, Renn went hunting.

Maybe it was the offerings she'd made to the Lake, or maybe it was the pair of ravens she saw overhead, but her luck was good. Another duck, this time a goosander. She cooked it the way her father had taught her long ago: rolling it in mud and burying it in the embers, then cracking it open to get at the juicy meat.

After they'd eaten, Bale sat on the pine-needles, smoothing one of the new ash paddles with horsetail stems, while Renn set the goosander's innards on the blade of the other paddle and tipped it into the Lake as an offering. It was a warm, still evening, and frogs were piping in the reeds.

From the west came the howling of wolves.

Bale lifted his head. 'There they are again.'

Now and then, they'd heard them; but although Renn thought she recognized Wolf's howl, she couldn't make out Torak's. She felt a stab of worry. How could Torak be without Wolf?

The ravens were back, flying high and turning their heads from side to side to look down at her. She wondered if they were a good sign to set against all the bad ones.

'You're very quiet,' said Bale.

She turned to speak – then froze.

'What is it?' said Bale.

'The first morning, after the storm, you walked from those pine-needles where you are now, down to the water's edge.'

'So?'

'It wasn't far. It only took you about three paces to get to the water. Try it now.'

Puzzled, he did as she asked. Then he did it again, to make sure. He stared at her. 'Five paces. The Lake. It's sinking, just like the Otters said.' His face turned grim. 'Seshru.'

Renn nodded. 'She's getting stronger.'

TWENTY-SEVEN

'Uff!' barked Wolf, warning Torak not to go any further. But Torak couldn't turn back now, and Wolf couldn't come with him.

Torak cast him a reassuring glance and pressed on through the reedbed, jumping from tussock to tussock. The sun was low, but with luck, he would reach the healing spring before dusk.

He couldn't wait till morning. The wound on his chest was burning, and had begun oozing yellow pus. The Soul-Eaters were reasserting their power.

'Uff!' barked Wolf from the edge of the trees.

Go back! Torak said in wolf talk. Through the reeds he saw Wolf running in circles, whining.

The rockface was as he remembered: steep, yet oddly enticing, with its waterfall misting the ferns. It was surprisingly easy to climb, with convenient footholds and bushes; but he was soon soaked in spray.

'Uff!'

Glancing down, Torak saw with a pang that Wolf was coming after him. But the rockface was too much for him. He leapt – clawed granite – and fell back with a yelp. It didn't help that Rip and Rek alighted on a ledge and laughed at him.

Go back! Torak told him. *I'm at the Den in the Light!* He hated not being able to explain that he would be back soon; but in wolf talk there is no future.

When he looked again, Wolf was gone.

Tiring now, Torak climbed on. He passed the creatures he'd seen before, hammer-etched into the rock. He was too close to glimpse more than fragments – an elk's sloping nose, a snake's forked tongue – but he caught their wet clay smell, and made sure not to touch.

At last he heaved himself over the top.

Except it wasn't the top, but a rocky hollow where part of the cliff had fallen away.

Before him lay a pool of luminous green, as bright as beech leaves with the sun shining through. Around it, purple orchids and black crowberries flourished in green clay: the same clay he'd seen on the faces of the Otters. As with the rockface, stone guardians thronged the encircling boulders. Stone elk raised antlered heads; stone waterbirds flew across stone skies, or plunged after stone pike who swam forever out of reach.

Torak couldn't see the spring itself, but he heard its echo and felt its power. It felt neither good nor evil; it had existed long before either.

He was only too well aware that he didn't know the proper rites, and he sensed the Hidden People watching.

Bowing to the pool, he offered what he'd brought with him: the wing of a woodgrouse wrapped in burdock leaves, which he buried under a rock, in case Rip and Rek came back.

Then he knelt, cupped water in his hands, and bathed his chest, asking the spring to heal him. The water was icy. He welcomed its clean, sharp bite on his burning flesh.

Tentatively, he drank. The water tasted flinty. So did the crowberries, which bore an odd greyish bloom.

He thought about smearing some of the green clay on his chest, but decided not to risk it. He'd only seen that clay on the Otters and on the posts among the reeds. It belonged to the Lake. He was of the Forest. It wouldn't feel right.

Rip lit down beside him with a loud 'rap rap rap'! – and he jumped. 'Rap rap rap'! croaked Rek, thudding down beside Rip and fluffing up her feathers in alarm. In the last rays of the sun, the spray on their wings glittered scarlet, like drops of blood.

'What's the matter?' said Torak. 'Do you want some berries?'

To his surprise, they refused to eat, and pecked angrily at the crowberry bushes, scattering twigs. Torak shooed them away before they could do much damage.

In the world below, an elk bellowed, and the wolves started their evening howl.

Torak yawned. His chest went blessedly numb, and an irresistible languor was stealing through him. He curled up in the ferns and shut his eyes.

Moon and stars whirled above him, trailing silver fire across a dark-blue sky. He felt giddy and tired, so tired.

He heard the hiss and spit of embers; the spring gurgling a song which had no end. Then another voice joined in, murmuring words he couldn't understand. It sounded like Renn.

It *was* Renn.

She sat with her back to him, tending the fire. In the gloom he made out her pale arms and her long, loose hair.

To make sure she was real, he put out a clumsy hand and grasped her wrist.

Her bones were light and small. Yes, real.

'I knew you'd find me,' he said. It didn't begin to express what he felt.

Her skin was warm and smooth; he didn't want to let go. *Smooth.*

No zigzag tattoos.

'I knew I'd find you too,' said Seshru the Viper Mage.

TWENTY-EIGHT

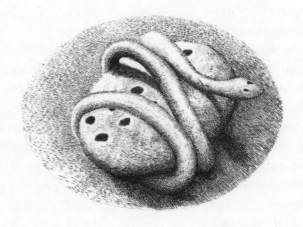

'How you've grown since last we met!' said the Viper Mage with her mocking sideways smile.

Her hair was a mantle of darkness, and the viper tattoo seemed to throb on her high white brow; but her beautiful lips were black.

Torak tried to move, but he couldn't. He wasn't tied up, his limbs simply refused to obey. He said, 'The crowberries. You poisoned them.'

Her eyes glinted. 'But I'm not going to hurt you.'

'Why would I believe that?'

'Because I would have done it by now. I could have cut out your heart and eaten it. Not even your wolves could have reached you up here.' She leaned down and whispered in his ear. 'But I want you alive!'

His heart was thumping so hard that she must be able to hear it. 'Why?' he said.

But she only laughed, and licked her lips with her little pointed black tongue.

As she twisted to tend the fire, her tunic of supple buckskin fell about her like water. It was fringed with snakeskin which caressed her naked arms and calves, shimmering with every move. Torak couldn't take his eyes off her. Fear and revulsion burned in him – this woman was evil, she'd helped kill his father – but he couldn't look away.

He watched her pass her hand over the lid of a basket, evoking a rustle from whatever lived within. He watched her twist a garland of herbs and set it on her brow, and paint long, wavering stripes on her arms: green snakes which wriggled to life on her pale skin. Fascinated and repelled, he watched – and she smiled her knowing smile, enjoying her power.

With a forked stick, she dropped a stone from the fire into a rawhide pot, sending up a hiss of steam.

'What's that?' he said.

Her lip curled. 'Hot water. I was a Healer, remember?'

Wringing out a piece of buckskin, she bathed his chest, then smoothed on a cooling salve. It felt good. The pain was gone.

'It won't fester any more,' she told him. 'I no longer need it to draw you to me. Though it's as well I summoned you when I did.'

I summoned you. The voice he'd heard in his sleep hadn't been Renn, but Seshru.

'What do you want?' he said between his teeth.

Rising to her feet, she went to the edge of the cliff and gazed down. 'All the tiny creatures,' she murmured. 'The

181

wolves, the frightened little Otter people. They belong to me now. They must submit – or I will empty the Lake.'

Torak thought of the pine-needles on the black beach. The Lake was draining away. He tried to stir, but managed only a twitch of his head.

The Viper Mage touched the green clay on her arm. 'This – this has power! When I wear it, those I meet see only a woman masked in green: sick, frightened, like them. Not even your wolf knows my scent.'

As if she'd called to Wolf, a howl rang out from below. *Come down!*

Seshru smiled. 'Now he knows me! I've shed my mask. He knows who has defeated him!'

Torak saw that the garland she wore was nightshade, which on a single stem bore purple flowers, green berries and ripe scarlet ones: a most potent herb, whose every part was deadly, like the Viper Mage herself. She was too strong. For a moment, he despaired.

He heard wings. Rip and Rek alighted on a boulder behind her.

'Ah, but you're strong!' said Seshru, oblivious. Kneeling beside him, she drew off his headband and gently pushed the hair from his forehead. 'To have spirit walked in an ice bear!' She stroked his temple. 'Brave, too. To cut out the mark of the Soul-Eater. Who taught you the rite? It must have been a Mage of great power.'

She was trying to flatter him. She wouldn't succeed. And yet – her touch was gentle. He struggled to keep his thoughts together.

'You – stole the red deer antlers,' he said. 'You poisoned the drink when I did the rite. You made me spirit walk in the elk.'

She smiled her beautiful, maddening smile. 'So strong.

And to fight off soul-sickness!'

His thoughts were darkening, her fingers reaching into his mind. 'The F-Far North,' he stammered. 'How did you get away? Where is the Oak Mage – the Eagle Owl Mage?'

She laughed. 'Ah, we're so alike, you and I! Both outcasts, both unimaginably strong. That's why the clans hunt us. The weak will always fear the strong.'

Rip and Rek flew away. Torak scarcely noticed.

'So alike,' breathed Seshru. 'Why fight it? Why not accept it?'

'No,' he said with an effort. 'We're not alike. You've killed people. You've broken clan law.'

'But that's all it is,' she countered, 'the law of the clans. Only the Soul-Eaters know the law of the World Spirit. That's why it delivered the spirit walker to me.' She paused. 'But why didn't I know you at once for what you are? How did you conceal yourself from me? The answer must lie somewhere.' With a supple movement, she reached for his gear.

The spell of her touch was broken. Torak hated seeing her handle his things.

'Your father's knife,' she said with distaste. 'A traitor's knife. Slate, antler, sinew. Nothing there. The axe, then. Not yours, I think.' Taking his hand, she measured it against the axehead. How clever she was! If the axe had been made for him, its head would have spanned from the heel of his palm to the tip of his middle finger. It was slightly longer.

'It has the Raven mark on the handle,' she mused, 'but the head is greenstone . . . They say that Fin-Kedinn lived with the frog-eaters for a time.'

She read the truth in his face. 'So it *is* his! You stole Fin-Kedinn's axe! *You* broke clan law!'

Next, she took his medicine pouch and drew out his medicine horn. Her lips thinned. 'Your mother's.' She set it down. 'Nothing. The answer lies elsewhere.'

With a shudder of relief, Torak remembered that the strand of Renn's hair was inside the pouch. Seshru hadn't found it. She was not all-powerful. She could make mistakes.

Seshru sensed the change in him, and her features turned colder than wind-carved ice. 'Do not imagine you can hide from me.'

Torak met her stare and held it.

With the speed of a striking snake, she brought her face close to his. 'You cannot defy me! Not while I have this!' In her fingers she held something small, caught in the coils of a green clay serpent.

Torak's belly turned over. The pebble he'd made for Renn.

'Have you any idea of the power this gives me?' she hissed. 'With this I blighted your souls! You have no will of your own. You belong to me!'

Her fist tightened on the pebble – and Torak's heart clenched.

She opened her fist – and he breathed again.

She laughed, and on her breath he smelt the carrion stink of the root which turned her mouth black. How could he have thought her beautiful? Her spirit was hollow, and where her heart used to be there was only a shadow, like the dark stain where a carcass once lay.

Now she was casting off the lid of the basket, and a viper was sliding over the edge. Silently, silently it flowed into her lap. Its zigzag markings were stark down its glistening silver length, and its lidless red eye was fixed on its mistress.

184

Seshru picked it up and it wound itself about her arm, its black tongue flickering out to meet hers. 'Keep very still,' she told Torak. 'Their bite is worse than any you will encounter in the Forest. Their bite can kill . . . '

A second viper, black as a moonless night, poured from the basket, and Seshru showed it the pebble. As its forked tongue flicked out to taste it, Torak gasped. He had felt that tongue on his skin.

'You wanted this, spirit walker,' breathed the Viper Mage. 'You put yourself in my power. You left the stone for me to find.'

'No,' he whispered.

Her eyes pierced his souls. 'Then why make it?'

'A – a present,' he stammered.

'For whom?'

'– A girl.'

'Why take it back?'

'To tell her I was gone.' He tried to push Renn's image from his mind, but the Viper Mage was faster.

'Her name is Renn,' she said. 'Who is she?'

With a huge effort, he dragged his gaze from hers – only to settle on the greenstone axe.

Seshru was on it in a heartbeat. 'Fin-Kedinn's. She's Fin-Kedinn's child.'

'– His brother's.'

There was a moment of stillness. Then the Viper Mage turned her back on him and sat, staring at the Lake, while the snakes in her lap twined their sleek coils about each other.

'– His brother's child,' she said tonelessly. 'Of course. He would have cared for his brother's child.'

Torak couldn't bear to hear her mention Renn.

But Renn is far away, he told himself. Renn is safe.

'No.' Seshru twisted round again. 'She is here on the Lake. I saw her in a boat with a boy, a tall boy with yellow hair. But they can't help you now.'

Was she telling the truth? Were Renn and Bale looking for him, or was it another of her lies?

'Why do you want me alive?' he said. 'What do you *want*?'

'You know what I want.'

'My power. You want to be the spirit walker.'

'I have that already. I can make you spirit walk whenever I wish. I want more. I want – the fire-opal.'

To hear her name it . . . Her voice breathed life into the image in his mind. He saw its pulsing red heart.

'It – it was lost in the ice,' he said.

'Don't lie to me,' said Seshru. 'I am a Mage, don't you think I have ways of knowing? When your father shattered it, three pieces were left – *three*! One held by the Seal Mage, one taken by the black ice. One remains. Your father must have told you before he died.'

'No.'

'He hid it. He hid it and he told you where, as he lay dying –'

'No –'

'– as he lay in agony, his life bleeding away, his guts ripped out by the demon bear –'

'No!' he screamed.

Clawing the nightshade from her brow, she flung it on the fire. Blue smoke wound about her, pungent, dizzying.

Powerless, Torak watched her open a pouch at her breast and dip in her finger. He tried to resist, but she held his jaw and smeared a stinking black sludge on his lips. Grasping the dark viper in one hand, the silver in the other, she brought them to her mouth and whispered a charm. Then she placed both snakes on his chest.

He didn't dare breathe. He felt their cool softness gliding over him; the tiny contractions as their scales gripped his flesh. He felt their tongues on his skin. Seshru observed his terror with the dispassionate gaze of a serpent watching its prey.

'Your body can't move, but your souls can. Your souls will go wherever I command. Your souls will do whatever I want.'

The black sludge was bitter in his mouth. Lights flashed behind his eyes, sickening spirals of light.

He saw the dark hair of the Viper Mage floating like snakes about her white face. He felt his souls ripped from his marrow. He screamed . . .

. . . silently, his black tongue tasted the air.

The last thing he heard before he became snake was the voice of the Viper Mage, commanding him to find Renn.

TWENTY-NINE

Faster than thought, the snake slithered down the rockface.

It tasted the scent of cricket and fern. It felt the scurrying of ant and shrew. Air, leaf, water, prey, light – it ignored them all. Its mistress had sent it after richer quarry.

The rocks burned with the heat of the vanished sun, and the snake took in that heat as it passed. Noiselessly, it slid off the rocks; the water enfolded it, and it took in the chill of the Lake.

The snake felt this change, but that was *all* it felt. No pleasure or discomfort, eagerness or fear. Those feelings it recognized, because it tasted them on the struggling prey and on the mountains of warm meat which shook the earth – but such feelings were not snake.

This made the souls of the snake very strong: pure

intent, unclouded by emotion. Torak would not have believed such strength could exist in so slender a body. His own souls were weak from the poison; he couldn't turn the snake from its purpose. He could only shiver inside its small, cold brain as it sped through the Lake, deadly as an arrow.

He felt the coolness of weed and water flowing over his coils. His lidless eyes knew the flash and flicker of fish. Then he was out in the heat again, and the scent of pine was thick on his tongue. The sand was rough, he gripped it with his scales. Raising his snake head, he tasted the scent of raven.

The hot bird swooped – its cries muffled by air, then piercingly loud as it thudded to earth. The snake darted into a hole and prepared to strike.

He felt the raven hop towards the hole. It smelt him, but it couldn't reach. Frustrated, it pecked the tree-root which sheltered him. The ground shuddered as it flew away.

When the threat was past, he emerged. He crested the mossy hillside of a log, slithered under bracken taller than trees. At last he caught the scent of slumbering male, and beyond it, the sweeter scent of female.

Torak's souls fought to get free – to turn the snake from its purpose – but it glided on, relentless. And now as he slid under leaf and over stone, he felt waves of heat from sleeping flesh.

Bite, bite. The voice of his mistress wove in and out of his snake mind.

Again the part of him that was Torak tried to turn the creature, but his muscles would not obey.

Bite, bite.

His coils gripped a naked foot, slid up a pale calf; over soft elk hide and rough wovengrass, into a band of warm

189

raven feathers heaving in sleep. His snake head recoiled from the markings on the wrist – so like his, yet different – but beyond, his cloven tongue tasted uprotected flesh.

No! shouted Torak in the cold snake brain. *No! This is Renn!*

The snake stretched its jaws wide – its fangs unfolded from the roof of its mouth and pointed down – they filled with venom, ready to strike . . .

Bite, bite.

Ψ

Torak woke.

Above him the clouds spun, jolting him on a sea of sickness. Gradually, he became aware of the sound of the spring. At his side the Viper Mage sat motionless, her face as white as bone. The vipers were gone.

'It is done?' she said.

He nodded.

She breathed out. Rising to her feet, she gazed across the Lake. Then she turned, and he could tell that she wasn't seeing him, but was looking through him to the power he could give her.

'Until now, 'she said, 'not even I understood the strength of the spirit walker.' Returning, she knelt, and her long hair brushed his chest as she brought her face close to his. 'Think what I can do with such power! I can learn the darkest secrets. I can bend all, all to my will!'

Torak shut his eyes. That made the churning worse. He tried to sit up – but although movement was returning to his limbs, he remained weak as a fledgling.

Seshru pushed the sweat-soaked hair back from his forehead. '*This* is the will of the World Spirit! *This* is why it sent such a gift to me! With the spirit walker and the fire-opal I shall rule! All creatures, all demons will fear me and obey!'

Sickness engulfed him. Clumsily, he raised himself on his elbow and retched.

With her icy hand, the Viper Mage pressed him to her breast. 'Great power is bought with suffering, I know. But now you understand. You belong to me.'

Exhausted, he slumped against her.

'Say it,' she whispered, and her breath was hot and foetid on his skin. 'Say that you belong to me!'

He gazed up at her, and she was very beautiful. Even her black smile was beautiful.

He said, 'I belong to you.'

THIRTY

Renn was shaken by her dream about the viper.

'What did it mean?' said Bale as they loaded the skinboat.

'I'm not sure. But it was in colour, so it must be true. I think . . .'

'Yes?'

'I think it means she has him now.'

Bale stopped with his paddle in his hands. 'You said the Magecraft had worked.'

'I said I *thought* it had. You can never be certain.'

He considered that. 'Well, I've got more faith in you. And in Torak.'

Renn didn't reply. She hadn't told him about the real viper she'd glimpsed as she'd started awake. What would have happened if those ravens hadn't chased it away?

Oh, Seshru was cunning! She'd cut Torak off from the clans, from his friends, even from Wolf – and now she had him to herself, on this Lake which she was taking for her own. Somewhere, she was laughing at them all.

It was a hot dawn, and with the wind at their backs they made good speed. Their islet turned out to have been much further west than they'd thought, and by mid-afternoon the Island of the Hidden People came into view.

As they bobbed in the shallows, Renn made an offering, asking leave to go ashore; then they landed the skinboat on a black beach backed by a watchful Forest. It had rained recently, and a steamy haze rose from the trees. A smell of decay wafted from a band of reddish pine-needles which reminded Renn of a snake.

'No sign of Torak,' said Bale, returning from a search further up the beach. 'But I found other tracks.'

When Renn saw them, her heart quickened. 'A wolf.' She blew her grouse-bone whistle, but got no answer. Her unease deepened.

As soon as they entered the Forest, the wind dropped and the heat settled on their skin. Clouds of midges whined in their ears. The rasp of crickets was loud, but there was no birdsong, except for the brief warble of a redstart.

Wading through springy lingonberry scrub, they followed a rivulet upstream. They passed man-high nests of wood-ants, and hunched boulders mantled with steaming moss. Over her shoulder, Renn caught the glint of the Lake between the trees; then the pines closed in and she saw it no more. The presence of the Hidden People was strong. She saw Bale touch his seal-rib amulet.

They reached a clearing where the stream had been dammed by branches. Brown pools spread amid gnawed stumps and piles of wood-chips. The air was fresh with the tang of tree-blood.

'Beaver,' they said together.

Bale gave a lopsided smile, and Renn's unease lessened. If the Hidden People allowed beavers on their island, then maybe Torak . . .

Again that redstart.

Renn froze. 'Torak?' she called softly. 'Is that you?'

Bale raised his eyebrows, and she explained that it was a signal they sometimes used.

Once more she called. The Forest tensed. Her heart raced.

'Maybe it's our weapons,' said Bale in a low voice. 'He'll be wary.'

Renn stared at him. 'Not of us!'

'Renn. He's been outcast a long time. Let's set them aside; and we should move into the trees. If it is him, he won't come into the open.'

Propping their weapons against a stump, they left the clearing and re-entered the Forest.

'Torak!' Renn breathed to the watching pines.

'We came to help you,' whispered Bale.

They hadn't gone far when they rounded a boulder and found their weapons neatly laid on a lingonberry bush – except for Renn's bow, which hung from a birch tree.

'Couldn't let it get wet,' said Torak.

There was no time for greetings.

Torak jerked his head at them to follow, and headed into the trees. 'Got to get deeper in, or she'll see us.'

'She's *here*?' cried Renn and Bale together.

'Up on the north cliff,' muttered Torak, 'that's her eyrie. I don't think she'll risk the island because of the wolves.'

Renn's skin prickled. 'You've actually seen her?'

'She lured me there. She thought I was going to help her. I – I got away.'

'How?' said Bale.

Torak's face closed. 'Even the Viper Mage has to sleep.'

'Not for long,' said Renn.

Torak didn't answer. His expression was taut and unsmiling, and he kept turning to listen for sounds of pursuit. There was a bruised look about his eyes that told of broken nights and not enough food. And Renn noticed with a pang that he no longer wore the rowanberry wristband.

She couldn't tell if he was glad to see them. She couldn't tell *what* he was feeling. She tried to overcome the awful sense that he'd become a stranger.

And he looked so different! He'd been a skinny boy when he left, but now he was as tall as Bale, and the veins on his arms stood out like cords. There was a scab on his chest where the mark of the Soul-Eater had been, and some puzzling scratches on his shoulders; and although he still wore the headband, it only reminded her of the outcast tattoo beneath, and of all the dangers he'd survived on his own. Without her.

They found a fallen pine and hid behind it while Bale shared out dried duck meat from his food pouch. Torak ate fast, like a wolf. He didn't say much about the past two moons, just told them briefly about Wolf joining a pack. Bale told how they'd met the Otter Clan and wrecked the boat, but to Renn's relief, he didn't mention her attempt at Magecraft. Throughout, Torak spoke mostly to his kinsman, and avoided looking at her.

Silence fell and she plucked up courage. 'You got rid of the Soul-Eater mark.'

He nodded. 'I did the rite, but I'm not sure it worked. I got sick. A kind of madness.'

'Soul-sickness,' said Bale.

'Is that what it was?' said Torak. 'Well. I got better.'

'How?' said Renn.

'I don't know. I just did.'

There was a whirring of wings, and a raven flew down onto Torak's shoulder. Wincing, he lifted it off. 'I told you not to do that!'

Renn and Bale exchanged startled glances.

Another raven alighted on a juniper bush. Torak gave each bird a scrap, and they flew to a nearby tree, where they eyed the newcomers suspiciously.

Renn was astonished. Ravens are supremely wary birds, but with Torak they behaved with perfect ease.

'Where did they come from?' said Bale.

'There was a hailstorm,' said Torak. 'They fell out of their nest, and I – I had to look after them. It's odd, but after that I got better.'

Bale caught Renn's eye and smiled.

She didn't smile back. She didn't *want* to be good at Magecraft. And she was a bit envious of the ravens.

'I call the bigger one Rip,' said Torak. 'The smaller one's Rek. Watch your gear, because they like to steal, and what they can't steal, they shred. And when Wolf's around, *don't* make a fuss of them. He gets jealous.'

Feeling self-conscious, Renn bowed to the ravens. 'Well met, little grandfathers, and thank you.'

Rek flapped her wings and croaked, 'Well met well met!' and Rip lifted his tail and spattered the ferns with droppings.

Torak glanced at Renn in surprise, but she didn't speak.

Let him think the ravens had come to him by chance.

Bale stood up and said he was going to hide the skinboat, and suddenly Torak and Renn were alone and the awkwardness was worse.

Torak frowned. 'Renn . . . '

'What?'

'That elk. The one that attacked you –'

'I know,' she said quickly.

'Do you?' His frown deepened. 'I was so worried. That's why I went back to camp, to see if you were all right.'

'I know. Torak – '

'She made me do it!' he burst out. 'She made me do terrible things! Attacking you, then Ak – the Boar Clan boy . . . '

'Aki?' Renn snorted. 'He's all right!'

He stared at her. 'He is?'

'Broken arm, but it's on the mend.'

'He's *alive*.'

'Actually, I wish it'd been a bit worse. Bale said that when he left, Aki was trying to get his clan to come after you.'

Torak wasn't listening. He had both hands to his temples, and he looked younger and more vulnerable.

Renn said, 'Maybe you haven't changed as much as I thought.'

He blinked. 'You're the one who's changed.'

'Me?'

He touched his cheek, to show that he'd noticed her moon-bleed tattoo. 'You seem older.'

She was embarassed. 'I *hate* sharing with Saeunn. She grinds her gums in her sleep. First time I heard it, I thought someone was sharpening a knife. But it went on *all night*.'

His lip curled. 'Does she smell?'

'Like a three-day-old carcass.'

He grinned. And suddenly he wasn't a stranger any more.

Bale returned, looking worried. 'I should have hidden the skinboat earlier, she might've spotted it.'

'Whatever you do,' said Torak, 'she'll soon know you're here. She knows everything.'

Renn went cold.

'But what does she *want*?' said Bale.

'She wants to crush the Lake into submission,' said Torak. 'She wants me to help her find the last piece of the fire-opal. She wants to rule.'

'How would she get you to help her?' said Renn, feeling breathless.

Torak hesitated. 'That pebble I made for you? She has it.'

Renn shut her eyes. She'd been dreading this.

'But – I still got away,' he said uncertainly. 'And I fought off the soul-sickness. And when she made me spirit walk in the viper, I fought back.'

No you didn't, thought Renn. The ravens woke me in time. Out loud she said, 'She'll make you do it again, Torak. Or she'll think of something else. She's like a snake. If she meets an obstacle, she slithers around it.'

Torak stood up. 'Then we'll have to find the fire-opal before she does. Come on. We'll be safer with the wolves.'

Everything was happening too fast, Torak couldn't take it in.

First his flight from Seshru: scrambling down the rockface, splashing through reeds, crashing into the Forest. Fearing at any moment to feel a viper's fangs sinking into his calf; to come face to face with that all-seeing, all-powerful gaze.

And now suddenly, Renn and Bale.

He should have been elated, but he was too churned up. Renn looked so different! The birch-seed freckle was still there at the corner of her mouth, but the red bar on her clan-tattoo made her seem older, less like his friend. It was a stark reminder that the life of the clans had gone on without him; that he'd been left behind.

It was a shock, too, to see her with Bale. As they moved through the Forest, he saw how easily they fell into step together. He watched Bale hold a branch out of the way of her bow, and felt a twist of jealousy. The Seal boy had taken his place.

Renn, though, didn't seem to notice. She wanted to know everything Seshru had said and done when he'd been with her at the spring, and she listened with the same intense concentration which she brought to hunting.

'She'll find some way to get you,' she said. 'If only we knew what she was doing.'

Bale watched Rip alight in a pine. 'Torak could spirit walk in a raven, and find out.'

'I thought of that,' said Torak, 'but I can't. In the Far North, I promised the wind I'd never fly again.'

'How she'd laugh if she knew that,' Renn said bitterly.

The light was failing as they reached the water lily lake. The denning place was quiet.

Torak gave two short barks. *I am here!*

No answer.

He ran to search the Den.

No cub-watcher. No cubs.

'They've gone,' he said in disbelief. 'The pack is gone.'

Renn stood with her hands on her hips, looking about her. 'Where would they take the cubs?'

Torak thought for a moment. 'When they get big enough,

the pack takes them to a new place, to learn to hunt.' He breathed out. 'Yes, that must be it.'

'Will it be far?' said Bale, his voice strained.

'A day's lope, maybe more.'

'So – it'll be off the island?' said Renn.

'Yes,' said Torak. 'But Wolf will come back for me, or we'll find each other by howling – '

'Torak,' cut in Bale, 'don't you see what this means? If the wolves have left the island, it means – '

'Yes,' said the Viper Mage, 'it does.'

THIRTY-ONE

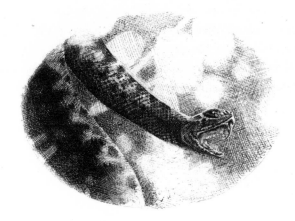

She sat cross-legged on the boulder above the Den, gazing down at them with her mocking sideways smile. 'The wolves are gone,' she told Torak. 'I sent them all away.'

'Don't listen to her,' said Renn.

'Why, what harm can I do?' said the Viper Mage without taking her eyes off Torak. 'It's three against one, and I have no weapons.' Her voice was as smooth as water that wears away stone, and she made him feel as if she spoke to him alone: as if they were the only ones here in this hot, airless dusk. 'No weapons,' she murmured, 'not even a knife.'

Torak felt the sweat starting out between his shoulder blades. He darted a glance at his friends. Bale stood transfixed, his axe forgotten in his hand. Renn gripped bow and arrow, but did not take aim.

'Not even a knife,' repeated the Viper Mage, drawing his gaze back to her. At her breast the medicine pouch softly rose and fell. In the failing light her eyes were black, unblinking as a snake's. 'You lied to me,' she told him. 'You deceived me and ran away. I thought you were braver than that.'

Torak swayed. 'You can't make me go with you,' he said with an effort.

'Ah, but I can.' She touched the pouch. *You know I can. I have your stone, caught fast in the coils of the green clay serpent. You cannot defy me!*

'Don't listen to her,' snarled Renn again.

'So this is Renn,' said Seshru, leaning back on her hands and regarding her with amusement. 'What a little vixen! It was you who helped him resist me, wasn't it? You must have some small talent for Magecraft.' She paused. 'But of course you do! And we both know why.'

Shakily, Renn nocked an arrow to her bow.

Torak grabbed her arm. 'Renn, no!'

'You can't, she's not armed!' cried Bale.

Seshru laughed, baring her white throat. 'Oh, she won't shoot! She can't. Can you, Renn?'

Trembling from head to foot, Renn lowered her bow.

'I knew she wouldn't,' said the Viper Mage with contempt. She turned her gaze on Bale. 'To kill a weaponless woman . . . who could do such a thing? Could you?'

Her beauty caught him in its web, and his axe slid from his grasp.

'I didn't think so,' she said. 'That would be the mark of a weak man, and you're not weak. You're a Seal Clan hunter. You're strong.'

Bale shook himself and drew a deep breath, as if coming up for air. But his arms hung limp at his sides.

The Viper Mage withdrew her gaze from him, and again Torak felt its force. It was like staring at the sun.

'Don't look at her,' said Renn. 'Don't listen to her!'

Torak gripped his knife-hilt till his knuckles were white. This knife had belonged to Fa. Fa had had the strength to resist the Soul-Eaters. So must he. 'I – won't go with you,' he said at last. 'I won't help you find the fire-opal.'

'Oh, but you will,' said Seshru, and her lips parted in noiseless laughter. 'When you know the truth, you will!'

'No.'

'You see,' she continued as if he hadn't spoken, 'I can make you leave your friends – I can cut you out from your safe little herd – just as easily as snapping my fingers.'

'No,' whispered Torak.

'She's lying,' said Renn in an odd, pleading tone. 'That's what she does, Torak, she lies! She takes credit for things she didn't do; she denies the crimes she did. You can't believe anything she says!'

'Some things you can,' Seshru told Renn, her voice tinged with venom. 'We both know that, don't we, Renn? Although I must say, I'm surprised that you never told him. If he's your friend – if you care for him as much as he cares for you – and he does care, he really does . . . Not to have told him! *Such* a mistake! But then,' she added slyly, 'you already know it was a mistake. Don't you, Renn?'

Torak saw that Renn's face had gone chalk-white. 'Renn?' he said. 'What's wrong?'

Renn's eyes were shadowy hollows, her expression unreadable. 'I was going to tell you,' she said in a strangled voice. 'But I could never . . . It was never the right time.'

He began to feel cold. 'Tell me what?'

'Haven't you guessed?' said Seshru, leaning forwards and watching him with the fixity of a snake closing on its prey.

'Guessed what?' said Torak. 'Renn, what is it?'

Seshru smiled her carrion smile. 'Tell him, Renn. Tell him!'

Renn opened her mouth, but no sound came.

'*What?*' shouted Torak.

The Viper Mage licked her black lips and hissed, '*She is my daughter!*'

THIRTY-TWO

Renn wished Torak would say something – anything – but he just stood there, staring at her. And that was worse.

'I wanted to tell you,' she said. 'It was never the right time.'

He looked as if he'd been kicked in the chest. He looked as if he didn't know who she was.

She said, 'I couldn't tell you in the beginning. You would never have been friends with me.'

'Two summers,' he said quietly. 'You hid this for two whole summers.'

She felt cold: a deep inner cold that went beyond shivering. 'I thought maybe you'd guessed. When you spirit walked in that elk. And the viper. I thought you were angry.'

'No. You hid it too well.'

She flinched. 'You – you hid things too,' she faltered. 'You didn't tell me about the Soul-Eater tattoo. But I got over it. I understood.'

'That was for two moons. Not two summers.' He took a few steps away, then turned and confronted her. The blood had left his face. His lips had a greyish tinge. 'The first time I met you,' he said slowly. 'I felt there was – something. I didn't trust you.' He paused. 'Turns out I was right.'

'How can you say that?' she burst out. 'Of course you can trust me!'

He was shaking his head in disbelief. 'Two whole summers. I was your friend and you lied to me, every single day.'

'You're still my friend!' she cried. 'I'm still Renn! Still the same person!'

Bale stepped between them. 'Torak. She never meant to hurt you.'

'What do you know?' snapped Torak. 'Keep out of this, it's got nothing to do with you!'

'Torak, *please*,' said Renn. 'I *know* I should've told you . . .'

'Get away from me!' His face worked. 'I never want to see you again! Just – get away!'

She turned and fled.

'Renn, come back!' shouted Bale. 'No – Torak – don't you go too! *Renn*! We've got to keep together! This is just what she wants!'

Renn tore through the bracken, not caring where she went. As she ran, she saw that the Viper Mage was gone from the boulder. She had scattered them just as she'd said she would: as easily as snapping her fingers.

4

Torak's only thought was to be on his own. He could hear Bale crashing after him, but the Seal boy was no match for him in a darkened Forest, and he was soon left behind.

At last, Torak reached the shore and had to stop. The reeds stood deathly still, like a thicket of spears. He hardly saw them. It was a hot, still night and the sweat was pouring off him, but he was shaking with cold.

Images from the past flashed before him. Renn's talent for Magecraft. Her reluctance to practise it. Her refusal to explain why.

She and the Viper Mage even looked alike! The same pale skin and high-boned, regular features. Why hadn't he seen it?

But what hit hardest and hurt the most was that she'd kept this from him for so long. That she could be capable of such deception. It turned her into someone else, someone he didn't know. And that was the worst, because it meant that he'd lost her. He was alone again, just like when Fa was killed.

No, he thought, not alone. Never alone, while you've got Wolf.

Wolf never lied to him. Wolf wouldn't know how.

Putting up his head, Torak howled. *Come to me, pack-brother! I need you!* Reckless of the Viper Mage, he shut his eyes and put all his pain and loneliness into his howls.

At first, he heard nothing. Then, very faint, came an answering howl.

At least – Torak *thought* it was Wolf, but it was too far away to make out. Maybe it wasn't Wolf at all, but one of the others. Maybe it was nothing to do with him.

Bereft, he wandered along the shore.

Much later, he found himself sitting at the southern tip of the island, gazing over the Lake. He had no idea how he'd got there. He only knew that he was very, very tired.

Far to the south, he made out the lights of the Otter camp; nearer, to the west, the glimmer of campfires. Distractedly, he wondered what that meant. Maybe the clans were coming after him. He couldn't bring himself to care.

On the Lake, a shadow slid towards him.

He couldn't summon the strength to hide. With his axe in one hand, he rose to his feet.

Whoever it was moved skilfully, nosing towards him as silently as a pike.

'Torak. Get in.' Bale spoke quietly from the gloom.

Torak didn't move.

'Torak! Come *on*, the Viper Mage could be anywhere! And judging from those campfires, half the clans have come after you!'

When Torak still didn't move, Bale sighed. 'I know this is hard, but there's no time! We'll head for the north shore, they won't dare hunt us there; then we'll look for Renn.'

'No,' said Torak. 'You do what you like. I'm going to find Wolf.'

'Wolf will find you, but Renn's out there alone, and that – creature – could be anywhere!'

'I don't care.'

'Yes you do. If anything happened to Renn, you'd never forgive yourself – and neither would I. Now get in!'

208

The Bright White Eye was shining in the Up as Wolf paced the ridge.

During the Light, he'd told himself that all was well: that once he knew the cubs were safe at their new resting place, he could race back and fetch Tall Tailless. Then, far in the distance, he'd heard his pack-brother's desperate howl.

The other wolves had heard it too, but to his dismay, they'd hardly stirred. The cubs lay in an exhausted heap, and the full-growns – tired from the journey – sprawled, whiffling, in their sleeps. Tall Tailless was their friend, but he wasn't of the pack, as Wolf was of the pack.

This troubled Wolf. He wanted everyone to be together, as they had been on the island.

Trotting down to Darkfur, he snuffle-licked her muzzle. Sleepily, she raised her head and thumped her tail, then slumped back on her side. Soon her paws were twitching in her sleep.

The lead wolf felt Wolf's worry and woke.

Wolf dropped his ears and wagged his tail, apologizing for leaving. Then he started down the ridge.

It helped to be on the move. He would hurry back to the Den and find Tall Tailless. Then he would lead him to the pack, and everything would be all right.

For a while he gave himself up to the whisper of the grey flowers against his fur and the sweet breath of the slumbering trees; but the part of him that was always on watch noted that this Dark, smells and sounds were keener than usual. His pelt was tight, his pads tingled. The Thunderer was restless. There was going to be a storm.

Reaching flatter ground, he slowed. He smelt dogs. Some he knew, many he didn't. Keeping downwind, he crept past the great Dens of the taillesses, which clustered by the Wet like a herd of aurochs. So many taillesses! Here were ones who smelt of boar and raven and even of wolf; but he couldn't stop to explore.

Beyond the Dens, he quickened his pace, weaving through the reeds, following the ancient trails known only to wolves and Hidden Ones. As he loped, he glimpsed them: silent, swaying. He ignored them, and they let him pass.

At last he reached the denning place, and suddenly everything was wrong wrong wrong. It stank of Viper-Tongue!

Wolf smelt that Tall Tailless had been here, and to his surprise, he also caught the scent of the pack-sister who smelt of ravens, and of the pale-pelted male who was their friend. *But they had fought!* Wolf smelt rage and pain and biting sorrow. He smelt Viper-Tongue's dreadful pleasure.

A breeze woke the birch trees, and in the distance, Wolf heard howls. The pack was singing its joy at having found a safe place for the cubs.

Wolf lifted his muzzle to tell them he was coming back – but suddenly, he stopped.

A terrible certainty came to him. It hurt more than strong teeth tearing into his flank. *A wolf cannot be of two packs.*

Wolf saw now that Tall Tailless couldn't be with the pack, because that wasn't what he was for. Fighting bad taillesses was what he was for; just as hunting demons was what Wolf was for.

Pain sank its teeth into Wolf's heart. Not for him to run with the pack and teach the cubs to play hunt-the-lemming. Tall Tailless had rescued him when he was little; and later, he had braved the Great Cold to save him from the bad taillesses. Tall Tailless was his pack-brother. A wolf cannot be of two packs.

Something pecked Wolf's tail.

Wake up! cawed the ravens.

With a half-hearted snap, Wolf chased them away.

The ravens perched on the rock, then flew to earth and stalked him again. Now that they'd found him, they weren't going to leave him alone.

They were right.

Swallowing his sorrow, Wolf cast about, untangling the scent trails. He soon found that of Tall Tailless, and followed it into the Forest.

He hadn't gone far before he reached the Big Wet. He smelt fish-dog and pine-blood and the pale-pelted tailless. He sat on the shore and whined. Tall Tailless had gone with the pale-pelt in the floating hide. Those floating hides were Not-Breath – Wolf knew that because he'd chewed one once – and yet they swam faster than a blackfish. It would be useless to swim after Tall Tailless. He was gone.

Again Wolf cast about for scents. He caught that of the pack-sister. *Yes.* Now he knew what to do!

Once he'd found the pack-sister, he would find his pack-brother. They wouldn't stay apart for long.

THIRTY-THREE

Renn didn't care which way she ran. The dark pines watched her impassively, but the junipers snagged her clothes, telling her to slow down. She ran on.

Torak's voice echoed in her mind. *Get away from me – I never want to see you again!* The look on his face . . . Retreating into himself, like a wolf licking its wounds.

She had done that to him. It was her fault.

The sound of a waterfall broke through to her, and she found herself at a narrow stretch of reeds backed by a looming cliff-face.

Her fists clenched. Somewhere up there was the woman who had ruined her father's life and overshadowed her own; who had burdened her with unwanted powers and robbed her of the only friend she'd ever had.

Leaping from tussock to tussock, she made her way to

the foot of the cliff and stood, craning her neck. She could climb up and confront the Viper Mage; but that might be just what she wanted. She could set some kind of trap and capture her alive – or dead – she didn't care which.

With a cry, she turned and ran.

She found a trail which tracked the north shore. She hadn't gone far before she felt eyes on her and spun round.

'Bale?' she whispered. 'Torak?'

No-one. No-one was coming after her. She was back where she'd been before Torak. Friendless.

At last she reached a little bay that glowed dark-blue in the summer night. Driftwood lay in piles, bleached silver by wind and rain. At the head of the bay, three posts stood guard. They had misshapen clay heads, and their white eyes stared over the Lake. Renn caught the faint, high whine of their power, and clutched her clan-creature feathers. She edged behind them, so as not to be seen.

At the eastern end of the bay, screened from the posts by pines, she found a small deerhide boat tethered in the shallows. Maybe it belonged to the Viper Mage. She didn't care.

Quickly, she unlashed the mooring and jumped in. The boat lurched, but she dug in the paddle and headed off. She had no idea where she was going; she just needed to be on the move.

Something made her glance back.

The Viper Mage stood at the water's edge, watching her.

Terror washed over her. As if caught in an invisible net, she brought the boat about, and they faced each other across the shimmering water.

'What do you want?' Renn said, hating the way her voice shook.

'Nothing you can give,' said the Viper Mage, her face livid in the moonlight.

'Then why are you here?' said Renn. 'Haven't you done enough?'

The black lips parted. 'You disappoint me, daughter. I'd hoped for less passion. More control.'

'I hurt him. I hurt my best friend.'

Seshru tossed her head in scorn. 'What a pity, you have your father's heart! Although – ' her lip curled as she indicated the stolen boat, 'you have your mother's courage.'

'I have *nothing* of yours!' spat Renn.

'Ah, but we both know that isn't true. You have my talent for Magecraft. You did well to help the spirit walker resist me. Perhaps I should be proud of you.'

Renn's chest tightened with hatred.

'He belongs to me, daughter,' warned the Viper Mage. 'He is my reward for the long winters of waiting.'

'He belongs to no-one but himself.'

'Don't fight me. It would be fatal to pit your power against mine.'

'Maybe. But you're not invincible. Saeunn's power was less than yours, and yet she triumphed over you once.' That struck its target. Renn saw the white fists clench.

'Not in Magecraft,' Seshru said thinly. 'She was nothing but a thief. She stole you from me.'

'She saved me!' Renn flung back. 'I was a baby and you were going to sacrifice me!'

'Is that what she told you?' Seshru drew herself up, like a snake recoiling to strike. 'Why would I carry you for nine long moons, if only to kill you? No, you were destined for greater things.' Her black mouth twisted. 'You were to have been my finest creation – you were to have been my tokoroth!'

Renn no longer heard the frogs or the lapping of the Lake.

'I could have done it,' said the Viper Mage. 'The fire-opal would have drawn the mightiest demon – a very elemental – and I would have trapped it in my newborn child! *My* thing, *my* creature! With such power, what could we not have achieved!'

For a moment, she stared past Renn at visions of impossible glory. Then she dragged herself back and regarded her daughter with contempt. 'Instead, the old crone "saved" you. And there you sit: weak, powerless, wondering if you have the courage to kill me.'

'I could,' said Renn between her teeth. 'I could shoot you right now.'

Seshru laughed. 'Never make a threat you can't carry out, daughter! Against me you have no power. You cannot vanquish me and you cannot kill me! Remember that.' Stretching her arm towards the boat, she twisted her wrist so that her palm faced down. Renn jerked back as if she'd been struck, and nearly lost her balance.

When she looked again, the Viper Mage was gone.

ꝑ

The stink of Viper-Tongue bit Wolf's nose as he raced along the edge of the Big Wet. But the bad tailless was out of reach on the rocks, so he ran on, following the scent of the pack-sister.

He passed the bay where the Hidden Ones gathered to drag things from the Wet. He loped through a stand of watchful pines and out the other side. As he ran, he caught the distant smell of the Great White Cold. He sensed its restlessness. He heard the Thunderer stirring in the Up.

After many lopes, he found the pack-sister. She was crouching by the Wet, near a floating hide which stank of Viper-Tongue – but to Wolf's astonishment, she didn't seem to care. She had her head in her forepaws and she was shaking and yowling as taillesses do when they are very, very sad.

Cautiously, Wolf padded towards her. Then he sat down and licked her knee.

She raised her head and blinked. Then she said something miserable in tailless talk and flung her forepaws round his neck, and buried her face in his scruff. Wolf didn't like this much, but he let her do it, because he sensed that she was breaking inside.

At last her yowls changed to snufflings, then gulps. To Wolf's relief, she let go of him. Leaning against each other, they sat, looking out over the Wet. This time, when Wolf licked her toes, she gently batted him away, and he knew she was feeling better.

Raising his muzzle, he snuffed the air, but of Tall Tailless he caught no scent. Wolf was puzzled. His plan to find his pack-brother wasn't working.

Renn hadn't cried like that since her father had died. It left her feeling empty and brittle as an eggshell.

Wolf had helped a lot. He'd left as suddenly as he'd come, but she could smell his strong, sweet wolf smell on her clothes and skin, and that was extremely comforting. She wasn't entirely without friends while she had Wolf.

After washing her face in the Lake, she thought about what to do next.

Torak no longer wanted her for a friend, but maybe she

could still find a way to help him. 'So think,' she said out loud. 'What does the Viper Mage want?'

She wanted Torak and the fire-opal. And she'd thought she had him, until the ravens came.

That made Renn feel better. After all, her Magecraft *had* worked. She was the one who'd sent the ravens.

She began to pace the pebbles. The night was breathless and sticky, and a ring around the moon told her that the World Spirit was not at peace. There was a storm on the way. For now, though, the Lake was quiet, except for a pair of diverbirds skimming the water. Thoughtfully, she followed their flight.

All of a sudden, they swerved and headed straight for her.

Startled, she ducked.

They sped overhead, so close that she heard the whisper of wings, and caught the glint of a scarlet eye. With ear-splitting cries they veered and vanished into the reeds.

Renn stayed where she was on the pebbles. This was another sign, she was sure of it. Twin fawns. A two-headed fish. The Otter twins. Two birds. Everything in pairs. For a long time now, the spirits had been trying to tell her something. If only she could see the pattern.

Slowly, Renn got to her feet.

To read the signs, she would have to open her mind completely. No matter what the cost.

The moon had fled across the sky and still Renn sat, grinding the white pebble on the black as Saeunn had taught her. All night she had rocked back and forth, grinding the pebbles, working herself deeper into the trance.

The juniper smoke made her head spin, and the alder juice stung her eyes, forcing them shut. That was part of it. She had to remove herself from the outer world, to see with her inner eye. She had to empty her mind so that the answer would come.

Her muscles ached. The scrape of stone on stone filled her thoughts, drawing her into darkness.

'Spirits of Lake and Mountain,' she breathed, 'spirits of Forest and Ice, I ask for guidance. You've sent me signs and I thank you. Now help me find their meaning.'

Suddenly she felt a strong will buffeting hers. Frightened, she nearly opened her eyes.

Seshru.

Gritting her teeth, Renn went on grinding, retreating behind the shell of sound.

I see you . . . Seshru's mind reached for hers. *I know the limits of your power* . . .

The pebble in her hand was heavy as a boulder, she could hardly lift it. She forced herself to keep going, shutting out the Viper Mage.

I am the reed and the storm, the thunder and the wind . . . *You cannot prevail* . . .

Her muscles burned, her head swam. She felt Seshru's will surging towards her: stronger than the tempest which fells the mightiest oak.

The grinding of stones grew louder. And now it was a buzzing like bees, many bees, and she was floating on the sound and travelling down, down into the deep of the Lake. Far away in the upper world, a howl of fury faded as she sank deeper.

Cowering at the bottom of the Lake, she felt its pain soughing through her, its unimaginable age.

Now she was hovering above the healing spring, watching the hands of the Viper Mage clawing the sacred clay.

Now she was bobbing on the water at the edge of the ice river, craning her neck at the ice wall glittering in the sun: such a fierce, hard, cruel blue. So *blue* . . .

With a cry, Renn awoke.

Her cramped muscles screamed as she lurched to her feet and staggered to the water's edge.

'I've got it wrong,' she whispered. 'It's not Seshru. It's the *Lake* that kills!'

THIRTY-FOUR

The moon had set when Torak and Bale put in at a bay on the north shore of the Lake.

Three staring posts warded them off, and only the hope of finding some trace of Renn made them risk going ashore – after Bale had first offered a scrap of dried duck meat on his paddle.

Searching the island by night had proved hard even for Torak, and the only sign they'd found had been one of Renn's prints near the reeds, and another on the Lake's northern shore. At the eastern end of the bay, he found more.

It was Renn's, he would know her footprint anywhere, but she hadn't been alone. Another track overlaid hers: slender, high-arched, the same shape as Renn's – but longer. Seshru.

Torak rubbed a hand over his face. Renn had confronted the Viper Mage alone and at night, in this haunted place.

'What happened to her?' said Bale in a low voice. 'Did Seshru – '

'I don't know,' snapped Torak. 'Let me think!'

They'd hardly spoken all night, except for brusque exchanges to determine where to search next, but Torak could feel Bale blaming him. He forced himself to concentrate on the tracks.

The trail of the Viper Mage led back into the Forest, then disappeared. More encouragingly, the upper part of the shore was criss-crossed with paw-prints. From the look of it, Wolf had been casting for scents.

'Wolf was with her,' said Bale. 'That must be a good sign.'

'Maybe,' muttered Torak. He scanned the shore.

Oh, Wolf, where are you?

He didn't dare howl, for fear of drawing Seshru. Her presence hung in the air, like the smell of smoke which lingers after a fire.

'But if Renn was here,' said Bale, 'where did she go?'

Head down, Torak traced her trail from the trees at the eastern end of the bay to where it ended. Then he did it again. Same result. The trail ended in the Lake.

Shutting his mind to the worst, he continued his search.

Over here, something had scraped through the mud into the shallows. Near it he found an alder sapling, its bark slightly worn in a narrow band, as if by rope. 'A boat. She found a boat moored to this tree.'

Bale blew out a long breath. 'That means she could be anywhere.' He flexed his shoulders. 'We need to rest. Start again when it's light. Otherwise, we'll make mistakes.'

I started doing that a while back, thought Torak.

To get away from the guardian posts, they took the

skinboat round a spur of pines and put in at the next bay, then carried the boat a good distance up the wooded slope beyond the shore. Bale shared out a few strips of dried duck meat, and they ate in prickly silence.

Dawn wasn't far off, but the Forest was strangely hushed. No frogs, no crickets. And no birds, thought Torak uneasily. Only Rip and Rek, who were making a nuisance of themselves picking at his gear.

From where he sat, he saw the flicker of campfires on the western shore. He guessed that the Raven Clan would be among them. Fin-Kedinn would have come in search of Renn.

'Torak,' said Bale, cutting across his thoughts.

'What,' he replied.

'I know she should've told you sooner.'

Torak set his teeth. For Bale to mention Renn was like ripping off a scab.

'But the fact that her mother is . . . I mean, it doesn't change that she's your friend.'

'What changes everything,' said Torak, 'is that she didn't tell me.' But inside, he was finding that harder and harder to believe.

'To carry such a secret.' Bale shook his head. 'What a burden.'

Torak picked up a stone and threw it at a tree-trunk. He missed. The ravens raised their heads and gave him reproachful stares.

'Although,' Bale went on, relentless, 'she's tough. Brave, too.'

Torak turned on him. 'All *right*! You've said what you want, now leave me in peace!' Snatching up his things, he moved off a few paces, then threw himself down with his back to Bale.

Wisely, the Seal boy left him alone.

Torak wasn't hungry any more, and although he was exhausted, he knew he wouldn't sleep. To make matters worse, Rip and Rek were being particularly annoying. Rek kept fluttering her wings, pretending to be a fledgling in desperate need of food, and Rip was pecking at his knife-hilt.

'Stop it,' Torak told him. Of course that didn't work.

He tossed Rip a scrap of meat. The raven ignored it and made another attack on the knife.

'*Stop* it!' said Torak in a hoarse whisper.

'What's the matter?' Bale called softly.

Torak didn't reply.

Rip was staring up at him: not asking for food, just staring. His eyes were black as the Beginning, and his raven souls reached out to Torak's.

Torak glanced from Rip to the sinew binding on the hilt of his knife, then back to Rip. He turned his head and stared at Bale. He tried to speak, but no sound came.

The Seal boy saw his expression and came towards him.

Still without speaking, Torak drew the knife from its sheath and picked feverishly at the binding. It was tight – Fa had renewed it the summer before he was killed – and not even raven beaks had made much impression.

Without asking for an explanation, Bale handed him his own knife. 'Cut it,' he said.

Once the sinew was cut, it was easier to unpick. Torak's heart raced as he peeled back the final layer.

The trees stilled.

The Lake held its breath.

Sweat streamed down Torak's sides as he beheld the thing which had lain concealed for so many summers in the hilt of his father's knife. He tilted the knife, and out it

223

fell onto his palm, from the hollow which Fa had cut to hold it. As Torak stared at it – at this thing which was no bigger than a robin's egg, yet possessed the power to enthrall the demons of the Otherworld – the sun crested the ice river and a blazing shaft of light struck deep into the cold red heart of the fire-opal.

Bale drew in his breath with a hiss. 'All this time.'

Torak did not reply. He was twelve summers old again, kneeling beside Fa.

'Torak,' gasped Fa. 'I'm dying. I'll be dead by sunrise.'

Torak saw the pain convulse his father's lean brown face. He saw the tiny scarlet veins in the light-grey eyes, and at their centres, the fathomless dark.

'Swap knives,' Fa told him.

Torak was aghast. 'Not your knife! You'll need it!'

'You'll need it more.'

Torak didn't want to swap knives. That would make it final. But his father was watching him with an intensity that allowed no refusal . . .

'Oh, Fa,' whispered Torak. He felt the fire-opal burning his palm with a searing cold. He stared into its fiery, pulsing heart.

Bale's brown hand covered the stone, shattering the spell. 'Torak! Cover it up!'

Torak blinked.

'She'll see it!' hissed Bale. *'Cover it up!'*

Roused from his daze, Torak replaced the fire-opal in its nest, and wound his headband around the hilt to hold it in place. Only when it was safely concealed did they breathe again.

At last Bale said, 'How do we destroy it?'

Torak frowned. How could he think of destroying something so beautiful?

'Torak! How?'

Of course Bale was right. 'You've got to bury it,' Torak said in a cracked voice, 'but only earth or stone will do. And . . .' he broke off.

'Yes?' said Bale.

'It needs a life buried with it. Or it won't stay dead.'

They didn't meet each other's eyes.

Torak thought about Renn, and how, in the Far North, she had been ready to give her life so that the fire-opal would be destroyed. He wondered if he would ever find the courage to do that.

He thought about all the times she'd risked her life to help him.

Suddenly, Rek gave a loud 'kek kek', and both ravens lifted into the sky with a clatter of wings.

Torak leapt to his feet.

'Listen!' whispered Bale. 'There's something down by the Lake!'

Straining his ears, Torak caught a faint trickling of water. Then a dragging sound, as if something were crawling out of the Lake – then a squelching, stumbling tread.

Clutching their knives, they crept through the trees.

There, twenty paces below them in a shadowy clump of alders, something moved.

Torak felt Bale grip his arm as the thing lurched to its full height. Weeds dripped from its limbs and its streaming hair.

Bale turned to Torak, his lips bloodless. 'What is it?'

Torak glimpsed the pale arms hanging limp at the creature's sides. The band of rowanberries on one wrist. He rose to his feet. 'It's Renn!'

THIRTY-FIVE

Renn saw them running towards her, shouting her name. Her knees buckled and she went down. Bale caught her by the shoulders. Torak took her quiver and bow.

'It's coming!' she gasped. A spasm of coughing seized her and she sicked up swampy Lake water.

'Where've you been?' said Bale.

She tried to reply, but more coughing took hold. No time to tell of that terrible moment when she'd foreseen the disaster which threatened them all; of her frantic dash to warn the clans, while the boat did its best to thwart her: spinning, bucking, finally pitching her overboard. And now Bale was kneeling beside her with no idea of the danger, while Torak was drying her bow with a handful of grass, and avoiding her eyes.

'You're safe now,' said Bale.

'Nobody's safe!' She clutched his arm. 'Listen to me! *The flood is coming!*'

They stared at her.

'The ice river,' she panted. 'All spring it's been keeping back the meltwater! *That's* why the ice wall was so blue, *that's* why the Lake is sinking!' Again she broke off to cough. 'I kept seeing twins. *Two* lakes, do you see? This Lake – and the one *behind the ice!* Seshru stole the sacred clay, she made the Lake sick. And now there's a storm coming, and the World Spirit's going to shatter the ice wall! The flood will take us all!'

She turned to Torak. 'Whatever you think of me, you've got to believe me! You've got to warn the Otters! Get them into the hills, or they'll never stand a chance!'

Still without meeting her eyes, Torak set down her bow. 'It's not just the Otters.'

'What do you mean?' she said.

'Campfires on the western shore,' said Bale. 'We think it's the Boar Clan, after Torak. Maybe other clans too.'

Renn bit her knuckle. 'The Ravens. Fin-Kedinn will have come to find me. They'll be drowned.'

Torak spoke to Bale. 'We'll take the skinboat. It's the quickest way to reach them.'

Bale nodded. 'But not all of us, that'd slow it down; besides Renn couldn't make it.'

'Yes I could!' cried Renn.

'No you couldn't,' said Bale. Then to Torak, 'This slope's not too steep, I can get her up to higher ground, we'll be safe there. You take the boat. You warn them.'

'Me, take your boat? You never let anyone – '

'Torak,' cut in Bale, 'this is your chance to show them you're not a Soul-Eater!'

'If they don't shoot him first,' put in Renn.

Torak ignored her.

Within moments Bale had the boat in the water and Torak was ready, but suddenly he leapt out and ran back to Renn. Untying his knife-sheath, he pressed it into her hands. 'Keep it safe,' he muttered.

'But it's yours, you'll need it!'

'No time to explain. Bale will tell you.' Over his shoulder he added, 'She's after me *and* the fire-opal, she mustn't get both!'

The World Spirit was turning day to dusk as Torak made the skinboat fly across the water. Thunder growled. The air crackled with foreboding. The flood could come at any moment.

In his mind, he saw the creatures of Forest and Lake fleeing for safety. Elk, deer and horses racing for the ridges; beaver and otter scampering up the slopes as best they could; squirrel and marten seeking refuge in the sturdiest oaks. Even the fish would be hiding at the bottom of the Lake.

And the wolves? This must be why they'd fled the island, because they'd sensed what was coming. Torak hoped they'd taken the cubs high enough – and that Wolf was with them.

In the east, the sky was a boiling mass of storm clouds. Soon, lightning would lance the ice river, releasing the awesome fury of the waters behind. Torak pictured the flood engulfing the Lake: devastating islands, washing away the Otter camp and everything in its path.

The wind strengthened, and still he paddled. He was

almost spent when he reached the western shore and put in just south of the Axehandle river. No sign of boats or people. Only the reeds, flattened by the wind.

Leaving the skinboat on the shore, he slipped into a thicket at the foot of the ridge. The trees moaned, warning him back. For all he knew, the whole slope might be crawling with hunters on the lookout for him, and all he had was his axe. Not much use against arrows and spears.

Exhausted, he soon had to stop for breath. He was wondering which way to go when something leapt from the junipers and knocked him to the ground.

At last Wolf had found Tall Tailless!

In a snap, his sadness at leaving the pack was chased away, and he was covering his pack-brother's face in snuffle-licks.

I couldn't leave you! he told Tall Tailless. *I'm back now and I'm never leaving, just like you said!*

But Tall Tailless' greeting was rushed and urgent, and Wolf caught his mood. He smelt Viper-Tongue on his pack-brother. He sensed great worry and danger. *What do I do?* he asked.

Find the ravens, Tall Tailless replied.

That made Wolf cross. *Why them?*

No, said Tall Tailless, *not the birds. Wolves that smell of raven. Find the pack leader!*

Now Wolf understood. Giving his pack-brother a nose-nudge to acknowledge this, he raced off through the trees.

The great denning place of the taillesses wasn't many lopes away, and he was soon in the bracken at its edge. Stealthily, he padded forwards to find the pack leader.

The denning place seethed with anger, and Wolf heard much snarling among the boar, wolf, and raven packs. Then he caught the quiet, strong tones of the raven leader. This tailless never yowled loudly. He didn't need to. He had the respect of all the others.

Placing his paws with care, Wolf crept closer.

The dogs were restless, but on the way, Wolf had rolled in a pile of auroch droppings, so he approached un-smelt. When he'd got as far as he could, he crouched down to wait.

Soon, the raven leader felt his stare and saw him.

Ah, he was cunning! Like a normal wolf, he grazed Wolf's glance with his own, then looked away, so the others wouldn't notice. A little later, he left the denning place: calmly, so as not to awaken suspicions.

When Wolf knew he was following, he headed off to find Tall Tailless.

When Torak glimpsed Fin-Kedinn striding through the willowherb, it didn't occur to him to hide. He rose to his feet and stood in the open. The Raven Leader saw him, and his face lit up. Torak's heart twisted. He'd missed Fin-Kedinn more than he'd realized.

'Torak!' Fin-Kedinn gripped his shoulder. He glanced behind him. 'Come. We're too close to camp, and Aki's nosing around after you.'

With Wolf trotting after them, they moved into a wind-tossed thicket. The Raven Leader's sharp eyes searched Torak's face, and took in the scar on his chest. 'Where's Renn?'

'Safe with Bale on the north shore. Fin-Kedinn, you've

got to listen!' As briefly as he could, he told the Raven Leader of the coming flood. Fin-Kedinn heard it without question or interruption.

'You've got to get the clans to higher ground,' said Torak. 'Right now! The flood could come at any moment!'

The Raven Leader's face was unfathomable as ever, but Torak knew from the glint in his eyes that his thoughts were racing. 'Everyone's in camp,' he said, 'arguing about the best way to hunt you. That'll make them easier to move.'

'I've got a skinboat,' said Torak, 'I'll find the Otter camp and warn them.'

'No. They'd shoot you before you got the chance.'

'But someone's got to.'

'I'll see to it.'

'And the clans?'

'I'll get them up to the Hogback.' He jerked his head at the ridge behind them. 'You get up there too, fast as you can. Try to reach the south side, there'll be fewer people.'

Torak nodded. But as he made to go, Fin-Kedinn held him back. 'Where's the Viper Mage?'

'I don't know. On the north cliff, I think.'

Fin-Kedinn looked grim. 'She hasn't finished with you yet. I know her, Torak. Never underestimate her. Never forget that she might be closer than you think!'

Torak hadn't told him of the fire-opal and he didn't now, but as the Raven Leader turned, he said, 'Fin-Kedinn. You wouldn't be here – in danger – if it weren't for me. I'm sorry.'

A shadow crossed the Raven Leader's face. 'I cast you out. You're not the one who should be sorry.' He touched Torak's arm. 'Get as high as you can. Go!'

The wind screamed in Torak's ears as he scrambled up the slope, while Wolf raced ahead. The Forest was dark as night, and the trees thrashed and groaned.

He was halfway up when he had to stop, bent double, chest heaving. Slumped against a pine, he told Wolf to go on without him.

Wolf hesitated.

Lightning flared. Thunder crashed directly overhead. Rain pattered on the leaves – and swiftly became a downpour.

Torak saw Rip and Rek take cover in an oak tree. Yes. Climb the tree. No time for anything else. Maybe the Forest would protect him, too.

Go! he told Wolf again, and Wolf – sensing what he meant to do – turned and sped to safety.

In the distance, Torak heard a deeper reverberation behind the thunder: an echoing boom that he'd heard before, in the Far North. The boom of breaking ice.

He stumbled for the oak – tripped – and fell headlong in the mud. Lightning flickered on a footprint by his hand. Behind him, a branch snapped. He rolled sideways just as Aki's axe thudded into the root where his head had been.

'Got you at last!' bellowed the Boar Clan boy. With his good arm he tugged at his axe, which he'd buried in the root.

'Aki, are you mad?' shouted Torak against the wind. 'The flood is coming! We've got to get into the trees!'

'I said I'd get you and I will!' yelled Aki.

More lightning, more thunder. The ice river boomed across the Lake.

As he struggled to his feet, Torak saw that Aki wasn't driven by hatred, but by fear of failing his father – and against that there was no reasoning. Leaving him yanking at the axe, Torak raced for the oak and leapt for the lowest branch. Desperation lent him strength, and he was soon ten paces up.

'Aki!' he shouted. 'Leave the axe! Climb!'

Another boom from the ice river – and suddenly Aki let go of the axehandle and ran for the oak. But he was heavier than Torak, he couldn't reach the lowest branch.

'Grab my hand!' Torak leaned down as far as he could.

Not far enough. And Aki couldn't climb with only one arm.

Through the rain, Torak saw the Boar Clan boy's right arm strapped to his chest: the arm that he, Torak, had broken when he'd sent Aki crashing into the rapids.

With a snarl, Torak leapt from the tree and linked his hands to make a step. 'Quick, climb!'

Aki was aghast. Then he put his foot on Torak's hands, and Torak boosted him into the tree with the last of his strength.

The roar came again, but this time it wasn't ice, Torak realized, it was the flood. Far in the distance he saw it: a giant wall of water powering across the Lake – obliterating islands, uprooting trees, coming for him.

Aki was shouting and leaning down to give him his hand, but now it was Torak who couldn't reach. He wasn't going to make it.

In the moment before the flood hit, he saw Wolf racing towards him. Torak staggered to meet him – he flung his arms around his pack-brother's neck . . .

. . . and the wave took them both.

THIRTY-SIX

Torak came to his senses lying on his back, with rain pattering on his face.

A dead fish hung in the birch tree above him. The storm had passed. The flood had thrown him onto a stony hillside strewn with broken saplings. There was no trace of Wolf. Torak prayed that he'd found his way to safety.

He raised himself on one elbow. He was battered and bruised, but otherwise unhurt.

He was also surrounded.

Behind a forest of spears – all pointed at him – he saw a throng of Boar and Wolf and Raven, maybe eighty strong. Some of them he knew – Thull, Raut, Maheegun – but they stared at him as if he were a stranger. To a man, they were filthy, frightened and eager for the kill.

An arrow thudded into the mud by his thigh. He got to

his feet. He was alone and weaponless. The flood had taken his axe.

Then he saw Wolf on the slope behind them, preparing to leap to his aid.

Stay away! Torak barked. *Too many!*

Wolf didn't move.

Agitated murmurs. They didn't like him speaking wolf.

A stone struck his temple. He managed to stay standing. If he went down now, it would be the end.

'No stones.' A familiar voice spoke, and the spears parted to let Fin-Kedinn through. Leaning heavily on his staff, he moved towards Torak, then faced the throng, shielding him with his body.

'Stand aside, Fin-Kedinn,' cried the Boar Clan Leader. 'I found the outcast! To me goes the honour of the kill!'

'No!' Aki pushed forwards. 'You can't do this! He saved my life!'

The Boar Clan Leader turned on his son, and Aki quailed – but stood his ground. 'He could have saved himself, but instead he helped me! Father, you can't kill him, it's not right!'

'Not right?' With his fist, the Boar Clan Leader struck his son a blow which sent him flying. 'He's an outcast! That's the law!'

'How can you say that?' shouted Bale, shouldering his way through. 'Torak saved you all!'

'He warned you of the flood!' panted Renn behind him. She looked bedraggled and furious. 'If it weren't for Torak, you'd have drowned, every last one of you!'

'Don't listen to her!' cried an Otter man, the only one Torak could see. 'All this is his fault! The outcast angered the Lake, *he* caused the flood!'

'No, Yolun,' said Fin-Kedinn. 'Not Torak. The Viper Mage.'

'The Viper Mage!' sneered the Boar Clan Leader. 'So you say, but where is she? *There's* the Soul-Eater!' He jabbed his spear at Torak.

'He's no Soul-Eater,' said Fin-Kedinn. 'He cut out the mark, you can all see the scar.'

But the Boar Clan Leader had the support of the crowd, and it lent him courage. 'He's an outcast! The law says an outcast must die!'

'Then the law must change!' retorted the Raven Leader.

'Why? Because you say so?'

'Because it's right.'

'He's a Soul-Eater and an outcast –'

'He's my foster son!' roared Fin-Kedinn.

Ravens flew up from the trees. People shrank back.

Nervously, the Boar Clan Leader licked his lips. 'Since when?'

'Since now,' snapped the Raven Leader.

'Fin-Kedinn!' called Renn. 'Catch!' She threw him Torak's knife and Fin-Kedinn caught it, then drew the blade across his forearm, raising beads of blood. Grasping Torak's wrist, he did the same to him, and they clasped hands as the Raven Leader spoke the words of fostering. Then he turned on the crowd and his blue eyes blazed. 'If he stays outcast, then so do I! Kill him – and you'll have to kill me too!'

The Boar Clan Leader gripped his spear, but made no move.

No-one stirred.

But Torak sensed that not even the Raven Leader could hold them for long. He saw the violence in their grimy faces; the desperation with which they clutched axes and spears. They'd just survived a disaster, they needed someone to blame. And if Fin-Kedinn stood in their way – or Bale or Renn – they would get themselves killed.

Taking his knife from the Raven Leader, Torak said quietly, 'I don't want your blood on my hands.'

The Boar Clan Leader taunted Torak. 'Hiding behind your foster father?'

'Fin-Kedinn,' urged Torak, 'I've got to face them on my own.'

Reluctantly, the Raven Leader moved aside.

'Where's your courage now, outcast?' jeered the Boar Leader.

'Right here,' said Torak.

It was a strange relief to be confronting them at last. 'No more hiding, I'm sick of it!' he cried as he circled the ring of spears, his arms spread wide. 'Here I am! You can kill me if you want! Who *cares* if I'm the wrong target? Who *cares* if this is what the Soul-Eaters want? The Oak Mage – the Eagle Owl Mage – the Viper Mage – they're still out there! Kill me, and you solve *nothing*!'

'This is a trick,' spat the Boar Clan Leader. 'Don't listen. *He's* the Soul-Eater!'

'I *was* a Soul-Eater,' Torak flung back. 'They made me one against my will.' With his fist he struck his scar. 'I cut out their mark – with this!' Brandishing his knife, he flicked a glance at Renn, and her lips parted as she guessed what he meant to do.

'My father gave me this knife as he lay dying!' Torak told them, 'and here's how I choose to use it: to prove to you – once and for all – that I'm no Soul-Eater!'

There was a ringing in his ears as he unwound the headband which bound the handle. The last layer came away, and he let fall the buckskin and tilted the hilt to drop its dreadful burden into his palm. The cold red light of the fire-opal blazed out.

The Boar Clan Leader gasped.

Fin-Kedinn's hand tightened on his staff.

Terror and awe filled every face.

'The fire-opal,' said Torak, holding it up for all to see. 'The heart of Soul-Eater power. This is the last fragment of the one my father shattered. *My father,*' he glared at Maheegun, 'who defied the Soul-Eaters and broke their power! And now it's *mine!*'

A soft voice spoke. 'Give it me.'

Torak turned.

The Viper Mage stood on the ridge above him, twenty paces beyond the ring of spears. Her face and limbs wore the sacred clay of the Otter Clan, and calmly she gazed down upon them: inhuman, invincible.

A shiver ran through the crowd. *'The Soul-Eater . . . The Viper Mage is come . . .'*

'Stay back,' warned Seshru, stretching out her green hand and sweeping them with her forefinger. 'Death shall come to any who attempt to harm me.'

Such was the power of the Soul-Eaters – such the terror the Viper Mage inspired – that not one of them moved.

'Give it me,' she said to Torak, and her words were a caress meant only for him.

He fought to look away from that perfect green face.

A movement caught his eye. Some distance behind the Viper Mage, Wolf stood watching. Silently, Torak warded him back. The Soul-Eater was too strong even for Wolf.

'Give it me,' repeated Seshru.

Unable to resist, Torak met her gaze. He forgot the spears, he forgot Bale and Renn and Fin-Kedinn and Wolf. Nothing existed on this ruined hillside except the Viper Mage and the fire-opal, hot and heavy in his hand.

'I will,' he said at last. 'I will give it to you.'

Everyone gasped.

Stooping, Torak placed the fire-opal on a boulder between himself and the Viper Mage. 'Take it,' he said. 'It's yours.'

Seshru's black lips parted in a triumphant smile.

Still stooping, Torak snatched a lump of granite in his fist. He raised it high, and the eyes of the Viper Mage widened in horror. As she whipped out her knife and leapt towards him, he shouted, 'Take it! Take the fire-opal!' He saw Renn nock an arrow to her bow and aim at her mother; Bale grab the weapons from her hands and take aim in his turn. He saw Seshru give a terrible scream and fall with an arrow in her breast as he brought the granite crashing down and shattered the fire-opal to fragments.

Silence rang from hill to hill.

The granite fell from Torak's hand as he stared at Bale. The Seal boy stood panting, Renn's bow in his hand.

Still alive, the scarlet fragments of the fire-opal glittered in the mud.

Still alive, the Viper Mage reached for them: writhing like a snake that has been cut in two.

Renn burst through the throng. Clawing the fragments of the fire-opal in a handful of mud, she pressed them into Seshru's palm and clenched the green hand in a fist around them, then tied it shut with Torak's discarded headband. 'There,' she breathed. 'You've got what you wanted! The fire-opal dies with you!'

Seshru gazed at the scarlet light bleeding through her fingers, and bared her teeth. 'This – is not the end,' she hissed. Blood trickled from her mouth. Her eyes glazed. As her souls left her body, the red glow between her fingers flickered and died.

Grimly, Fin-Kedinn raised his staff. 'The Soul-Eater is dead,' he declared. 'Let all bear witness: the outcast shall be outcast *no more!*'

After a moment's hesitation, Maheegun bowed his assent.

Then the Boar Clan Leader.

Then Yolun for the Otters.

Then all the others.

Renn stayed on her knees by the Viper Mage, watching the rain wash away her blood in muddy rivulets.

She's too close to the body, thought Torak. The souls of the Viper Mage must be perilously near.

Quickly, he took Renn's medicine horn and poured earthblood into his palm, then grasped her hand and, making sure that she still wore her finger-guard, dipped her forefinger in the ochre and helped her draw the Death Marks on her mother's forehead, heart and heels. Then he pulled her gently away from the corpse.

The crowd parted to let someone through.

Wolf's hackles were raised, his lips peeled back in a snarl as he walked stiffly towards the corpse, stalking something no-one else could see.

As the rain fell, Torak watched his pack-brother leap – snap the air – and race off into the Forest, chasing the souls of the Viper Mage away from the living.

THIRTY-SEVEN

The pack is leaving without him, and Wolf knows this must be so – but it hurts.

The full-grown wolves tread neatly in the paw-prints of the leader, but the cubs jostle one another, pouncing on interesting bits of moss.

Digger and Snap see that Wolf isn't following, and scamper back to fetch him. *Come on! Don't get left behind!*

Mournfully, Wolf wags his tail.

The lead female gathers the cubs and they trot after her, looking back in puzzlement.

Darkfur is the last to leave. A wistful glance over her shoulder, then she too disappears.

Wolf woke with a jolt. Lying in the mud, he felt sorrow press upon him. The pack was gone.

Through the trees came the sound of the taillesses

beginning to stir. Wolf padded along the rise to sniff the scents.

Since the Big Wet had come roaring through, everything had changed. The Thunderer was gone, and the Big Wet was at peace, although it had grown, and there were fish in the trees, which was odd. The Hidden Ones were quiet, as they had their island to themselves; and the taillesses were no longer hunting Tall Tailless, but had welcomed him back. Wolf didn't understand why.

Tall Tailless had changed, too. Over the past Lights and Darks, his scent had altered and his howls had become deeper. Wolf *did* know the reason for this. Unlike wolf cubs, tailless cubs take an extremely long time to grow up, but even they manage it eventually. Tall Tailless was almost full-grown.

Right now, he was in the Den with the other taillesses, having one of his endless sleeps. Wolf wished he would wake up, and sense that his pack-brother needed him.

But he didn't come.

ıl

'Time to go back,' said Fin-Kedinn, and Renn, sitting on a rock above the healing spring, nodded, but didn't move.

Nearby, a group of Otters was returning the sacred clay to the Lake by washing it off their faces. Bale stood at the cliff edge, lost in thought, and Torak was searching the ferns for his name-pebble.

Renn wanted to help, but she couldn't muster the courage. He hadn't really talked to her since he'd found out about her mother. She wasn't sure if they were all right again – or if everything had changed.

The Otters had arrived in their reed boats at dawn. It

242

turned out that they hadn't needed warnings of the flood, as their Mage had read the signs and led them to safety. That was why Yolun had been sent to the Forest clans' camp: to warn *them*.

Nor had the Otters seemed surprised when Fin-Kedinn told them of the Viper Mage. They'd accepted it as they'd accepted the flood which had destroyed their camp – then quietly taken over the funeral rites.

After bearing the body to a remote bay on the north shore, they'd washed the corpse, laid it on a Death Platform, and covered it in juniper branches so that it wouldn't walk. Then they'd led everyone to the spring, to be purified. They'd gently insisted that Renn should keep a little apart, because, as she'd put the Death Marks on the corpse, she would be unclean for the next three days. She didn't mind. It was a relief. That's what she told herself.

'She left no trace,' said Torak, making her jump.

He stood on a boulder behind her. She couldn't see his face for the sun.

'You didn't find the name-pebble?' she said.

He shook his head. 'What should I do about that?'

She noted that he said I, not we, and wondered if that meant something. Out loud she said, 'We'll ask Saeunn. She'll know.'

The Raven Mage had remained at the new camp on the Hogback, and although Renn would never have admitted it, it was reassuring to know she was there. If Magecraft was needed, Saeunn would do it.

Torak looked over the Lake. 'The only thing I found was her snake basket. Empty.' He paused. 'They didn't feel evil, those snakes. Maybe they'll like being free.'

Renn broke off a fern frond and tore it to bits.

Why can't you just say it, she thought. Torak, I'm sorry I

243

never told you. But it doesn't change anything, does it? Not really?'

But Torak mumbled something about helping Bale look for the wreckage of the skinboat, and then he was gone, and she'd missed her chance.

Fin-Kedinn came and sat beside her.

Renn said, 'He knows about the Viper Mage. I mean, about me.'

'Yes, he told me.'

'Did he? What did he say?'

'Just that he knows.'

She scrunched up the fern and threw it away.

Fin-Kedinn asked her who else knew, and she said, only Bale. Fin-Kedinn said he thought some of the older Ravens had recognized the Viper Mage despite the green clay, and that Renn should tell them when things had settled down, and she said she would.

Fin-Kedinn said, 'Are you sorry she's dead?'

'No. – I don't know.' She scowled. 'I hated her for so long, and now she's gone. Somehow it feels worse.'

He nodded.

He looked tired. Renn saw the grey hairs flecking his dark-red beard; the lines at the corners of his eyes. With a twist of terror, she realized that he was getting older. People died when they were younger than him. But he was Fin-Kedinn, he couldn't die.

'Why can't things stay the same?' she cried.

Fin-Kedinn followed a damselfly skimming the water. 'Because that's how it is. Everything changes, all the time. Mostly, you don't notice.' He turned to her. 'The thing to remember, Renn, is that not every change is bad.'

She drew a breath that ended in a gulp.

Fin-Kedinn said, 'Torak was outcast. Now he's not.

244

That's a good change. But it'll take him a while to get used to it.' Using his staff, he rose to his feet. 'We'll go back now. You're exhausted.'

'No I'm not,' she lied.

He snorted. 'When was the last time you had a proper meal?'

ılı

That night, the clans held a feast to give thanks for surviving the flood.

The fish had mysteriously returned to the Lake, and although the Otters didn't dare remark on this aloud for fear of chasing away the good luck, there was a lightness in them as they bustled about, directing the preparations.

Like everyone else, Torak and Bale had to help, but Renn, being unclean, wasn't allowed. She hung around the camp, trying not to look spare, then went to find Wolf. She didn't, but she heard him howling. He sounded sad. She guessed that he was missing the pack, and resolved to take him a treat, to cheer him up.

Before the feast could begin, the best of everything was placed in a reed boat and taken to the Lake; then everyone settled down to eat. It was a cool, still night, and they sat around a long-fire: Otter and Boar Clan, Wolf and Raven. All except Renn, who'd been given her own little blaze at the edge of camp.

The food was better than she'd expected, and Fin-Kedinn was right, she was ravenous. There was stewed elk and succulent bream roasted over alderwood fires; toasted trout cheeks and crisp golden cakes of reed pollen with sweet, sticky gobbets of reed gum; and the thickest, smelliest stickleback grease, which the Otters had taken with them when they'd abandoned camp. This Renn avoided, but she saw Torak – who didn't know any better – struggling to compose his features after his first mouthful.

He sat in the place of honour with the clan leaders, looking uncomfortable with the attention. Renn saw him self-consciously touching the outcast tattoo on his forehead, but either he didn't see her, or he was avoiding her. She told herself not to worry.

Not far from Torak sat Bale. He caught Renn's eye, and seemed about to smile, but checked himself. They hadn't yet spoken of what he'd done, and she guessed that he wasn't sure how she felt. She gave him a brief smile, and he looked relieved.

When the eating was over, the Otters collected all the fish bones which were too small to be useful and took them to the Lake, so that they could be born again as new fish. Then the Otter Mage twins stood up and started to sing.

Like a silver stream falling into a pool of clear water, their voices dropped into the listening silence. In her head, Renn saw the dark of the Beginning, when all the world was water. Then a diverbird dived to the bottom and scooped up a speck of mud in its beak, and flew back to the surface – and made the earth.

Now they were singing a new song. This time, Renn saw the viper who stole the sacred clay and made the Lake sick. The Lake sought the aid of the World Spirit, who loosed the waters behind the ice and washed away the evil; and the Forest people would have been swept away too, if they hadn't been warned by the Clanless Wanderer. Then the boy from the Sea killed the viper, and peace returned.

When the song was over, everyone bowed to Torak, and he went red. The Boar Clan Leader's bow was grudging, but Aki's was whole-hearted. Standing up to his father had given him new respect for himself, and he'd relaxed a lot. Maheegun and the Wolf Clan bowed lowest of all.

By now it was nearly dawn. Surely, thought Renn, the feast must be over soon. Food had made her feel braver. She would simply march up to Torak and say what had to be said.

But now the Otter Leader was giving gifts, so once again she had to wait.

Bale was given a diverbird claw as an amulet – so that, like the most skilled of water creatures, he would always stay afloat.

Torak got a wristband made from a pike's lower jaw sheathed in elkhide, so that he would be as skilled a hunter as the pike. And his knife had been repaired; in the hole left by the fire-opal lay a piece of greenstone, precisely cut to fit.

Just when Renn was feeling left out, Yolun came and laid something at her feet. He bowed, murmuring his thanks for the part she'd played in saving his beloved Lake. His gift was a beautiful little beaver-tooth knife with a hilt carved like a fish's tail.

Dawn came, and at last people went off to sleep. Suddenly there was Torak, coming towards her.

Renn stood up, scattering her bowl and spoon, which she'd forgotten were still in her lap.

Torak helped to retrieve them, and gave her an awkward nod. 'Renn . . . '

'Yes?' she said, more sharply than she'd intended.

'Ah, Torak,' said Fin-Kedinn, coming over to them.

For once in her life, Renn was *not* glad to see her uncle.

'Come with me,' said the Raven Leader, unperturbed. 'There's something we need to do.'

Torak opened his mouth, then shut it again.

'Where are we going?' said Renn.

Fin-Kedinn motioned her back. 'No, Renn,' he said gently, 'just Torak. This isn't for you.'

Torak threw her a glance that could have meant anything. Then he followed the Raven Leader into the Forest.

THIRTY-EIGHT

Torak bit back his impatience as he followed Fin-Kedinn.

Now that he was no longer outcast, he'd hoped that he and Renn and Wolf could be together again, but maybe he was wrong. Wolf hadn't come near the camp since the flood, and with Renn there was a great awkwardness of things unsaid.

And now Fin-Kedinn was leading him along an elk trail without even telling him why. He moved fast, leaning on his staff, and he had a rawhide pouch slung over one shoulder.

They hadn't gone far when Fin-Kedinn halted. Setting the pouch under a hazel tree, he told Torak to lie down.

Torak asked why.

'I need to fix your tattoo. You can't live the rest of your life with the mark of the outcast.'

Torak had been wondering about that, but now he was apprehensive. 'Are you going to cut it out?'

'No,' said Fin-Kedinn. 'Lie down.'

Torak lay on his back and watched the Raven Leader take from the pouch a bone needle, a small antler tattooing hammer, a grindstone and a buckskin bundle. This he unwrapped to reveal lumps of earthblood, white gypsum and green tufa stone.

'I've sent Bale to find the woad,' he said, as if that explained anything. 'Now keep still.'

Mounting a needle in the hammer, he stretched the skin of Torak's forehead between finger and thumb, and began the rapid piercings which you need for a good tattoo, pausing occasionally to wipe away the blood.

At first it hurt a lot. Then it simply hurt. To keep his mind off the pain, Torak fixed his eyes on the hazel tree. The nuts were still green, but a squirrel was busily foraging, stopping now and then to churr at the intruders below.

After a while, Torak shifted his gaze to Fin-Kedinn.

His foster father.

He felt honoured and pleased, but also perplexed. 'There's something I don't understand,' he said.

Fin-Kedinn did not reply.

'When I first met you – when you found out who my father was – you were angry. Since then, sometimes I've thought you liked me. Sometimes not.'

Placing the earthblood on the grindstone, Fin-Kedinn crushed it with a piece of granite.

'I know you were angry with my father,' Torak went on carefully. 'But my mother . . . You didn't hate her too?'

Fin-Kedinn carried on grinding. 'No,' he said. 'I was in love with her.'

Birdsong echoed through the Forest. Bees buzzed among the meadowsweet.

'But she loved me as a brother,' the Raven Leader went on. 'Your father she loved as a woman loves her mate.'

Torak swallowed. 'Is that why – why you hated him?'

Fin-Kedinn sighed. 'Growing up can be a kind of soul-sickness, Torak. The name-soul wants to be strongest, so it fights the clan-soul telling it what to do. You've got to find a balance, like a good knife. It took me a while.' Dipping a corner of buckskin in earthblood, he rubbed it into Torak's forehead. 'I stopped being jealous of your father a long time ago. But I went on blaming him for your mother's death. I still do.'

'Why?'

'He joined the Soul-Eaters. When she gave birth to you, she was in hiding, far from her clan. If he hadn't put her in danger, she might still be alive.'

'He didn't mean to put her in danger.'

'Don't ask me to forgive him,' warned Fin-Kedinn. 'For her sake I took you in. For her sake, and yours, I've made you my foster son. Don't ask for more.' Cleaning the grindstone with a clump of moss, he crushed the tufa stone.

Torak studied the features of the man he'd come to love. 'Did you never find a mate?'

Fin-Kedinn's lip curled. 'Of course I did. There was a girl in the Wolf Clan. But after a time she said we should part, because I still thought of your mother. She was right.'

Silence. Then Torak said, 'What was my mother like?'

Fin-Kedinn's face tightened. 'Your father must have spoken of her.'

'No. It made him too sad.'

The Raven Leader was quiet for a long time. Then he said, 'She knew the Forest like nobody else. She loved it. And it loved her.' He met Torak's gaze and his blue eyes glittered. 'You're very like her.'

Torak hadn't expected that. Until now, his mother hadn't been truly real to him: just a shadowy woman of the Red Deer Clan who'd made his medicine horn – and declared him clanless.

Fin-Kedinn stared unseeing at the hazel tree. Then he squared his shoulders and resumed his work. 'In a way, it's because of your mother that you survived as an outcast. Those creatures who helped you. Beaver, raven, wolf. The Forest itself. Maybe they saw her spirit in you.'

'But why did she make me clanless? Why did she *do* that?'

Fin-Kedinn sighed. 'I don't know, Torak. But she loved you, so –'

'But how do you know? You didn't even know that she'd had a son!'

'I knew her,' Fin-Kedinn said quietly. 'She loved you. So she must have done it to help you.'

Torak couldn't see how being clanless was any help at all.

'Maybe,' Fin-Kedinn added, 'the answer lies where she came from. And where you were born.'

'The Deep Forest.'

A breeze stirred the trees, and they nodded agreement.

'When should I go?' said Torak.

'Not for a while,' said the Raven Leader, grinding gypsum. 'There's trouble among the Deep Forest clans, they won't let in outsiders. And it would be foolish to venture in when Thiazzi and Eostra could be anywhere.'

Bale came through the bracken. His face was grave as he handed Fin-Kedinn a small horn cup containing the woad. 'I heard you talking about the Soul-Eaters. I don't think you'll find them in the Deep Forest. I think they're in the islands.'

Torak sat up. *'What?'*

'Something Renn said, a while back. She said the Seal Mage had a fragment of the fire-opal, and it went down with him in the Sea.' He shook his head. 'I don't think it did. He always kept what he needed for spells in a seal-hide pouch. He didn't have it when he was killed. Later, when we burnt his shelter, it wasn't there.'

'That could mean anything,' said Torak uneasily.

'Before you came to the islands,' said Bale, 'when he was simply our Mage, we would sometimes see a red glow on the Crag. We didn't know what it was. I do now.'

'The fire-opal,' said Torak.

'And before I left for the Forest,' Bale went on, 'there were disturbances – in the woods and around our camp. As if someone were searching for something.'

Torak thought of the last words of the Viper Mage. Then he noticed that Fin-Kedinn didn't seem surprised.

'Think about it, Torak,' he said as he applied the woad. 'If the fragment in your father's knife had been the last, why was only the Viper Mage after it? Why not Thiazzi and Eostra, too?'

'So we've achieved nothing!' cried Torak. 'It's all to do again!'

'Not so,' said Fin-Kedinn. 'Step by step. Remember?'

Torak made to reply, but the Raven Leader was gathering his things. 'Time to go back,' he said firmly. 'And Torak – we won't tell Renn of the fire-opal just yet. She's got enough to think about.'

When they reached camp, Renn was waiting for them. She glanced at Torak's forehead and nodded. 'Ah. I see.' Then to Fin-Kedinn, 'Although the white bit isn't really white, is it?'

The Raven Leader shrugged. 'He's too brown. But it'll do.'

'What *is* it?' said Torak. 'What have you done?'

Fin-Kedinn grasped his wrist and raised it high, then spoke to the others who were gathering round. 'Each of you bear witness,' he said in his clear voice. 'This is my foster son: the one who was outcast, but is outcast no more. He's clanless – but from now on, because of this mark he bears, he is for *all* the clans!'

There were smiles and murmurs of assent, and Torak could see that whatever the Raven Leader had done, it had worked.

Bale explained it to him. 'He's divided the circle of the outcast into four: one for each of the four quarters of the clans, then he's filled them in. White for the Ice clans, red for the Mountains, green for the Forest, and blue for the Sea. It looks good.' He grinned. 'Well. Better.'

Torak was still taking that in when Rip and Rek swooped out of nowhere. Rek made a barking noise that drove the camp dogs wild, and Rip – who was carrying something in his beak – dropped it in the mud, narrowly missing Bale. Then they were off, somersaulting over each other with raucous caws.

Bale picked up what Rip had let fall, and his eyebrows rose. 'Here.' He handed it to Torak.

It was his name-pebble. His "clan-tattoo" could still be seen – but every speck of the green clay serpent had been pecked off.

Torak and Bale had gone with Yolun in a reed boat, and when they'd reached the deep part of the Lake, Torak had dropped his name-pebble over the side and watched it disappear into the dark-green water.

Yolun was pleased. 'The Lake will keep it safe for ever.'

Torak thought so too. At first he'd been frightened of the Lake, but he'd come to understand that it was neither good nor bad; just very, very old.

On reaching land again, Bale and Yolun went off to talk about boats, and Torak was finally free to go in search of Renn.

He found her on the shore, oiling her bow. He sat down beside her, but she didn't look up.

After a while she said, 'It's had so many soakings, I think it may be warped.'

He glanced at her. 'If Bale hadn't done it – would you have killed her?'

She rubbed more oil into the wood, which was already gleaming. 'Yes,' she said between her teeth. 'When you smashed the fire-opal, whose life were you going to give it?'

'I don't know,' Torak admitted. 'And I don't know why Fa gave it to me. I suppose he guessed that some day I might need it.'

'But why keep it at all? He could've destroyed it along with the rest.'

Torak had wondered about that too. In his mind, he saw the awful beauty of the fire-opal. Maybe Fa just couldn't bring himself to do it.

He turned to Renn. 'Your mother. Have you always known?'

A flush stole up her neck. 'No. Fin-Kedinn told me after Fa was killed.'

'So you were – seven, eight summers old.'

'Yes.'

'That must have been hard.'

She glared at him, repudiating pity.

He scooped up a handful of sand and poured it from palm to palm. 'How did it happen? I mean, how did she come to . . .'

Renn chewed her lip. Then she told him, staring at the sand between her bare feet, and spitting out the story like poison. 'When she left my father for the Soul-Eaters, she changed her name. People thought she was dead. Not my father. Fin-Kedinn told him to forget her. He couldn't. Then she came back to him in secret. The clan never knew. She needed another child, a baby. My brother was too old for – for her purpose. So she got one. Then she left my father again. She broke his heart. She didn't care. She bore me in secret. Saeunn found her and took me from her, I don't know how. I was very small. I hadn't been named.'

'Why did Saeunn take you?' said Torak. 'It can't have been out of pity.'

Renn smiled mirthlessly. 'It wasn't. She needed to stop the Viper Mage using me . . .' She took a breath. 'Anyway. Saeunn told everyone that Fa had mated with a woman in the Deep Forest, who had died; she said that woman was my mother. They believed her.' Her fists clenched. 'Saeunn saved me. Sometimes I hate her. I owe her everything.'

Torak was silent. Then he said, 'Why did the Viper Mage need a baby?'

Renn hesitated. 'Can I tell you later?'

He nodded, pouring sand from palm to palm. 'Who else knew?'

'Only Fin-Kedinn and Saeunn. He said it would be my secret, to tell when I wanted.' Laying down her bow, she turned to him. 'I *was* going to tell you, I swear! I'm *so* sorry I never did!'

'I know,' he said. 'I'm sorry too, for all those things I said. I didn't mean them. You know that, don't you?'

Renn's face worked. Then she put her elbows on her knees and buried her head in her hands. She didn't make a sound, but Torak could see the tension in her shoulders.

Awkwardly, he put his arm around her. For an instant she resisted; then she relaxed and leaned against him. She felt small and warm and strong.

'I'm not crying,' she muttered.

'I know.'

After a while she straightened up and wiped her nose on the back of her hand, and wriggled out from under his arm. 'You're lucky,' she sniffed. 'You never knew your mother.'

'Well. But I remember my wolf mother.'

Another sniff. 'What was she like?'

'She had soft fur and a tongue like hot sand. Sometimes her breath smelt of rotting meat.'

Renn laughed.

Side by side, they gazed across the Lake. Torak heard the plop of a watervole; the distant tail-slam of a beaver. An otter broke the surface and regarded them, then dived underwater, trailing bubbles.

Watching it, Torak felt his spirits lift. If only Wolf were with them now, he could cope with anything.

As if in answer, a mournful howl rose from the Forest.

Torak turned and gave two short barks. *I am here!*

'Poor Wolf,' said Renn.

'Yes. He misses the pack.'

'I think he misses you, too.'

'Come on, then.' Torak pulled her to her feet. 'Let's go and cheer him up.'

They didn't find Wolf; he found them some time later, under a stand of pines not far from the camp.

Listlessly, he wagged his tail as he padded over to greet Torak. His ears were down and the brightness was gone from his eyes.

Squatting beside him, Torak gently scratched his flank.

Wolf lay down and put his muzzle between his paws. *I miss the pack*, he told Torak.

I know, Torak replied in wolf talk. He thought of Wolf's delight in the cubs and his affection for the black she-wolf. Wolf had given up all that for him.

I am your pack, Torak said.

Wolf thumped his tail. Then he sat up and licked Torak's nose.

Torak licked him back, and blew softly into his scruff. *I never leave you.*

Wolf's tail lashed from side to side, and his eyes gleamed.

Renn ran off, saying she had to fetch something from camp. Soon she was back, carrying a large alderwood bowl with otters carved around its sides. Torak helped her set it in the bracken. It stank. It was full of stickleback grease, speckled with mysterious black lumps.

'Yolun insisted I used this bowl,' said Renn. 'He said wolves are special, because they make strong music. There,' she told Wolf, 'I hope you like it!'

When they'd moved off a polite distance to give Wolf eating space, he went to sniff the bowl. Then he started to eat. He liked it. In a remarkably short time, he was licking the sides clean of the last remaining smears.

'What were the black bits?' said Torak.

'Dried lingonberries,' said Renn.

For a moment, Torak forgot about the Soul-Eaters – and laughed.

Outcast is the fourth book in the *Chronicles of Ancient Darkness*, which tell of Torak's adventures in the Forest and beyond, and of his quest to vanquish the Soul-Eaters. *Wolf Brother* is the first book, *Spirit Walker* the second, and *Soul Eater* the third.

AUTHOR'S NOTE

Torak's world is the world of six thousand years ago: after the Ice Age, but before the spread of farming to his part of north-west Europe, when the land was one vast Forest.

The people of Torak's world looked pretty much like you or me, but their way of life was very different. They didn't have writing, metals or the wheel, but they didn't need them. They were superb survivors. They knew all about the animals, trees, plants and rocks of the Forest. When they wanted something, they knew where to find it, or how to make it.

They lived in small clans, and many of them moved around a lot: some staying in camp for just a few days, like the Wolf Clan; others staying for a whole moon or a season, like the Raven and Willow Clans; while others stayed put all year round, like the Seal Clan. Thus some of the clans have moved since the events in *Soul Eater*, as you'll see from the amended map.

When I was researching *Outcast*, I spent time around Lake Storsjön in northern Sweden. There I was lucky enough to hear elk bellowing as I wandered the springtime forest, and to find a whole clearing and dam system made by beavers. I also got muzzle to muzzle with some elk (called moose in north America) at an elk refuge, including some adorable five-day-old calves and a mournful yearling who'd just been abandoned by his truly enormous mother.

The inspiration for the stone carvings at the healing

spring came from the hugely evocative rock carvings at Glösa, near Storsjön, which are believed to have been made by people who lived in Torak's time. While there, I was also able to view some superb reproductions of Stone Age clothes, musical instruments, weapons and an elkhide canoe.

To get closer to wolf cubs, I got to know some very young ones at the UK Wolf Conservation Trust, where I bottle-fed them, played with them and – more importantly – watched them at play among themselves, as well as observing their startlingly rapid development, in just a few months, from tiny bundles of fluff to large, extremely boisterous wolves.

To get the feel of snakes, I met some at Longleat, where I handled a very beautiful cornsnake and two regal, curious and extremely strong royal pythons. I hadn't understood just how beautiful and fascinating snakes can be until I held one, and felt the flicker of her tongue on my face as she inspected me.

ψ

I want to thank everyone at the UK Wolf Conservation Trust for letting me make friends with the cubs while they were growing up; Sune Häggmark of Orrviken for sharing his extensive knowledge of elk and for letting me get close to his rescued elk and elk calves; the friendly and enormously helpful people at the Tourist Information Centres at Krokom and Östersund, who made it possible for me to reach Glösa, then showed me round on a cold, rainy, but highly atmospheric day; Mr Derrick Coyle, the Yeoman Ravenmaster of the Tower of London, for sharing his extensive knowledge and experience of some very special ravens; and Darren Beasley and Kim Tucker of Longleat, for introducing me to some amazingly beautiful and fascinating snakes.

As always, I want to thank my agent, Peter Cox, for his unfailing enthusiasm and support; and my wonderful editor and publisher, Fiona Kennedy, for her imagination, commitment and understanding.

Michelle Paver

2007

THE WAYS OF THE LAKE

"'Eat," she said, ladling a grey sludge over Renn's gruel.'

The Otter Clan make their grease from the stickleback, a small freshwater fish. The Tsimshian and other peoples of the Pacific Northwest made grease out of the eulachon or candlefish, a sardine-like fish, which is a species of smelt. Grease was highly prized, and people ate it with fish, roasted roots and berries; in fact, pretty much everything. They made beautifully carved containers to hold their grease, and traded it with others. They also lavished it on their guests, just as the Otters do with Renn and Bale. Many people believed that to eat berries *without* grease was a mark of poverty.

Methods for making grease varied, but a simple one was to fill a wooden canoe with whole fish and leave them to rot in the sun for several days, often adding hot stones, to speed things up. When the fish were nicely rotten, the oil was extracted by pouring it off, squeezing the carcasses, heating, and straining. As you can imagine, the grease was *extremely* smelly, and took some getting used to; so it's hardly surprising that Renn, who is new to it, thinks it's horrible. It's an acquired taste, and some American Indian peoples still relish eulachon grease today. They have a point. Eulachon grease is rich in iodine and vitamins: just the things that many of us buy as supplements from health food stores, to improve our diet.

'When the eating was over, the Otters collected all the fish bones which were too small to be useful and took them to the Lake, so that they could be born again as new fish.'

Uncertainty was an ever-present part of a hunter-gatherer's life, and it remains so today. Will there be many reindeer or lingonberries or grouse this year, or will they mysteriously disappear, as sometimes happens? Such uncertainty is particularly acute when, like the Otter Clan, you live mainly on fish. Why is it that in some years, lakes and rivers are teeming with fish, while in others, nets are empty? To deal with this uncertainty, fishing peoples had a whole range of customs, taboos and ceremonies that governed every aspect of catching, preparing and eating fish. These were designed to honour the fish and make sure that they would return.

Returning fishbones to the water was a widespread custom. Bones are the part of the body that last longest after death, so it was natural to think that they held the secret of life. Many fishing peoples, including the Kwakiutl of the Pacific Northwest, held a feast to honour the first salmon of the year's catch. This was because they regarded these first fish as scouts, whose spirits would swim back to the others and report on how well they'd been treated. If the scouts told the others that the people were disrespectful, the rest of the fish would stay away. An important part of this feast was to return the bones to the water. The Koyukon Athapaskans of north America dealt carefully with the bones of all water-going creatures, including beavers. In contrast, we tend to regard the meat and fish we eat simply as "food", perhaps because we believe we'll always have an unlimited supply.

'The fish had mysteriously returned to the Lake . . . although the Otters didn't dare remark on this out loud for fear of chasing away the good luck.'

The American Indians of the Pacific Northwest considered it unlucky to comment on a good catch, in case a demon or bad spirit overheard and made mischief. Simliar beliefs are extremely widespread. At the beginning of the 20th century, the fishermen of the Orkney islands north of Scotland never asked each other the size of their fishing catch, for fear of incurring bad luck. Today, many people all over the world don't like to boast too loudly about any good fortune which has come their way, in case they "tempt fate".

'Now they were coming through the mist: three reed boats curved at stem and prow, like water birds.'

Like the Otter Clan, the Paiutes of the American Southwest made many things out of reeds, using in particular the cat's tail or cattail (*Typha latifolia*), which the Otters simply call "reeds". The Paiutes and others like them, such as the Coast Salish people further north, were and are amazingly skilled at basketry and all forms of weaving. From reeds they fashioned boats, shelters, ropes, cooking utensils, sleeping-mats and clothes; and like the Otters, they ate the reed stems, shoots and pollen. Paiute weavers were so skilled that they made water jars of tight-woven reeds that contained the water without leaking, while allowing just enough to seep through so that the contents stayed cool: very useful at the height of summer.

'Twins, thought Renn. Dread stole through her.'

To lots of traditional peoples, twins have special powers, such as the ability to summon the weather, or prey. To the fishing peoples of the Pacific Northwest such as the Nuxalk, twins and their families were believed to cause the all-important salmon run to start. Nuxalk twins would help this along by casting small offerings of carved salmon into the water. Until the last century in some parts of England, a surviving twin, known as a "left twin", was believed to have special powers, particularly the ability to cure certain throat infections by breathing into the mouth of the sufferer.

'Now the girl withdrew a long loop of twisted sedge and wove it between her fingers. Renn saw patterns form: a fishing net, a boat, a tiny Death Platform.'

The weaving of patterns with a looped cord, known in England as "cat's cradle", has a long history. Some Inuit still pass long winter evenings by weaving figures with a loop of string, sometimes illustrating stories, for example, the tale of the lemming who fell through the smoke-hole. However, "cat's cradles" weren't always simply for entertainment. In parts of Canada and Alaska, they were woven in the autumn as a means of keeping the sun above the horizon for a little longer, while in the spring, the loops were cut to bits, to allow the sun to rise higher in the sky.

Weaving patterns in string could be dangerous, too. Until fairly recently, Inuit children in some parts of the Arctic were forbidden from playing cat's cradle when the men went hunting, for fear of causing the harpoon lines to get tangled up. And in the Orkney islands in the early 20th century, a fisherman's wife would never wind wool while her husband was out fishing, in case he got caught in the lines and thrown overboard.

'We will ride with the spirits on the voice of diverbird and reed.'

The English name for the Otter Clan's diverbird is the red-throated diver or loon (*Gavia stellata*), a bird revered throughout the northern world for its strange, haunting cry. This and the fact that it is equally at home in the sky, the water, or the forest, led many to believe it has supernatural powers. In the Pacific Northwest of America, some Kwakwaka'wakw shamans (Mages) thought loons were powerful spirit helpers who could help them contact the spirit world. To the Inuit, the diverbird is the bird of eloquence and song, and the Copper Inuit wore caps of loon skin for their ceremonial dances. To many Inuit, the skin, claws or beak of the diverbird were valuable amulets for health, happiness and skill at kayaking. So when the Otters give Bale a diverbird claw, they are giving him an amulet of great power, and one well suited to his talents.

Michelle Paver, 2008

CHRONICLES of ANCIENT DARKNESS

Six adventures. One quest.

There are six books in the Chronicles of Ancient Darkness, and all feature Torak, Renn and Wolf.

In *Wolf Brother*, Torak finds himself alone in the Forest, when his father is killed by a demon-haunted bear. In his attempts to vanquish the bear, Torak makes two friends who will change his life: Renn, the girl from the Raven Clan, and Wolf, the orphaned wolf cub who will soon become Torak's beloved pack-brother.

In *Spirit Walker*, a horrible sickness attacks the clans, and Torak has to find the cure. His search takes him across the Sea to the islands of the Seal Clan, where he encounters demons and killer whales, and gets closer to uncovering the truth behind his father's death, as well as learning of his own undreamed-of powers.

In *Soul Eater* Wolf is taken by the enemy. To rescue him, Torak and Renn must journey to the Far North in the depths of winter, where they brave blizzards and ice bears, and venture into the very stronghold of the Soul-Eaters.

Outcast takes place on and around Lake Axehead. Torak is cast out of the clans, and has to survive on his own, separated from Renn, and even from Wolf.

In *Oath Breaker* one of Torak's closest friends is killed, and he tracks the murderer into the mysterious heart of the Deep Forest. Here the clans are at war, and punish any outsider venturing in. In the Deep Forest, Torak learns more about his mother, and about just why he is the spirit walker.

Ghost Hunter is the final adventure. Set in the High Mountains, it tells of Torak's battle against the most fearsome of all the Soul-Eaters, Eostra the Eagle Owl Mage, who seeks to rule both the living and the dead.

A legend for all time.

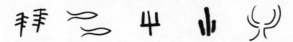

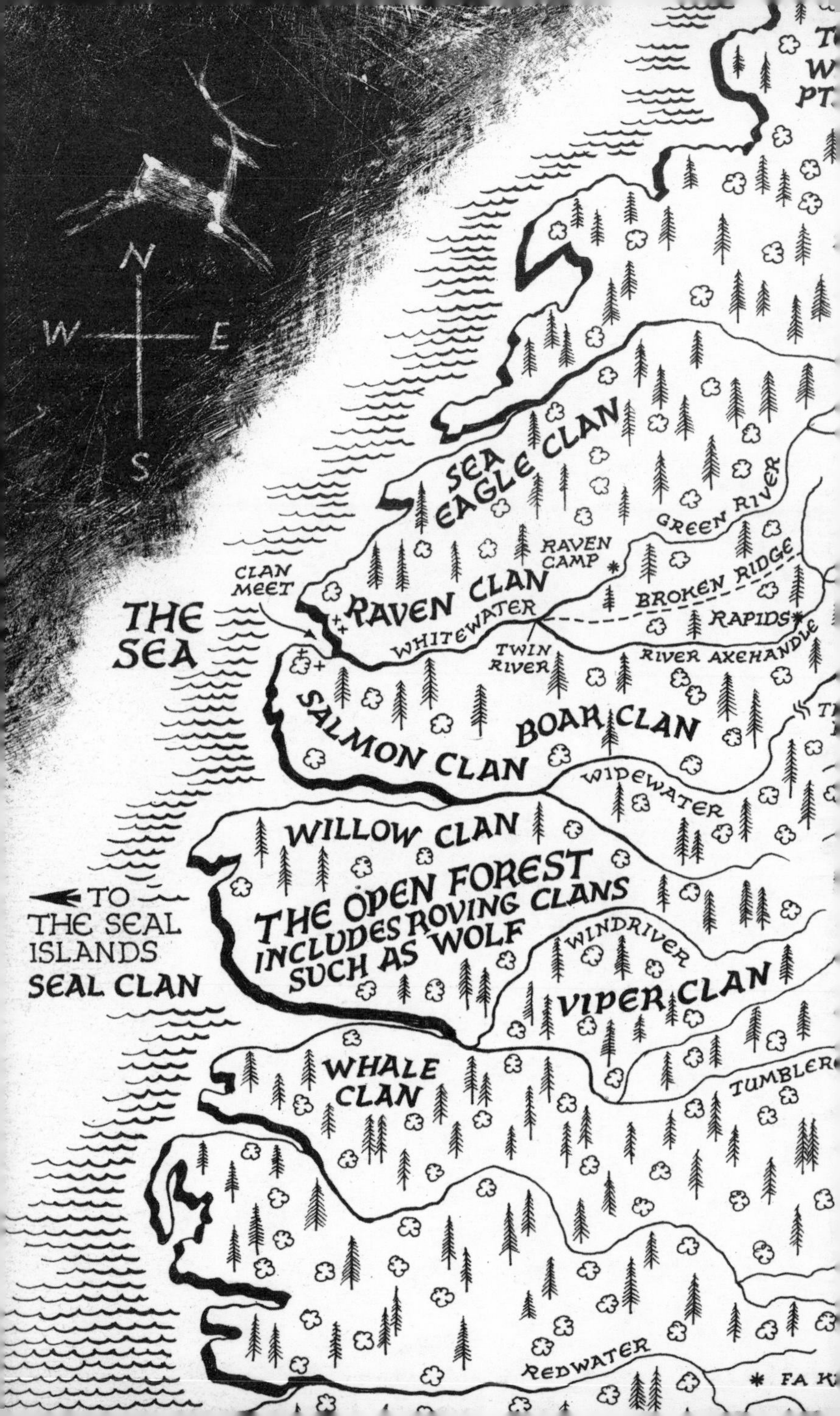
N
W
E
S
THE SEA
CLAN MEET
SEA EAGLE CLAN
RAVEN CAMP
RAVEN CLAN
GREEN RIVER
BROKEN RIDGE
WHITEWATER
RAPIDS
TWIN RIVER
RIVER AXEHANDLE
SALMON CLAN
BOAR CLAN
WIDEWATER
WILLOW CLAN
THE OPEN FOREST
INCLUDES ROVING CLANS
SUCH AS WOLF
WINDRIVER
VIPER CLAN
TO THE SEAL ISLANDS
SEAL CLAN
WHALE CLAN
TUMBLER
REDWATER